MORAY DALTON

DEATH IN THE FOREST

With an introduction by Curtis Evans

DEAN STREET PRESS

MORAY DALTON
DEATH IN THE FOREST

Katherine Dalton Renoir ('Moray Dalton') was born in Hammersmith, London in 1881, the only child of a Canadian father and English mother.

The author wrote two well-received early novels, *Olive in Italy* (1909), and *The Sword of Love* (1920). However, her career in crime fiction did not begin until 1924, after which Moray Dalton published twenty-nine mysteries, the last in 1951. The majority of these feature her recurring sleuths, Scotland Yard inspector Hugh Collier and private inquiry agent Hermann Glide.

Moray Dalton married Louis Jean Renoir in 1921, and the couple had a son a year later. The author lived on the south coast of England for the majority of her life following the marriage. She died in Worthing, West Sussex, in 1963.

Moray Dalton Mysteries
Available from Dean Street Press

One by One They Disappeared
The Night of Fear
The Body in the Road
Death in the Cup
The Strange Case of Harriet Hall
The Belfry Murder
The Belgrave Manor Crime
The Case of Alan Copeland
The Art School Murders
The Condamine Case
The Mystery of the Kneeling Woman
Death in the Dark
Death in the Forest
The Murder of Eve
Death at the Villa

WHAT HAPPENS IN SAN RINALDO STAYS IN SAN RINALDO?

MORAY DALTON'S *DEATH IN THE FOREST* (1939)

As a mystery writer Moray Dalton certainly was not lacking in imagination, some of which admittedly falls rather strikingly on the outré side. Several of Dalton's mysteries involve witchcraft, while another one concerns, literally, the end of the world. It is not unfair to say that stern traditionalist aestheticisms of the detective novel like T. S. Eliot and S. S. Van Dine would have frowned upon Dalton's occasional exoticisms. To be sure, some of her wilder novels are standalones, like *The Wife of Baal* (devil worship in Italy) and the aforementioned apocalyptic sci-fi mystery *The Black Death* (likely a genre unto itself, although Ellery Queen once took time with his father Inspector Queen to solve a murder problem at a country mansion on the verge of being consumed by a cataclysmic forest fire)—the latter necessarily. However, Dalton's series sleuth Hugh Collier has some notably bizarre detective episodes of his own, like previously republished *The Belgrave Manor Crime* and the novel which follows this introduction, the deceptively innocuously titled *Death in the Forest*.

Forest opens quietly and traditionally enough in the dear old quaintly rural England beloved by several generations of Anglophile Golden Age mystery readers now. Young Roger Frere has returned to live with his dying bachelor uncle at Frere Court, the grand ancestral mansion of the Freres located at Swain Green in southwest Hampshire at the edge of the New Forest, although the old man will not at any price have the rest of Roger's family— his stepmother and his two half-siblings—settle in with him at Frere Court, on account of his opposition to his younger brother's second marriage. Not long after his arrival at Frere Court, Roger meets lovely Celia Holland, daughter of the impecunious widowed local vicar. Celia, who taught at a girls' school in Sussex, divulges to Roger that she shortly is headed out to the South American republic of San Rinaldo, "one of the smaller and more backward of the South American republics," where she has taken a post as governess to two young girls, the daughters of the Don Juan Romero and his wife, one of the little country's wealthiest couples.

The next seven chapters of the novel take place from the perspective of Celia in San Rinaldo at the palatial mansion of the Romeros, which bears "about as much resemblance to the usual country house as Hardy's *The Dynasts* does to an average West End drawing-room comedy." The estancia Romero comes complete with a proper English butler, Metcalfe, and the children's indigenous nursemaid, Catarina, who resentfully deems Celia an interloper. After two years in San Rinaldo, Celia ends up returning home under rather extraordinary circumstances, and she finds herself immediately plunged into weird local mysteries. Out of the frying pan into the fire, one might say.

An unknown man recently has been discovered dead in the New Forest, having apparently expired from some overwhelming fright in the night. (The man had a dicky heart, it seems.) Roger, now married, sits as master of Frere Court, his uncle having passed away, and there he has installed with himself and his bride Nina his grasping stepmother Rhoda and his "blond, exquisite and languid" half-brother Cedric. (His half-sister Sibyl died tragically in a car accident in the New Forest not long after arriving at Frere Court.) Also new in the neighborhood is Major Enderby, a solitary individual lately retired from distinguished service in India and a chess-playing compadre of Reverend Holland. Invariably accompanied by his large, loyal Airedale, Jock, the Major has an enigmatic air of seeming to know more than he lets on about strange events in the neighborhood. These include, in addition to the recent death of the unknown man in the forest:

> Creepy nocturnal prowlings by some creature of the night which frighten the New Forest ponies
>
> The poisoning murder of a seemingly inoffensive maid at Frere Court

A vicious attempt made to dispose of Celia Holland by means of a deadly gift of dates sprinkled with ground glass.

Just what the devil is going on at lovely little Swain Green? Ultimately Superintendent Cardew of New Scotland Yard sends Inspector Collier and Sergeant Duffield to find out, a great many of the local cops being down with flu. (Collier here is described on entrance as "a youngish man with a lean active figure, brown hair turning grey at the temples, and very shrewd blue eyes. Not . . . a policeman of the narrow hide-bound type.") Perhaps the case is not one of Collier's greatest deductive triumphs, but then in defense of the man he gets presented with a truly extraordinary problem, one which should baffle and enthrall the devoted Dalton reader.

Curtis Evans

Chapter I
THE FRERES

"I FEEL now that I did wrong in not having you down here before, during my son's lifetime," said Mr. Frere, breaking a long silence.

Roger Frere said nothing for a moment. He was spending his first week-end at Frere Court and finding the experience somewhat overwhelming. His uncle was a stranger to him. He had arrived late the previous evening. A car had been sent to meet him at the nearest main line station five miles away. He had dined alone with his host in an oak-panelled parlour hung with portraits of dead and gone Freres, his ancestors, Nicholas Frere in doublet and ruff, Rupert Frere with a collar of lace over damascened steel—"by Sustermans" said his uncle. Since he left school he had lived with his stepmother and his half-brother and sister in a cheap boarding-house. He worked in an office in the basement of a block off Southampton Row, and in winter seldom saw daylight from Monday until Saturday. His stepmother often boasted of her late husband's connections. "An old county family. We are the new poor—" Roger had never really believed her, though he knew, of course, that he had an uncle living somewhere on the borders of the New Forest who had paid for his education.

Mr. Frere's sunken eyes had rested on him thoughtfully more than once during the meal. Later, when the butler had brought the coffee in the library whose windows opened on the moat where swans floated, silent as ghosts, in the starlight, he said,

"You see the likeness, Watkins?"

"To—to master John? Yes, sir. It's—it's really striking to my mind," he turned to the young man. "If you'll excuse me, Master Roger, you're a Frere all right."

Mr. Frere smiled for the first time. "He has paid you the highest compliment he knows."

Now they were walking across the park on their way to church.

Mr. Frere moved slowly and leaned heavily on his stick. He paused on a stone footbridge crossing the stream that fed the moat and turned to look back at the grey stone walls covered with magnolia and Virginia creeper.

"I like this view, don't you?"

"It's the most beautiful thing of its kind I've ever seen," said Roger.

"A good answer," approved his uncle. "You haven't seen much, of course. No opportunities, eh?"

"No."

"You know why your father was estranged from the rest of the family?"

"I think I can guess, sir. You didn't like his second marriage."

"Right. Never did, and never shall. His financial difficulties were no fault of mine. He had enough to live on, but he would speculate. That's the church. You can just see the tower through the trees."

"Yes, sir."

"You know—or perhaps you don't know—that the estate is very strictly entailed. Since John was drowned in the Solent—he was a fine swimmer but the current there runs like a mill race—what was I saying? I looked forward to his succeeding me here, and his son after him. As it is, you are the next heir. You'll need some training to fit you for the position. Would you be willing to come and live with me here?"

Roger was taken by surprise and showed it, but he met his uncle's searching gaze steadily. "Yes, sir. I'd love to. I—I would do my best. But you'd have to make allowances—I mean I'm not used to—a lot of servants and all that."

"You've got the knack, I fancy. Watkins is favourably impressed," said the old man with his faint half smile. "But one thing must be clearly understood. I mean you. Not the others. I can't prevent you from bringing them here when I'm gone, though you won't, if you're wise."

"I'm very fond of Sybyl."

"That's your half-sister? Well, that's your affair. But they don't come here while I live. That won't be long, I daresay. You might give me your arm up this slope. I can't manage hills nowadays."

The bells had stopped ringing as they passed under the lych gate, a little group of villagers moved to one side to let them go by. Mr. Frere touched his hat in answer to their "Morning, Squire,"

"Morning, Mr. Frere—"

Roger followed his uncle into the Frere Court pew which was raised above the chancel like a box at the theatre and furnished with faded crimson cushions. The small choir of men and boys passed up the aisle, their thick boots clattering on the stone pavement and over the worn brass of a Frere who fought at Agincourt. A girl was playing the organ. Roger found himself watching her while the vicar, a gentle old man with a hesitating manner, droned through the service. There was something unusual about her. For one thing, she wore no make up, and her straight shining fair hair owed nothing to art. She looked very earnest and efficient and absorbed in her job, and once during the sermon he saw her lean forward to admonish one of the choirboys who had started a surreptitious game of marbles. After the service Mr. Frere waited in the porch until she came out and she was introduced to Roger.

"Celia, I know your father does not care to dine out on Sunday, but I hope he will make an exception this evening. I want him to meet my nephew Roger, and he has to go back to London by a very early train. I'll send the car to bring you both over after the service."

She shook hands with Roger. Seen at close quarters her round, good-humoured face was decidedly attractive, though she could not be called pretty.

"We'll both be delighted to come, Mr. Frere. I must rush away now. I have to give that Tommy Cantle a good talking to. Those imps are the bane of my life when I'm at home. They listen to old Minns because he's a man, but he does like a holiday from the organ—"

"That's a good, sensible little girl," said Frere when she had left them and they were returning to the Court by the short cut across the park. "Clever too, though she doesn't put on any airs. She's been teaching at a big girls' school in Sussex."

"She looks little more than a schoolgirl herself."

"Celia's not so young as she looks. She's round about twenty-two. She got her L.R.A.M. last year through sheer hard work. She has to earn her own living. The vicar's stipend can't go very far."

After lunch Roger went for a tramp through the forest leaving his uncle to doze over the *Sunday Times*.

He was glad of the opportunity to think over Mr. Frere's unexpected offer. So far as he could see there was only one fly in the ointment and that was that his half-sister Sybyl was not to be allowed to share his good fortune. He would miss her companionship and he knew that she would miss him. His stepmother, of course, would be unsparing in her criticism of any action he took. He was used to that. He would send her half of any allowance his uncle made him. Even then he knew that she would not be satisfied.

Later, when they were having tea in the shade of the cedar on the lawn, Mr. Frere asked him some questions about his half-brother Cedric.

"You've been working in an insurance office, I understand. What does he do?"

"Nothing, at the moment."

Mr. Frere grunted. "How old is he?"

"Just over twenty-one."

"Hasn't he ever had a job?"

"No. He's supposed to be delicate."

"I see. A young wastrel."

"I don't know about that, sir, it isn't easy to get work. He hasn't been trained for anything. Sybyl works. She's a typist. I—I think you'd like her," ventured Roger. "She—she really has rather a thin time, I'm afraid. Mother's devoted to Cedric, but she's rather hard on Sybyl. Sometimes I think she resents her being young and pretty—"

Mr. Frere nodded. "That sort of woman. I know the type. Greedy and selfish. I'm sorry for the girl, but I won't have her here, Roger, and I don't want to hear about them in future. Is that clear?"

Roger opened his mouth to speak and thought better of it. He had caught a warning look from Watkins behind his master's chair. The old butler waylaid him as he was going upstairs to dress for dinner.

"If you'll excuse me, Master Roger, I'm glad you're so considerate. Mr. Frere's heart is in a bad state. He ought not to excite himself."

"I understand," Roger assured him. "I'll be careful."

The vicar and his daughter arrived punctually at eight. Celia looked very well in a blue lace frock. Mr. Frere was openly admiring. "Charming, my dear. Quite a creation—"

Celia laughed. There was no other woman present to detect the fact that her best evening frock was a reach-me-down from an Oxford Street bargain basement. After dinner she went into the garden with Roger while her father and Mr. Frere settled down to finish a game of chess.

"Are you coming to live here?"

"My uncle has asked me to."

"I thought he might if he liked you. I'm so glad. Poor Johnnie's death was a terrible blow. He'll never really get over it, I'm afraid," the girl said sadly. "I've been so worried. I'm fond of him—he's a dear in spite of that abrupt manner—and I was fond of Johnnie. You see, I was afraid he might hate you for taking his son's place. He was so wrapped up in him and he loves the old house, too. It's a mistake to care so much for anybody or anything, but I suppose one can't help it if one is made that way."

"It would have been quite natural," Roger said, "if he had hated me, I mean. I was simply dithering when I first arrived last night, but he's been frightfully decent."

"You are very like Johnnie—has he told you? You gave me quite a shock when I saw you in church. Only he was on a smaller scale, I think. He only topped me by a couple of inches, and I'm only just up to your shoulder."

They paused on the drawbridge, looking down into the moat at the dim white shapes of the swans floating on the dark water. "I say," said Roger, with satisfaction, "I am glad you're here. I shall rely on you to advise me."

"I shan't be here long."

"You teach in a school, don't you? Uncle told me. But you'll be home for the holidays?" said Roger hopefully.

"I used to be, but I'm going abroad, and I suppose I shall be away for at least two years."

"Oh"—said Roger, damped by this information. "How's that?"

"Well, I was leaving Toledene. I didn't like it much. A young South American couple came there one afternoon last term and I had the job of showing them round the place. They told me they thought of sending their two little girls there, and when I heard their ages were five and six I felt I had to tell them I thought they should be kept at home a bit longer. They said they were relying on me to look after them. They had heard of the school from Signora Giannini, the opera singer. Her little girl is there and she was very homesick at first and I rather took her under my wing, if you know what I mean. It seems they met her at their hotel in Paris and she mentioned my name, and that was why they asked specially for me to take them round. I had to tell them I was leaving at the end of the term, so that was that. But weeks later, when I had come home, I had a letter from Señor Romero. He said they had decided not to bring their children to Europe just yet, but would I go out to San Rinaldo, where they live, as their governess. He offered a perfectly enormous salary, besides paying my fare out and home again, if I didn't like it after three months. I didn't much like the idea of leaving Father, but he doesn't really need me. Mrs. Bond looks after him and is very trustworthy. And apart from that I'm simply thrilled. I've always longed to travel and see the world."

"So have I," said Roger. "But isn't South America rather—I mean, is it safe for a girl?"

"I know—and I have had a few qualms—but I wrote to the Minister for San Rinaldo in London and he wrote back and said the Romero family was well known and much respected in the Republic, and that it was quite all right. And besides," added Celia airily out of the depths of her inexperience, "I think girls who get into trouble abroad have generally been asking for it."

"Well—I hope you're right," said Roger. "I wish you weren't going, but that's pure selfishness on my part. I wish you luck. It seems rather topsy turvy, though."

"What do you mean?"

"My staying at home as a companion to an elderly relative, while you go out to the wide open spaces."

They both laughed and then relapsed into a companionable silence, leaning side by side over the oak hand rail of the bridge and seeing their shadows faintly mirrored in the moat below. After a while Roger said, "When are you going?"

"In ten days."

"So soon? I see—"

She was silent. After a minute he turned to her to ask if she felt cold.

"Not really. Someone walked over my grave."

She shivered again. "That's rather a gruesome superstition, isn't it. Perhaps we had better go in."

On their way home in Mr. Frere's car the vicar said, "Well, we've seen the young man. How would you sum trim up, Celia? I always think you're a good judge of character."

"I like him," she said. "But I'm afraid he is the sort that gets put upon. Almost too good-natured and unassuming."

"A good fault," said her father comfortably, "and there isn't much danger that he will be put upon, as you call it, here. I can see Frere is very taken with him. Of course he's inclined to be masterful, and the boy treats him with a rather charming defer-ence. He was in better spirits to-night than he has been since the tragedy of poor Johnnie's death." Then, as his daughter made no reply, he said, "Are you tired, my dear?"

"A little."

When they reached home she went directly to her room, leaving her father to see that the windows were fastened and to extin-guish the lamp in the hall. She was wondering, rather drearily, if something she would have valued had not slipped away from her for ever while she and Roger Frere stood talking on the bridge while they watched the white breasts of the swans reflected in the dark water. Had she, through no fault of her own, through the fact that in a few days she was sailing for the other side of the world, missed her chance of happiness? There was nothing to be done about it. Her passage was booked, all her arrangements made. In any case she was probably building far too much on a small foundation. She had always had a wholesome contempt for girls who imagined that every man who treated them with ordinary civility was falling in love with them.

"Celia," she admonished her reflection in mirror as she brushed her hair, "don't be a fool."

CHAPTER II
THE ENGLISH MISS

A STOUT man, whose only concessions to a thermometer registering ninety-six in the shade were a black alpaca jacket and a broad brimmed, straw hat, had been standing a little apart from the vociferous group of hotel porters who were preparing to scramble for the patronage of the seven passengers who were landing from the liner in the harbour. There was only one woman among the new arrivals. The stout man stepped forward with majestic deliberation, remarking in bad but intelligible Spanish that he had come to meet the señorita. The representatives of the Grand and the Splendide, who knew who he was, set down the suitcases they had snatched from her and withdrew sulkily, like jackals frightened away from their feast by the lion returning to his prey.

Celia adjusted her hat, which had been knocked sideways in the scuffle, with hands that shook a little.

"Are you—" her fragmentary Spanish failed her.

"It's all right, miss," said the stout man soothingly in English. "They didn't mean to harm you. They're excitable in these parts. You've got to make allowances. These suitcases and that trunk. Is that all your luggage, miss? I'll have it strapped on the back of the car."

"You—you came to meet me?"

"I am Señor Romero's butler, Metcalfe, miss. If you'll get in, miss, we can be off."

"Have we far to go?"

"Not as the crow flies, but the road is very bad outside the town."

The bare-footed loafers on the quay dispersed to make way for the car. A gaudy official breathing garlic waved aside Celia's proffered keys when he heard that her destination was the estancia Romero. She began to realise that her employer was indeed a person of some note in San Rinaldo. She had been rather damped on the voyage out by the lack of interest displayed by her fellow passengers in the republic. It was, she had gathered, not only one of the smaller, but one of the most backward of the South American States. The elderly French woman with whom she shared a state-room had shrugged her shoulders. She was a buyer for a big drapery store in Buenos Aires. "Get as much money as you can, and go home," she advised. "These South Americans can be charming—but don't fall in love. They are like their towns, a thin slice of Paris plastered over the primeval mud—"

Celia recalled that phrase as the car left the sun-baked squalor of the dockside and entered the main stream of traffic in a wide avenue with shops glittering with plate glass and handsome public buildings on either side. The wide pavements were shaded by trees, and there were cafés, with striped awnings, where dark-skinned, lean men in strange enveloping blue cloaks were sipping iced drinks and playing dominoes. Others, lounging on the terrace of the Grand Hotel, were dressed in white linen suits. Celia noticed that there were very few women, and those she did see were just going into a church. They passed public gardens with a bandstand and a bronze statue of an agitated gentleman draped in a flag and flourishing a sword. At one street corner, just opposite a cinema where a crowd of swarthy school children was being marshalled in to see a Silly Symphony, a black moving mass on the road proved to be a flock of vultures feasting on a dead horse. Celia shrank back, horrified. Metcalfe swerved to avoid the nasty mess and spoke to her without turning his head.

"Very crude here in some ways, miss. Shocking, I thought, when I first came. But you get used to it."

"Those dreadful birds—"

"Yes, miss. But very useful."

The wide, metalled road traversed a public park outside the town and then, after diverging to the right, ceased abruptly and became a deeply rutted track over which the car bumped painfully in a cloud of red dust. At frequent intervals they passed hovels built of old petrol cans and enclosed by fences made of barbed wire attached to what Celia thought were branches of very gnarled trees. Later she learned that wooden fences would have been eaten by white ants and that where there were no iron posts the peons used the bones of cattle that had died on their way down to the stock yards farther along the coast. For a few weeks after the rains that strip of low lying land between the foothills and the sea was green, and served to pasture the herds being driven to higher ground where there would still be grass when the plain was parched and arid. During the rest of the year it was deserted by all but its scanty population of outcasts who had erected crazy shelters for themselves by the roadside and who lived, apparently, by begging from the passing cars. A pack of naked, dusky children came scampering out of some of the dingy patches of garden where skinny fowls rooted in garbage, and Metcalfe threw them some small coins. They were left behind fighting in the ditch. A little farther on an old man grotesquely swollen with elephantiasis, leaned against a gate and watched them pass. In the red light of the setting sun the sinister fences of barbed wire and bones made a fantastic pattern of shadows on the ground.

Metcalfe spoke over his shoulder. "They say these parts were under water not so long ago. The sea receded after an earthquake. They are called the Bad Lands and they've got a bad name. It wouldn't be safe to be out here alone after dark, or so they say."

"'I see," said Celia. "And is this the only way to the town from the estancia Romero?"

"Yes, miss. But it's nothing with a car, and we have three, and two of the native servants can drive. You can be run in any time you wish so there's no need to feel shut off from the world. Señor Romero is very anxious that everything possible should be done to make you feel happy and at home here."

The English butler had the voice that should proceed from all stout, red-faced men. It was rich, fruity, and reassuring. Those soothing accents laid the foundations of the confidence Celia was to feel in Metcalfe.

And just then the road forked and they took the turning to the left and soon had left the plain and were climbing by a winding track through dense woods. They turned again under an arch of carved stone and passed between high banks of flowering shrubs to stop at the foot of a flight of marble steps. Metcalfe got out and opened the door of the car for Celia. "This is the place, miss."

Celia gasped. "I thought estancia meant farm."

"The house was rebuilt and the gardens laid out by Señor Romero's grandfather, miss."

The architect had apparently made his plans with an eye on the Grand Trianon, combined with a lurking weakness for the Alhambra and the Parthenon. The result was undeniably impressive and bore about as much resemblance to the usual country house as Hardy's *The Dynasts* does to an average West End drawing-room comedy.

Metcalfe picked up Celia's suitcase and walked with her up the steps. "An Englishman who came up here when Señor Romero sold his horses said it was by Daydream out of Blank Cheque." Celia laughed rather absently. She was wondering if one or both of the parents of her prospective pupils would come out to welcome her. But when the great double doors were opened they disclosed only the unwieldy figure of an Indian woman, with the blank face of a Buddha cast in bronze, leading by the hand two very small children dressed in pale pink chiffon and lace, who, at the sight of Celia, came fluttering forward like a pair of butterflies, uttering shrill cries of delight.

"Well, they aren't shy. That's one comfort," said Celia.

Metcalfe beamed. "I took the liberty of telling them you'd play games with them, miss. Their nurse is devoted to them, but she's not much for play."

"I suppose not," murmured Celia, uncomfortably conscious of the Indian woman's hard, black stare. Her heart sank a little as she foresaw that the nurse would inevitably be jealous of any influence she might acquire over her charges. She hoped, however, that she might be able to placate her.

"This is the Señorita Maria," said Metcalfe, "and this is the Señorita Pilar—"

The two children sidled closer, extending bony little hands and gazing up at the new governess with enormous brown eyes. Celia was struck by their fragile beauty. Their tiny, perfectly modelled features had the yellowish pallor of old ivory. They seemed to her to be ridiculously over-dressed. Were they wearing party frocks in her honour? That would be rather touching.

"They've learnt a bit of English from me," said the butler.

"When we help to clean 'im de silva, yes," explained Maria.

"That's splendid," Celia smiled at them both. "And does the nurse—"

Metcalfe lowered his voice and rather pointedly avoided looking towards the impassive figure waiting in the background. "Catarina? Not a word. She's none too pleased, between you and me, miss. But she has her orders from Señor Romero and she'll carry them out. She isn't what you'd call a pleasant, chatty sort of person, but she's faithful."

"Well, that's all right," said Celia, hoping it would prove to be so. "I suppose the Señor or the Señora will be telling me how much of the care of the children I am to leave to her."

The butler cleared his throat "As to that—they'd better stay with her while I show you your room, miss—"

She heard the children chattering excitedly in Spanish while the nurse led them out on the terrace, and noted that Catarina herself had not uttered a word. It struck her that Metcalfe, hitherto so blandly equal to any demand made on him, was showing a trace of embarrassment.

Her room was on the other side of the house where the trees had been cleared to give a view across the plain to the sea. It was large and airy, with windows opening on a wide balcony. The brief twilight of the tropics had given place to darkness. Celia could see the lights of the liner she had left—could it be less than three hours ago—in the harbour.

"This is lovely," she said.

"I'm glad you like it, miss. The little girls and their nurse are in the adjoining room. The Señor's instructions were that Catarina would attend to their clothes, dressing them and so on, but they were to have their principal meal with you and be with you during the day."

Celia turned to him. "When shall I be seeing him and the Señora?"

"I was afraid there might be some misunderstanding on that point, miss, from what you said just now. They aren't here. They are in Paris and there's no talk of them coming back at present. You see, miss, the Señora suffers from nerves and has done ever since—" he broke off and resumed. "I've been some years in Señor Romero's service and he relies on me to keep everything as it should be here. He wrote to me that you are to have a free hand with the little girls. Catarina would let herself be cut in pieces for them, but she can't teach them to behave like little ladies. You won't have any trouble with them, Miss Holland, I do assure you. They only have to be shown—"

"Do you mean that they have been left quite alone here? Isn't there an aunt or a grandmother, or anybody—"

Metcalfe looked at her gravely. "Only the servants, miss. I agree with you that it don't seem right—but—well, that's how it is. And the Señora has been so much better since they have been in Paris. And it's not as if there was any danger of a change of Government. The country seems quite settled under this President."

"What difference does that make??"

"Well, Señor Romero is one of his principal supporters. Shall I send up some tea to your room, miss? The maid Rosina has orders to attend to you. She'll answer the bell at any time and get your bath water, and anything you require. Dinner will be at eight."

"Thank you," said Celia.

He was leaving the room but he turned back at the door. "I'm afraid this has been rather an unpleasant surprise," he said. "But I do hope you will stay on, miss, for the sake of the two little girls. I've done my best, but they need a lady like you—"

He went out softly, closing the door after him. Celia remained standing at the window. At dawn, she knew, the liner would be moving out again to sea. Within a few hours her hull would have vanished over the horizon, and she would be left to shoulder a responsibility for which she had been unprepared. She could, she thought, rely on Metcalfe, though, after all, she knew no more of him than he had chosen to tell her. But beyond him she visualised a circle of enigmatic brown faces, of eyes like jet beads, like those of the nurse Catarina, watching her every movement. She wondered about the sentences the butler had left unfinished. Why, for instance, did Señora Romero, whom she remembered as very young and exquisite to look at, suffer from her nerves? On the other hand the two children were charming, as engaging in their way as a pair of baby antelopes with their great, velvety eyes, nuzzling confidingly at her hand.

"If I go," she thought "it must be at once, before I get too fond of them—"

The door opened and the maid Rosina came in with the tea tray. Maria and Pilar followed, peeping shyly round her solid stunted figure. Both were carrying stiff little bunches of flowers. Maria nudged Pilar, who swallowed hard. "Please—do we to play soon?"

Celia smiled at them as she poured out her tea. "Of course. You shall help me unpack. Are those flowers for me? How nice—"

CHAPTER III
FOOL'S PARADISE

THE shadowy fears that had haunted Celia during the first few hours after her arrival at the estancia Romero were soon almost, if not quite, forgotten. She frankly enjoyed the luxurious background to which she was quite unaccustomed. Metcalfe was as good as his word and upheld her authority. Though she never felt quite at her ease with the native servants she had no cause to complain. They were invariably respectful and attentive. She failed to establish friendly relations with the nurse, Catarina, but, on the other hand, she had contrived to avoid any open breach. Catarina never spoke to her and never smiled, but she was almost equally silent when she was alone with her two small charges. She followed them about and watched over them a dog-like fidelity. Celia sometimes fancied that the other servants were afraid of her.

The routine of her life was orderly and uneventful. Maria and Pilar had breakfast in their nursery and came to her at at half-past nine. There were lessons until noon when lunches was served, sometimes under an awning on the terrace. There were always two men servants in attendance in case a snake or a poisonous spider escaped the vigilance of the gardeners and found a way into the house. During the heat of the afternoon they rested in one of the great reception rooms, darkened by sunblinds and kept comparatively cool by electric fans, and Celia told the children fairy stories or helped them with jigsaw puzzles. Later, when it was possible to play more active games they brought out their dolls and their toy trains and rearranged the furniture in their doll's house. An hour before sunset they played with a ball on the hard tennis court that Señor Romero had laid down just before he took his wife to Europe. At seven Catarina came to take the little girls upstairs to have their supper and be put to bed. Celia dined by herself, in state, at eight o'clock, and afterwards read a novel or wrote letters.

Once a week, they were taken down to the town in the most gorgeous of the three cars, by Metcalfe. The little girls and their governess had lunch at the Grand Hotel and went afterwards to the Marionette theatre or to a cinema while the butler paid the weekly bills and drew a cheque at the Bank for current expenses. On the following day he forwarded an account of his stewardship to his employer in Paris. Celia also wrote regularly once a week. "Maria and Pilar are making good progress. Pilar is quicker but Maria is more persevering. They send their love and very soon, I hope, they will be able to write to you themselves."

Celia had been nearly a year at the estancia when she heard through her father of Mr. Frere's death.

"His nephew, Roger, whom you met, I think, just before you sailed, has been a great comfort to him during these last few months when his health has been failing. I must say I like what I have seen of the boy and I think he became sincerely attached to

his uncle. Now, however, the rest of the family have come down to the Court and I am afraid we shall see changes for the worse. Frere, as you know, disapproved violently of his brother's second marriage and would never have thing to do with his sister-in-law and her children. I must say that I feel it would have been in better taste on her part not to come down to the funeral, but that is a matter of opinion. She appears to be firmly established at the Court already. Roger, poor fellow, is, no doubt, in a difficult position. After all, she brought him up. He cannot remember his own mother. I have noticed that he seldom speaks of her, but he seems to be very fond of his half-sister. I hear that she is to learn to ride, and that he is giving her a car. I have not actually met Mrs. Frere yet. She does not come to church, and when I called I was told that she was engaged. I hear that some of the old servants are being pensioned off and that others are giving notice. I miss my old friend more and more. But—to end on a more cheerful note—the White Cottage, after standing empty so long, has been taken by a Major Enderby, retired from the Indian army. He lives alone, but for an Airedale dog. Mrs. Binns goes there daily to cook and clean for him. He plays chess and sometimes he comes to the vicarage and occasionally I go to him for a game. He gave me three pounds the other day towards the cost of having the hymn books rebound, which I thought very kind. They were beginning to fall to pieces. I am glad that you are happy in your present post, my dear. And it is nice for you to be earning so much money. I can't help wishing you were not quite so far away, but don't worry about me. My health is excellent and Mrs. Bond takes good care of me. She sends her love.

Your loving Father.

Celia had known that old Mr. Frere could not live very long, but the news of his death came as a shock, nevertheless. It saddened her to realise that she had seen him for the last time that evening that she dined at the Court with her father a few days before she left England. The following morning he had sent her a little pearl pendant as a keepsake. She had not many ornaments and she wore it nearly every night.

She knew that he had feared that Roger would be exploited by his needy relatives, but there had seemed no way of preventing that. She had realised as she watched his eager sensitive face, so like his cousin Johnnie's, that he would probably be defenceless against certain forms of attack, to appeals to his generosity, to his sense of gratitude, of fair play. Well, Mrs. Frere had certainly lost no time.

Celia was inclined to be absent-minded that afternoon and to answer Maria and Pilar's questions at random. Roger Frere might need someone to stand up for him, but she was evidently not the person to do it and the less she thought about him the better for her peace of mind. He would find some girl—

"Miss Holland, sing to us—" the children chattered quite fluently in English now.

"What shall I sing?"

"Lord Rendal, my son—"

"That's not a very nice song."

"We like it," said Pilar. She always knew her own mind. "Especially the speckled and spotted bit. That's lovely. Why didn't she make his bed the first time he asked, Miss Holland? Why can't we have eels for supper, Miss Holland? What are eels?"

"Rather like snakes."

"There was a snake in your bathroom yesterday," said Maria. "Rosina told me. She called Manuel up to kill it. It came through that hole where the water runs out, gloogloo. It was a coral snake."

Celia twirled round on the music stool. "That settles it. I can't possibly sing Lord Rendal after that." She went on quickly, noting that Pilar's chin was trembling ominously. "We'll play hide and seek all over the house—except the nursery and the servants' quartets," she added hastily. The two children forgot their disappointment over the song. Hide and seek was a special treat. They trotted out to hide, and after a few minutes Celia roused herself and went to look for them.

The great rambling house was very silent, drowsing in the heat of the afternoon. Only a little light came in through the slats of the closed shutters in the long series of rooms on the first floor. The gilded legs of Louis Quinze chairs and sofas glimmered faintly in the dusk. Clocks in cases of onyx and crystal and clocks flanked by ineffably coy shepherdesses in Sèvres porcelain ticked on marble mantelpieces. Metcalfe saw to the clocks. He had once told Celia that there were twenty-seven in the house and several of them had to be wound up every day.

Celia walked down the long corridor, looking into every room as she passed. The door at the end was locked.

"Maria, Pilar, are you in there?"

There was no answer. Celia remembered that when they played hide and seek before the same thing had happened.

"I beg your pardon, miss," Metcalfe had come up behind her. She had not heard him. He always moved very quietly for so big a man. "No one is to go in there, miss. Señor Romero's orders."

Celia flushed a little. "Oh—very well. I was looking for the children—"

"I have to carry out my orders, miss."

"Of course," she said.

She was turning away when he said, "Just a moment, miss—"

"Yes, Metcalfe. What is it?"

"I was wondering, miss, if you could suggest to the Señora when you write, that you might take the little girls over to Paris to see their parents. If you could put it in the middle of the letter where it wouldn't attract attention—"

Celia gazed at him, wondering if she had grasped his real meaning. "I don't think I could do that. What reason could I give? Besides—" it struck her that his broad, florid face had lost some of its colour and was looking lined and worried. "Why the middle of the letter?"

He cleared his throat. "I have reason to believe that letters from the estancia Romero are being censored, miss."

"Censored," she repeated, "but we aren't at war—"

"No, miss. But I've heard rumours. When trouble comes here it comes suddenly—like that—" he snapped his fingers. "It may blow over just as quick, but while it lasts it's bad. You'd understand that better if you could see the other side of this door."

"You're being very mysterious, Metcalfe. Is it a store of hidden arms or something?"

"Oh, no, miss, nothing of that sort. I wouldn't stand for that. I'm all for peace. Live and let live is my motto. As soon as I've enough saved I'm going home. There's a small country hotel I know of, a place where anglers stay. The river runs at the bottom of the garden. I know how to make people comfortable. I don't stay here a day longer than I have to."

"I expect you feel the heat," she said. "You're not looking well. I'm sorry—"

"I don't sleep as well as I did," he admitted. "And you're paler than you were, miss. If I were you I'd tell the Señor you can't stand the climate. I'd book my passage home on the next boat. Send him a cable. Very likely he'll cable back that you can bring the children over with you. That'd be the best thing."

"You're mistaken," said Celia, "I really don't mind the heat. I like it here. And now I really must find the children. They'll be getting so impatient."

Maria and Pilar appeared at that moment at the far end of the corridor, hand-in-hand, and squealing with excitement, and turned to run as Celia started in pursuit.

It was Metcalfe's first departure from the bland omniscience of the well-trained upper servant. He was in the dining-room as usual that evening to pull back her chair and fill her glass with iced lemonade before he delegated his authority to a footman and retired to the seclusion of his own sitting-room. She had half expected him to resume their conversation where they had left off, but he only said: "Good evening, miss."

She understood that he had shot his bolt. If the subject was to be brought up again she must initiate it. She decided to wait a little, but she felt uneasy. She knew nothing of the political situation in San Rinaldo. There were, she knew, two local newspapers and she had sometimes seen the butler reading one after their weekly trip to the town. Metcalfe had told her once that they were both controlled by President Peralta. It was, she realised, unlikely that he would allow any reports of future trouble to be published by his press. She had seen him, more than once, pass in his black Lagonda while she and the children were having tea on the terrace of the Grand Hotel. A tall, lean, swarthy man with a black spade beard and huge sunken eyes. Quite recently she had learned that Señora Romero was his niece. Surely, she argued, if it was really inadvisable for the two little girls to remain at the estancia they would be warned from headquarters. She did not feel that she could make any move on her own responsibility, but she did, in her next letter to Señor Romero, suggest that it was a long time since Maria and Pilar had seen their parents, and that, if he wished, she was quite prepared to look after them on the boat. She added that the weather was unusually warm. "He'll get that in about three weeks," she thought, "and if he takes the hint he can cable."

Some days later she told Metcalfe what she had done. He looked at her quickly. "Well, that's a relief. I was afraid you hadn't quite caught on, miss."

"I hadn't," she said. "I still don't understand. But I saw you were upset, and you know this country better than I do." She was sitting in the small blue drawing-room which she used for the children's lessons and for her own occupation after dinner. The windows were wide open to admit the cooler air blowing in from the sea. Fireflies glimmered among the rose bushes in the garden. The silence of the night was broken at intervals by a long-drawn howl from some animal in the dense jungle from which Señor Romero's grandfather had cleared a space for the house of his dreams. Usually the young half-breed Indian footman, Manuel, brought in her coffee. The English butler, with a nice regard for his prestige with the native staff, was careful not to wait on her himself except occasionally and as a favour. But tonight he had entered with the little silver tray set out with the Sèvres coffee service and she had realised at once that he was giving her an opportunity which must not be missed.

"Know this country, miss? The longer I've lived here the less I feel I know. That howling, for instance. It kind of sends a chill down your spine, doesn't it. It's like the crying of a lost soul. I've heard it now and again ever since I've been in service here, that's going on for seven years, and I still have no idea what sort of animal it is."

"It sounds rather like a dog," said Celia.

"Señor Romero kept dogs when he lived here, but they were never allowed beyond the gates. He said if one escaped into the jungle it'd be dead within twenty-four hours from snake bite."

Celia stirred her coffee thoughtfully. "I can't think why they built a house so far from the town."

"It's cooler up here. His wife was delicate and the doctor said the air would be better on this spur of the hills. The building of the house and the laying out of the gardens cost a fabulous sum. Most of the materials were brought from Europe and conveyed up here in ox carts. But it was the height of the rubber boom and he had money to burn, I suppose. You wouldn't remember that time, miss. It would be thirty years ago and more. He made the road too, such as it is, from where it forks at the foot of the hill. It stops here, you know, for us, at any rate. There's a maze of tracks through the jungle for the natives, of course. Our servants here— they vanish once they are outside the gates as if the earth had swallowed them up. It's a queer mix up, isn't it, miss, with the telephone and the electric light plant, and the cars in the garage, and all that dark growth, full of things we can't so much as guess at, pressing up against the walls—"

Celia lit a cigarette. "You used to be so reassuring Metcalfe. You've changed. I haven't been a bit nervous, thanks to you. You made me feel safe. Have I been living in a fool's paradise all these months?"

"I've got my savings," he said. "They don't give such wages in England, nor in America—the States, I mean—I don't trust the banks here. I keep it all in notes in an oilskin bag. I could be away at five minutes' notice. It's just as well, miss, to be prepared."

Chapter IV
THE VISITOR FROM ENGLAND

"Oh, Mr. Frere—"

One of the daughters of a large and cheerful family with whom he had been friendly on the voyage met him as he was coming away from the purser's office.

"Have you been changing money too? They tell me there's nothing to buy but striped Indian blankets and native knives. At the dance last night the First said the Opera House is more or less like the one in Paris, but we mustn't miss the snake farm—"

Her father joined them. "You're coming ashore, of course? What about a cocktail at the Grand Hotel to begin the day?" Roger accepted the invitation, but the party, a very gay and noisy one, was joined on the way from the quay to the hotel by several other passengers, and he found it easy to slip away unnoticed.

He was much better for three weeks at sea. He did not shake or break into a cold sweat at any unexpected sound. He could write without having to steady his right hand with his left. He was getting over the shock as the specialist had prophesied he would, and it was too soon yet to have to think about what it would be like to go home.

He spoke to one of the waiters. "How do I get from here to the estancia Romero?"

Roger was no longer the rather shabby young clerk who had paid his first visit to his uncle's house in Hampshire. During the months he had spent under Mr. Frere's roof learning the management of the estate he had gained confidence. He still had a pleasant, friendly manner, but he knew how to give an order and see that it was carried out. The waiter seemed a sullen fellow. He shook his head and was turning away when Roger stopped him.

"You heard me. The way to the estancia Romero—"

"It is outside the town, in the hill country. A bad road. I cannot stay here, señor. I have to serve the customers, por Dios—"

Roger let him go. There were several taxis waiting outside the hotel entrance. He signalled to one of them. The driver leaned towards him cagily.

"I show you all the sights, señor, before boat go. Lovely girls, snake farm, all things—"

"I want you to drive me to the estancia Romero, wait there, and bring me back to the quay."

The man's face fell. "It is a long way, señor, and a bad road. Besides, there is nobody there. Don Juan Romero and his wife are in Europe—"

"Is your car likely to break down?"

"No, señor. She is a beautiful car, magnificent, colossal. Bump, bump. She no care."

"Then you can take me where I want to go. I'll pay you well—" Roger held up one of the ornamental but rather grubby notes he had got from the purser before he came ashore. "You shall have that over and above the fare. Compris?"

The little man licked his lips and his eyes glistened, but even then, as Roger was to recall later, he seemed to hesitate before making up his mind.

"Buenos," he reached down to open the door for his fare. "Enter, Señor."

Roger took a cigarette from his case as they swerved abruptly into the stream of traffic. He was pleased to find that his hands were quite steady. This was only the second time he had been in a car since the accident. Sybyl had been driving herself in the little two-seater that had been his birthday present. She had not passed the test yet and he was beside her, enjoying her pride and pleasure in her new toy. He had warned her not to accelerate. She had laughed at him. "You darling old tortoise—"

He bit his lip hard. He must not go through that again. They left the comparative coolness of the public gardens, the tree-lined avenues, the statues, the bandstand. The metalled road ended and the shabby taxi ploughed forward, rattling and grunting and raising a cloud of red dust. Roger hastily let down the windows and leaned back, closing his eyes to keep out the blinding glare of the treeless plain. Dark, naked children darted from the wayside hovels as the car came in sight and ran beside it for a little way holding out grimy hands for coins.

Then, after a turn to the left, they began to climb. The rood went up the densely wooded hillside in a series of hairpin bends. It was silent and deserted. They toiled up in a greenish twilight as through a tunnel burrowed out of malachite. The driver stopped with a grinding of brakes before a great gate of closely wrought iron set between stone gate posts in a high brick wall.

"The estancia Romero."

Roger got out. "You will wait here to take me back."

The man glanced about him uneasily. "How long will you be, Señor?"

"I don't know."

"We should leave here by four o'clock at the latest. It is not safe to cross the bad lands after the sun has gone down."

"Very well."

Roger rung the bell and a dark-faced man servant came out of the lodge.

Roger asked if Miss Holland was at home and proffered his card. The servant vanished and came hack in a few minutes to take him up a winding drive between banks of scented flowering shrubs to the house.

The house had its usual breath-taking effect. Roger gazed up at the bewildering conglomeration of colonnades, loggias and cupolas and murmured "Gosh!"

He entered a vast pillared hall with doors open at either end and mirrors in the panelled walls that reflected an embarrassing number of young men in pale grey slacks and lemon silk sports shirts, and found himself on the threshold of a small dining-room furnished in the style of Louis Quinze, shaking hands with Celia Holland.

"How wonderful to see you here," she said eagerly. "I could hardly believe it when Manuel brought in your card—"

"I'm on a cruise," he explained. "They've allowed the passengers a day on land here so I thought I'd look you up. In fact I promised your father I would if I was anywhere near."

"You can stay to lunch then? Splendid. These are my pupils. The Señorita Maria and the Señorita Pilar Romero—"

He shook hands gravely with the two fragile little olive-skinned girls.

They sat down to lunch, waited on by Metcalfe, large, dignified and impassive as if visitors from England arrived every day, and Manuel.

"How is Father—really, I mean—he always says he's quite well."

"You needn't worry about him, Miss Holland. He looked very fit when I last saw him. He felt my uncle's death, but there's a

Major Enderby at the White Cottage now. I believe they play chess together—"

"And—every thing is all right? I mean—you're settling down comfortably?" she ventured. She thought, he was looking thin and worn and she remembered her father's hints of possible difficulties that might arise after Mr. Frere's death.

He answered quietly without meeting her eyes. "I thought you might have heard—"

"I haven't had any letters for six weeks. The post has been very uncertain lately—"

He glanced at the two little girls who sat on her right and left, silent and attentive, and said, "I'd like to tell you later perhaps—"

She understood. "There's a summer-house on the lower terrace facing the sea. It's the coolest place in the afternoon. I sit there and read. Maria and Pilar are supposed to lie down. Run along now to Catarina, children."

They lifted small, expectant faces to be kissed before they fluttered out together like white butterflies in their short, lace frocks. Roger watched them go with some amusement.

"How solemn they are."

"They are terribly excited really. They've never seen an Englishman before—except Metcalfe, of course, and they've known him all their lives."

"Is that the butler?"

"Yes. He's a sort of steward and maggiordomo here. Señor Romero trusts him absolutely. He draws money from the Bank to pay all the current expenses, and runs the whole show. He approves of me fortunately, though at first I think he considered me rather young for my job here."

"Your employers—the parents of those two little girls—are still in Europe?"

"Yes. She had a nervous breakdown here. She says she can only breathe in Paris."

The gardens, laid out on the steep hillside, had been terraced and joined by flights of marble steps. "This place must have cost a packet," Roger said as he followed Celia down to the summer-house.

"It's marvellous, isn't it. Señor Romero's grandfather built it. He was awfully rich because of the rubber boom. There's a high brick wall all round."

"You don't get a shut in feeling?"

"No. I like to think it keeps the snakes out."

There were steel tubular chairs in the summer-house and shiny blue cushions. Celia took one of her visitor's cigarettes and sighed contentedly as she leaned back. "It's nice having someone from home to talk to."

"You must feel lonely at times."

"I'm very fond of the children," she said, "they are dear little souls, and very quick and intelligent. It's fun teaching them. And I've got books and a piano. And every luxury. I like that, I'm afraid. And I'm saving money that will be useful later on. That's enough about me. You were going to tell me something."

"Yes," he said. "I feel I can talk to you somehow, though we've only met once before. Do you remember that evening when you came to dine with the vicar? It was just before you came over here. Of course, your father has often talked to me about you—" he broke off and resumed, leaning forward, with his hands loosely clasped between his knees, and following with his eyes the wanderings of a tiny insect creeping about the white marble floor. "I never got on very well with my stepmother and my half-brother Cedric. I try-but everything I do is wrong somehow. But my half-sister Sybyl and I were always the best of friends. We were so poor—she didn't have much fun—I always looked forward to giving her a good time. We were going to do heaps of things together. You know my uncle wouldn't see any of them. He was adamant about that. Of course he knew they would come when he was gone. Well—I gave Sybyl a car for her birthday. She had learned to drive. We went out in it together. I drove for a bit and then she took over. I warned her to be careful, but she—I don't really know what happened. It was in the Forest and nobody saw. I fancy one of the ponies came out suddenly on the road and she swerved to avoid it—when I came to I was in a nursing-home in Southampton. I'd had slight concussion and some bruises. I asked after Sybyl. They wouldn't tell me at first. I knew what that meant. She was—killed outright. Thank God for that anyhow. She didn't suffer."

"How terrible for you," murmured Celia. "I'm so sorry—"

"I had grown very fond of my uncle," he said, "but apart from him Sybyl was the only person I cared about. I loved her. She and Cedric never hit it off, and her mother always seemed to think more of him. But after the accident she—my stepmother—came to see me. She—she was like a mad woman. She said I'd planned it, that I meant her to kill herself—that she hoped the thought of what I had done would haunt me to my dying day—"

"She didn't mean it," said Celia quickly, "she didn't know what she was saying. The shock—you must forget it—"

"I'm trying to. That's why I came on this cruise. She's living at the Court with Cedric. I can't turn them out, and I can't go back and live under the same roof with them while she's in such a state—" he said hopelessly.

Celia was indignant. "But it wasn't your fault. And it is your house."

"You see," he said laboriously, "when we started, Sybyl and I, I was driving. Later on we changed places, but it seems there was nothing to show as we were both thrown clear, only I landed in the bracken and Sybyl was flung against a tree. My stepmother refuses to believe that I wasn't still at the steering wheel, that I wasn't entirely responsible for the accident."

"But even if you had been—accidents happen and the drivers aren't always to blame—" argued Celia.

"I know. But she said that I was deliberately trying to shift the blame on to my—my victim, and that such meanness would be incredible to many, but it wasn't to her, knowing me so well."

"She sounds—horrible," said Celia. "I don't see why you should have to live with her after this. Can't you make her an adequate allowance on condition that she leaves the Court?"

"I don't know," he said hopelessly. "She likes it there. And I suppose she has some excuse for being bitter. After all, she was my father's wife, and her son is the next heir. We're on fairly civil terms normally. Perhaps when I get back it won't be so bad. She must know perfectly well that I would have done anything in the world to save Sybyl. The fact is she was jealous of our being such pals."

"She was just raving," said Celia. "I'm sure you needn't reproach yourself—"

Roger looked at her gratefully. "You're helping me a lot." He talked on, encouraged by her eager sympathy, and neither of them noticed the passage of time. Roger exclaimed in dismay when at looked at his wrist watch.

"Five minutes to four, and my driver said we must leave then at the latest. I can't tell you how much—" he broke off as the butler came round the side of the summerhouse to the open colonnade facing them.

Celia looked up at him. "Metcalfe—what's the matter? What has happened?"

He looked like a man recovering from a heart attack. His breathing was heavy and his usually florid complexion had faded to a sickly yellowish grey. "Will you come up to the house at once, miss, and you too, sir—"

Celia sprang up. "What is it? The children? there been an accident?"

"We can't waste time talking," he said thickly. He stumbled as he turned to go back and Roger took his arm to support him.

"All right. Take it easy. We're coming with you—"

As they went up the long flight of steps to the upper terrace he said: "Thank you, sir. I'm a bit shaky about the knees. I'm glad you're here for Miss Holland's sake—"

"If you could give us some idea of what the trouble is—"

"I don't know for certain myself, sir. I can only guess. I went to my room as usual when the lunch was cleared away and lay down. When I woke from my nap I rang. One of the servants always brings up a cup of tea. I waited and I rang again, but nobody came. I went down to the servants' quarters and found that the dirty dishes and saucepans had been left piled up in the sink and that they had gone. What's more, they've taken their belongings. The cook's picture of the Holy Virgin in a gilt frame that she sets such store on, Manuel's dominoes that he keeps in the dresser drawer—"

"What does it mean?" asked Roger. "Are they striking for higher wages or something?"

Metcalfe shook his head. "No. They were very well paid. They'd no cause for complaint."

"Well, then—"

"They're afraid, sir, because of what happened here before."

Before Metcalfe could answer Celia said, "Not Catarina. She wouldn't leave the children. I'll run up to the nursery and make sure. That's the first thing—"

She was gone before they could stop her. The two men remained in the hall.

Roger was unpleasantly impressed by the deathly silence of the great house and by the butler's only too evident terror. He said, "What did happen here? We don't want to alarm Miss Holland, but now's your chance to be a little more explicit."

Metcalfe moistened his lips and glanced about him uneasily. "When the last revolution broke out Señor Romero's grandparents were living here with an unmarried daughter and the old lady's widowed niece and the family chaplain. Don Juan was away in Europe. A part of the army had revolted under the leadership of Carlo Fernandez. There has been a blood feud between the Fernandez family and the Teraltas and Romeros for generations. Some of the insurgents arrived here. The household was taken by surprise. Some of the servants escaped into the jungle and perhaps a few were in league with the attackers. One never knows. The rest were driven with the family into a room at the end of that corridor. The murderers wanted to save their ammunition, so they were battered to death with the butt ends of their muskets."

"Good God!" said Roger. "How ghastly."

"Like the Tsar and his family," said Metcalfe. "I've often thought that. The insurrection was soon put down, and the president sent a party up here as soon as he could to find out what had happened. The bodies were taken away and burned in the Campo Santo on the other side of the city. Don Juan cabled orders that the room should be left as it was. He had an altar set up there and a priest comes up every year on the day it happened to celebrate a mass for the souls of all who died there. It's kept locked up, but the Señora persuaded her husband to let her go in once. It was a mistake. It upset her nerves so that he had to take her away and they've been in Europe, barring a couple of flying visits, ever since. It's a part of my duties to go in once a year to air the room before the priest comes. It's not a nice thing to see, sir." Metcalfe licked his lips again and the whites of his eyes showed like those of a frightened horse as he glanced over his shoulder. "The walls," he whispered, "splashed with blood up to the ceiling."

And he's left his children here alone, with only you and a girl to look after them," said Roger incredulously.

"He—everyone said there was no danger of it happening again. Only just lately there have been rumours. Besides, we're on the telephone now."

"Of course. The telephone. We'd better ring up the police, hadn't we—"

He went to meet Celia who was coming down the stairs.

"Catarina and the children are gone. What shall we do?"

Metcalfe joined them. "Any—any signs of a struggle?"

Celia shook her head. "No. Some of their clothes have been taken. Pilar's favourite doll isn't there and Maria's teddy bear—"

Metcalfe drew a long breath. "That's something. I don't think we need worry about them at the moment. Catarina wouldn't let them come to harm, and the Indians have plenty of bolt holes. They'll be safer with her than with us, I daresay. We've got to think of ourselves now."

"Is it another revolution?"

"It looks that way to me, miss. I'd better see if I can find out what's going on in the city."

He went over to the telephone and took down the receiver. "Hallo, Hallo . . ."

"Can't you get anybody?" asked Roger when they had waited some time.

"No. The line's as dead as mutton. I expect it's been cut. It cost Señor Romero a good bit having it brought up here."

"I'd better find out what's happened to my taxi driver," said Roger. "He hasn't been paid so he's hardly likely to have left. I shan't be a minute—"

He ran down the drive between the high banks of flowering shrubs. The great wrought iron gates were closed but not locked and there was no key. The taxi had gone, apparently before the servants left, for the marks of tyres in the soft red dust were partly obliterated by the prints of bare feet going not down the road but across it to be swallowed up in the dense undergrowth of the jungle. Roger noticed a small blue object stuck in a patch of petrol and picked it up. It was a doll's blue kid shoe. He picked it up and went back to the house.

He found Celia alone in the hall. "Metcalfe's gone to the garage to see if the cars are all right. He thinks we'd better try to get down to the city, but I don't like the idea of leaving without knowing what has become of the children," she said anxiously. "What does your taxi man say?"

"He's bunked. Look, I found this just outside the gate."

She took the shoe from him. "Yes. That belongs to Pilar's doll. That shows they're not hidden anywhere in the house—"

"I suppose this butler fellow is on the level?"

"Oh yes—" she broke off as the door that shut off the hall from the servants' quarters swung open and Metcalfe rejoined them. "The two cars in the large garage are out of action. The petrol has been run off and the tyres slashed with a knife. Señor Romero has always allowed me to keep the Ford in the little garage for my own use. I've been keeping it locked lately as I fancied the petrol was going quicker than it should since Fernando's been here. We'll have to use that. She'll need more juice before long, but there may be just enough to get us into the town."

Celia hesitated. "We're in charge here. Couldn't we lock the gates and barricade ourselves in the house and hold it until help comes? We don't even know that we shall be attacked."

"It might even be safer here," said Roger, "if they are fighting in the streets and raking the plaza with machine-guns. I'm inclined to agree with Miss Holland, Metcalfe."

"What about the boat, sir? She'll be sailing tonight. Will they wait for you?"

"No. They warned us about that. They run to schedule. Probably if there's trouble in the city the passengers have been rounded up and taken on board by this time. But I'm travelling alone. There's nobody to get the wind up if I miss the bus."

"It's one of these pleasure cruises, isn't it, sir? Not ordinary passengers?"

"Yes. Why?"

"Miss Holland and I are British subjects. The Captain couldn't refuse to take us. Is that agreed, sir? If we get separated the ship is our goal. What's her name?"

"The *Cerne Abbey*. It's the Abbey Line."

"Have you a dark coat, miss, to wear over that light dress? Will you get it now? I don't suppose we've over-much time."

"Oh dear," said Celia. "Are we doing the right thing? I'd rather stay, and Mr. Frere thinks as I do—though I don't want to make him miss his boat—"

"He doesn't know these people, miss, and I do. You'll have to do as I tell you if you want to save your skins," he added roughly.

Roger could not blame him. The veneer of the well-trained servant was cracking under the strain, and whether his growing panic was justified or not, there was no doubting that it was genuine. "All right," he said. "Somebody must lead, and you know the ropes. We'll come. Fetch your coat, Celia." He waited for her at the foot of the stairs while Metcalfe went off to get the car. He glanced about him at the painted ceiling, the gilt chandeliers, the velvet curtains screening the entrance to the corridor, running the length of the house, to the secret room with the walls caked with dried blood that lay at the core of all this display of wealth like a canker at the heart of a rose. The silence was unbearable. He knew that, whatever befell them outside, the butler had been right. They could not wait there with those memories, like crowding ghosts, behind a locked door.

Chapter V
ESCAPE

NIGHT had fallen swiftly, like a black curtain while they were still going down the winding road to the plain. Metcalfe was driving very slowly and with what seemed to Roger, excessive caution. He leaned forward to say, "You're using up a lot of petrol this way—"

Metcalfe answered curtly, keeping his eyes on the road. "I'll get a move on when we get away from the trees. It'd be easy for these devils to fasten a rope to the trunk of a palm and take it across."

But when they were out of the wood and on level or comparatively level ground their progress was still exasperatingly slow. Roger and Celia sat looking out of the windows and seeing nothing but their own reflections in the glass. The girl had hardly spoken a word since they left the house. After a while the car stopped.

"What's wrong?" asked Roger. "Engine stalled?"

Metcalfe made no reply. He got out heavily and came to them after a moment to report: "We've run out of petrol. I was afraid we might. I'm going to switch off the headlights now. We'll be safer in the dark—"

Roger helped Celia out and they all stood together by the roadside. He could hear the butler's stertorous breathing on his right, and on his left a quick sigh from the girl. "Is it always like this? I can't see my hand before my face."

"There should be stars, but clouds have come up. Let's hope it doesn't rain," said Metcalfe. "I've seen some of these dry river beds turned into raging torrents in twenty minutes. Now I'll tell you—we're some miles out of the city, but we should be able to cut across country from here to the coast and find a fisherman who'll be only too glad to row us out to the *Cerne Abbey*. I've been thinking over what you said about getting mixed up in street fighting, sir. We can't do better than make our way to the beach and hire a boat."

"Won't it be very rough going for Miss Holland?" said Roger doubtfully.

"At the end of the dry season it's nothing but waste ground. Lots of gulleys, of course. We might get into one and follow it down to the sea—but the Indians say they're full of snakes," muttered Metcalfe.

"Anyway—I've been thinking," said Celia. "I'm not going to leave the country until I know what has happened to the children. I'm going to the town for help."

"You're right," said Roger. "We can't do a bunk and leave them to it. Aren't there any filling stations along this road, Metcalfe?"

"There is one about a mile on from here," said the butler after a pause and with evident reluctance, "but the fellow who keeps it may be on the other side. He's a surly brute at any time. I'm as fond of those little girls as anyone, you should know that, Miss Holland, but they'll be safe with Catarina in one of the Indian villages hidden away in the jungle until the troubles are over. If the army has revolted the city will be in the hands of Fernandez and his lot, and if they shot us out of hand we'd be lucky."

"We'll have to chance it," said Roger. "We'll go straight to the British Consulate. I agree with Miss Holland. The children may be all right. I hope they are. But so long as we don't know we can't leave. I'll walk on and wangle a tin of petrol if you stay here. I daresay I can make them understand what I want."

"No, sir. If you're determined about this—and I think, if you'll excuse the liberty, you're being foolish—you'd best remain here along with Miss Holland, and I'll go."

"Very well," said Roger. "Tell them I'll make it worth their while if there's any difficulty."

"Very good, sir." Metcalfe who, for a while, had been a fellow human being, had clearly withdrawn, resentful that they were not taking his advice. They were left with a well-trained servant carrying out an order. They heard the faint creaking of his shoes grow fainter as he moved away and cease as he stopped.

"Miss Holland—"

"Yes, Metcalfe?"

"I wouldn't sit in the car if I were you. Take a couple of cushions and go a little off the road. And if I'm not back within an hour don't wait any longer. Carry on as you think best."

Oh, Metcalfe, shall we come with you? We will—"

"No, miss. I expect Mr. Frere will be able to take care of you better than I should. Goodbye, miss, and good luck. You and me got along together very nicely—"

She called to him again but this time there was no answer. "Oh dear," said Celia with tears in her voice. "He sounds as if he felt sure he would be killed. Ought we to go after him? I don't like this one little bit."

"I think we had better stay where we are," said Roger. "I'll get out a couple of cushions as he suggested—" Fumbling in the darkness they got into a ditch and climbed over a bank and made themselves as comfortable as circumstances permitted. The heat was so oppressive that Roger, unused to the climate, was streaming with sweat even after that slight exertion. "I can't think how you've stood this country so long," he said as he wiped his face and neck.

"I've had electric fans and ice, and servants to wait on me. It's awful not to know what's happening, isn't it?"

"I suppose that dim, reddish blur on our right is what we're trying to make for?"

"It must be. The main street and the Plaza del Conquistador are always very brightly lit, and there are the cinemas. I believe there is an Italian company at the Opera House, too, this week. I saw the posters last week when I went in with Maria and Pilar. We saw a Silly Symphony at the Reale. Funny. It seems years ago, and it was only last Thursday."

"Listen—do you hear anything?"

In the ensuing silence they could both distinguish barely audible sounds, an intermittent crackling and a murmur no louder than the voice of the sea in a shell.

"We shall be all right," said Roger cheerfully. "Let them fight it out. We're English."

Celia said nothing. He felt her shudder as something rustled in the dust close to them. It might be a harmless lizard or a deadly coral snake. They had no means of knowing and they could only sit very still until the furtive movements ceased. "I suppose I'm a fool," whispered Celia with a shaky little laugh, "but I can't help imagining a python curled up on the edge of my skirt. I wish now that we'd stayed in the car. How long has he been gone?"

Roger looked at the luminous dial of his watch.

"Only just over forty minutes. Are you up in these local politics?"

"Not really. I know that General Peralta's party has been in power for several years. That's our side. Señora Romero is his niece. But the Romeros have not taken any active part in the government. They're young and like to enjoy themselves. The Señora's nerves go wrong directly they leave Paris. Next year I believe I'm to take the children to Europe. They'll be old enough to go to school."

"What do you know about the other side?"

"Nothing much. There was somebody called Fernandez who led the last rising. He was caught and executed when it was put down, but his son and his nephew escaped. I think Metcalfe must have heard rumours, that they had come back and were stirring up trouble. He's been very worried these last few weeks. He says once things start here they are pretty bad because the mixture of Spanish and Indian blood makes people very callous about—about the infliction of pain—"

Roger felt for her hand and, having found it, gave it a reassuring squeeze.

"We'll be all right," he assured her. "Being English—as I said just now—"

"Poor old England," she murmured, "nobody minds her these days, but I've often wished I was home."

They were silent for a while. Then she said, suddenly betraying a feverish impatience. "How much longer?"

Roger, who had already surreptitiously looked at his watch, said, "He's been gone five minutes over the hour now."

"If he's been killed I shall feel we've sent him to his death."

"If you ask me," said Roger, "I don't think he meant to come back. He was peeved with us for not agreeing to make for the coast from here. I'm fairly certain that he's gone off on his own. I was rather struck at the time by the way he said goodbye. It would have been better if he had been frank about it, but you must blame his training for that. Butlers aren't supposed to argue, and they don't get any opportunity. They say, 'Very good, sir,' to their employer, even when they mean 'Lousy,' and they give orders to the other servants."

'Poor Metcalfe," said the girl, "he was frightfully upset. He's run the house so beautifully, and he's looked forward to going home and buying a country inn, and he's got his savings in notes in an oilskin bag. He doesn't trust banks. I do hope he'll get safely out to the ship before she leaves. You should have gone too. You stopped here because of me. Have I been a pig?"

"Don't be a little idiot. You were absolutely right. Anyway, here we are, and the question is what do we do now?"

"Walk along the road towards the town. He may have been delayed. We may still meet him coming back to us."

"Yes," he said, "That seems the best, the only thing."

He made her take his arm and they trudged forward, keeping to the fairly level ground between the deep ruts scored in the early spring by the passage of lorries bringing laden cases from the great meat-canning factory forty miles farther up the coast to be shipped from San Rinaldo. There were traces, too, of the passage of the herds on their yearly trek to and from the great upland pastures. Now and again one or other of them trod on bones that cracked under their feet like dead wood. Their eyes were, by now, sufficiently accustomed to the darkness to enable them to distinguish the posts that carried the barb-wire fences on either side of the track and an occasional gate, and after a while a low one-storey building loomed on their left behind an advance guard of robot like objects that proved to be petrol-pumps. There were no lights anywhere. The place appeared to be closed down and deserted.

"There was a dog," said Celia, "he was barking and dragging at his chain when we passed—"

They found the kennel with a length of chain attached, but the dog was gone.

Roger had struck three matches to help them in their search, and then, in stumbling over the rough ground, the box had been knocked out of his hand. He stooped and felt about for it but failed to find it.

"We had better go on, I think," he said, "and try to get to the town on foot. Do you think you a manage it?"

"Of course. I used to walk a lot at home in the Forest. Let's be going. This place is creepy."

Roger agreed. There was something he had not told her. When he was groping about on the ground for his matches his fingers had come in contact with some viscous liquid and then with a rough hairy hide. The dog's body had been lying behind the kennel. Neither of them referred again to Metcalfe. They both knew they must have met him on the road if he had meant to come back to them. They were about a mile farther along the road when a light was flashed in their eyes. They stopped instinctively but not before Roger had moved in front of Celia to shield her.

A hoarse voice addressed them with unctuous civility. "Anglisch, no? On ze feet, on zis road, at zis hour? You give explanation, sare, damn queek, and oblige?"

"If you'll stop blinding us with that torch," said Roger irritably. "Yes, we're English. Our car broke down, and there wasn't anybody at that garage a mile back. And who may you be?"

"I spik your talk good, vary nice, no?" said the voice complacently while the white ray of light moved deliberately over them both. "You come off boat zat landed passengers, no? 'Ow much you pay me to get you back before boat sail?"

"Have you a car?"

"'Ow much if I save your lives? I run great peril, too. You go a little more along this road and meet big crowd. Some have guns, all 'ave knives. Carve you, keep her for when zere is time."

"That will do," said Roger savagely. "We don't need your help. Come on, Celia—"

But the figure dimly discernible behind the light still barred their way.

"No, sare, please, sare, you got me wrong. I spik true," urged the voice, "I swear to you, por Dios, if you go on, you die."

"They daren't touch English people. We don't belong to either side—"

"To-morrow maybe zey'll be sober, and zen vary sorry for being so 'asty," the voice agreed, "but to-night tigers zat 'ave tasted blood. To-night zey kill and burn."

As Roger hesitated they all heard what had seemed before like the murmur of the sea in a shell; it was louder now and unmistakable, the roar of an angry mob.

"All right," he said, "five pounds when we're safe on board the *Cerne Abbey*."

"Too bally cheap," said the voice. "You pay on beach ten pounds."

"Very well."

"Buenos. Follow me. Keep close—"

The light was switched off. Their self-appointed guide was opening a gate. "I am Pedro, you no find anyone better, matador, waiter in first-class restaurant, chucker-out dance club. You know Shaftesbury Avenue? Vary nice part. I sorry to leave—"

Roger gripped Celia's arm. "My God. I've placed him. He was on the quay this morning—" He knew now why the oily voice had been vaguely familiar. He had taken a violent dislike to the sallow individual in the shiny black suit and bright yellow shoes who, seeing that he did not belong to a party, had pursued him for some distance offering to take him to see all the sights "vary curious, vary interestin'—" and trying to make him look at indecent postcards. Roger, losing patience at last, had thrust him aside rather roughly and had left him snarling curses in a mixture of Spanish and Italian.

"Isn't he—"

"I wouldn't trust him a yard. Quick. We'll run for it—"

They ran along the road, stumbling over the ruts in the darkness, ignoring the voice that now altogether ceased to be mellifluous as it shouted to them to stop. After their first spurt of speed, they settled down to a steady trot until Roger felt the girl whom he was supporting with his arm beginning to flag. He paused then, still holding her for he was afraid that she would fall. He could feel her heart thudding against his side as she leant against him. His own breath was coming in gasps and he was streaming with sweat.

"All right?" he muttered presently.

"Yes. What was—that noise—like the crack of a whip? I heard it—three times—"

"I think he was shooting, probably more to relieve his feelings than with any hope of scoring a hit. You see, I'd been ass enough to let him know I had ten pounds on me. I fancy we've got well away from him now. I should say he's playing a lone hand and is as anxious to keep away from crowds as we are."

They could hear the tumult and the shouting more plainly now and there was a flickering red light on the horizon in the direction in which they were going.

"What is it, Roger? One of these wayside shacks on fire? There are several a mile or two on."

"It looks more like some kind of torchlight procession marching to meet us. All right, my dear, we'll get off the road soon and find some place to hide until they've passed—"

They moved forward doggedly, not running now, but shuffling through the thick red dust.

"Don't mind leaning on me, Celia—"

"I hate to be such a drag on you," she gasped.

"Rot. You're going splendidly. We both need a rest. I say—was that a spot of rain?"

Celia felt another on her face and a gentle pattering in the dust. She had been long enough in San Rinaldo to know what that meant. "Quick. We must find shelter. It may not last long, but while it does—"

A blue flash lit up the plain. It only lasted a split second but that was long enough to show them a ramshackle one-storeyed building standing in a patch of waste ground behind a crazy fence made of bones and rusty barbed wire.

"I don't know—" said Roger. "I didn't much care for the look of the people living in these shanties—" He remembered the sullen slatternly girls, the yelling children, the old man swollen with elephantiasis. But the advancing crowd was nearer than he had realised, and the mongrel dogs he had noticed tied up near many doors had started a chorus of barking interspersed with long-drawn howls, with an occasional sharp yelp, presumably when the owners came out to kick them into silence. His heart sank as he realised how unlikely they were to get any help from the inhabitants of this sinister suburb. The men had probably joined the mob, and the women and children were entrenched behind bolted doors and shuttered windows. Their chief hope lay in the possibility that the hovel they had just seen, the first they had come to since they passed the filling station, was unoccupied.

"All right," he said. "It may be empty, and certainly doesn't look worth looting. We'll have to chance it—"

Celia caught at his arm. "Somebody went in—or came out—just then," she whispered. "I heard the gate creak on its hinges—"

"I didn't hear anything. The rain has stopped. I think we'll have to go in here, Celia—"

"Very well—"

They found the gate and Roger closed it after them and they went stumbling over the rough ground towards the squat building that loomed before them, a shadow among shadow's. They were both uneasily aware of a faint, mephitic odour of decay. "I wish—" began Celia, and broke off, biting her lip.

Roger felt his way along the house wall. "Here's the door—" His hope that they would find the place deserted faded as he saw a thread of light through a crack in the crazy structure. Somebody within had just lit a lamp or a candle. He hesitated again, with a sense that he was about to do something irrevocable, of great issues depending on a simple action, before he rapped on the panels.

There was complete silence inside the hut and but for that betraying gleam of light he would have been sure that the place was empty. As it was, after waiting, he rapped again and said in bad Spanish, "We are English, passengers from the liner in the harbour. We have lost our way—"

There was still no answer, and the light went out.

"Not a warm welcome—" began Roger.

"Let's go away," said Celia eagerly, and had some difficulty in suppressing a scream as something touched her on the shoulder.

"Don't be afraid, Señorita. I shall not hurt you. I, too, am a fugitive, trying to escape from this horde of drunken fools." The soft, drawling voice, speaking English with a strong foreign accent, reminded Celia of Señora Romero. She was conscious of an overwhelming sense of relief.

"Was it you who came in just now? I heard the gate. I thought—I was afraid it was a horrible man we met further down the road. Our car broke down—"

"There are two of you, yes? Let me come to the door and speak to the person inside. She knows me and she will let us in—" They moved aside and the newcomer knocked on the door and spoke rapidly in the Indian dialect. Her voice when she spoke the native tongue sounded harsher and more urgent. It became apparent to both Roger and Celia as they listened without understanding that she, too, was afraid. It was too dark to see her, but they knew instinctively that she was young and that she came of the class that is more used to giving than to carrying out orders. She was sure of herself to the point of arrogance.

The bolts were being drawn very slowly and fumblingly. The door opened inwards. The darkness within was profound and the stale air thick with the same choking odour of decay.

Celia's gorge rose. "I—I'd rather stay outside—"

"And wait and see what that crowd will do to you? The smell is bad, I know, but it won't hurt you. We need only stay here until they have gone by. Listen to me now. Stand still and be careful not to touch anything, not the furniture or the walls or the handle of the door. That is very important—"

They moved forward reluctantly. The voice spoke again in dialect, and the door was closed, shutting them in. The bolts were being pushed forward again not sharply, but with a series of dull thuds and to an accompaniment of shuffling sounds and of heavy breathing. So far the occupant of the hovel had not uttered a word. To Celia there was something pitiful in that silent and unquestioning obedience to a curt word of command, but she could not think about it clearly. Roger had slipped an arm about her and she leaned against him, thankful for his support as she tried to overcome the physical nausea induced by the appalling stench. The crowd was very near now. The shouts and yells had died down, but the tramp of marching feet shook the crazy structure.

The three fugitives waited silently until the sounds had grown faint in the distance. Then Roger said, "We have to thank you—"

"Yes. Conchita would not have opened her door for you. You could not have found a better hiding place. I know they would not dare come here. That scum would be afraid even when mad with drink as they are to-night, and for more than one reason. She was my nurse when I was little—"

"Why should they be afraid?" asked Roger curiously.

"Because of some things that you, who come from another country, would not understand or believe. You would say, 'Silly superstition'. And because she is a leper."

"Good God!" said Roger.

She laughed. "You believe in that? You English are so practical. Why did you think I warned you not to touch anything, not even the walls. Did you ask yourselves why she was clumsy over the drawing the bolts? All her fingers have dropped off. Shall I tell her to light a candle so that you can see her? She does not like to be looked at, but she will do anything for me."

"No. For heaven's sake, don't do that. Poor creature. Is money any use to her?"

"Yes."

"If I drop some on the ground she will find it—?"

"Then will you ask her to open the door and let us get out? Please tell her we are very grateful to her."

"Very well."

Another curt order in the guttural Indian dialect, followed by the painful laborious shuffling efforts of the crippled hands struggling with the rusty bolts. Roger bit his lip hard. He could feel Celia trembling. When they were outside he drew a long breath, the night air, tainted though it was by smells from the refuse heaps by the door, seemed incredibly sweet. A star shone, diamond bright through a rift in the black canopy of cloud.

"I suppose we can walk on to the town now," he said.

The drawling voice answered. "They will be fighting in the streets. It would be wiser to wait. The soldiers will shoot first and after that it will be too late for explanations. You come from that English liner in the bay?"

"Yes."

"We will go across country from here to the sea and steal a fisherman's boat," she said casually.

"Is that possible on such a dark night? We may wander round in circles," Roger objected.

She laughed. "I will show you. Follow me—"

She went forward unhesitatingly, with the ease of one who knows every foot of the way, stooping to creep under a barrier of barbed wire and flitting on again noiseless and swift as the shadow of a cloud passing over the earth. To the two who toiled in her wake, stumbling over the rough ground, there was something uncanny about her unerring progress across that deserted plain. The crowd had passed out of sight and hearing, following the road inland that would bring them eventually to the estancia Romero. Already they could hear the murmur of waves breaking on the beach.

"I suppose there must be a track though we can't see it," said Roger. "Is she going too fast for you to keep up, Celia?" Celia gritted her teeth. "No. But there's something very queer about this. Well brought up Spanish girls don't wander about like this at night. Roger, I don't like it. She can see in the dark—like a cat—"

"Lucky for us," he said. "Some people can."

The choking dust and the hard, sun-baked earth had given place to loose shingle, a cooler air with a salt tang in it fanned their faces. The sea lay before them like some huge, drowsy animal, hidden behind a black curtain, and moving a little in its sleep with a gentle stretching of sheathed claws.

Their guide was waiting for them.

"There is one boat here," she said. "I thought there might be. Presently we will push it down to the water. But first you may rest a little. You are tired, no? Out of breath—"

Roger, who had flung himself down on the sand, rolled over and looked up at her as she stood, a barely discernible figure, gazing out to sea.

"Aren't you? We've covered a couple of miles in record time, and it was rough going."

There was a lilt, a vibrant note of suppressed excitement in the soft, drawling voice when she answered, "I like to run and run in the night, to run and—" she broke off to listen. Far away a dog was howling. "Wait a minute," she said. "I will go and see if I can find the oars in José's shed-—" Roger lay back. "I must say she's marvellous. I wonder what the time is. The sea seems quite calm. When I think of all the gadgets of civilisation on board the *Cerne Abbey*. Shower baths, and one's steward bringing early tea. Celia, my dear, our troubles are nearly over. A long, long drink—"

"Don't," she said huskily.

"You've been wonderful. Cheer up, you won't have anything more to do," he said consolingly, "just sit in the boat while I row. It can't be far—just round the point. This was Metcalfe's plan. I wonder if he's been taken on board. I—"

He never finished his sentence. The black night crashed down on him, roaring, and a fountain of flame sprang up and was extinguished by a huge and overwhelming wave of pain.

Chapter VI
THE VALLEY OF THE SHADOW

CELIA sat alone on the beach staring stupidly at the red smears on the hand she had just lifted to her aching head. The hair on the nape of her neck was sticky and dotted and when her fingertips explored a little farther, passing gingerly over a lump that had not been there before, she felt a sharp stab of pain.

She was trying to remember what had happened the previous night. After leaving the leper woman's hut she and Roger had been brought across the plain by the girl. She had told them to lie down and rest on the sand while she went to find oars for the boat in which they were to make their way along the coast to the harbour. After that—what?

They had been followed and attacked, possibly by some marauders lagging behind the main body of the crowd, or even perhaps by the man who had accosted them on the road near the filling station. She had been struck on the head and had lost consciousness. What of Roger and the girl? There was a deep ridge in the soft sand down to the water's edge, showing that a boat had been launched recently. Another boat still lay where it had been drawn up above the tide level. Celia had been lying almost under it. As she struggled weakly to her feet she saw that it was half full of water and realised that it must have rained heavily and that but for the shelter it afforded she would have been drenched to the skin. She scooped up some water in the palm of her hand and sucked it up thirstily. It was brackish, but it seemed quite drinkable to her then. When she had drunk as much as she wanted she bathed her face and made some attempt to rinse the clotted blood out of her hair, but the effort reopened the wound on the back of her head and she had to tear a strip off her silk underslip and use it as a bandage. When she had tied it, she felt faint and had to sit down again and rest.

The sun had risen and already the heat was intense in that little landlocked bay. She knew that she would have to move very soon to find some shade. She would have to fend for herself now. She had no hope that Roger and the strange girl who had led them to that place would ever return. They had been murdered and their bodies thrown into the sea. Their assailants had gone away in the boat, and if they came back she would be killed, too. They had probably left her for dead.

Things like that happened while revolutions were going on, and no enquiries were made. Poor Roger. He had been very unhappy. He had been dreading going back to England. "But they'll need proof of his death," thought Celia dully. She stumbled to her feet again presently and wandered away along the beach until she came to the edge of a broad and shallow lagoon formed by the outlet of a stream flowing down one of the many deep ravines that broke up the coast line. She turned inland then, too thankful at first for the cooler air of that sunless cleft filled with the murmur of running water to notice its sinister likeness to the entrance to a trap. Her plan, so far as she had a plan, was to find her way back to the road they had left last night. She believed that in broad daylight she would be safe from attack and that if her strength held out and she was able to walk the three or four miles into the city, she could apply for help and advice at the British Consulate.

The plain, as she was beginning to realise, was not on the sea level. The walls of rock on either side of the stream soared up to a height of from sixty to a hundred feet, and after heavy rains the ledges on either side would be swept clear of the accumulation of refuse that covered them now by a rush of water coming down from the mountains to leave in its wake a fresh trail of uprooted trees and bushes and posts and rails festooned with straggling ends of broken wire and the bodies of drowned cattle and goats. The bones of last year's victims had been picked clean by the vultures, or perhaps by the piranha, the dreaded cannibal fish of the South American rivers. Celia, shuddering, saw a small green snake glide away between the white shining ribs of the carcass of an ox lying right across her path. A quarter of a mile farther on the walls of the cleft closed in and the river was spanned by a frail native bridge of twisted lianas swaying in mid-air like a thread spun from a spider's web. Celia had never seen one before but she had heard that the Indians could make one in a few hours and that it would then be used by any who cared to risk their lives on it until it broke.

While she stood looking at it and wondering if she would be able to screw up her courage to attempt to cross, a man emerged from a cranny in the rock near the bridge and, after pausing to light a cigarette, strolled along the ledge, which had been cleared of rubbish at this point, to meet her.

He was a seedy-looking individual dressed in dingy black and wearing a broad-brimmed hat tilted over his eyes. As he came nearer he bared strong teeth stained brown with tobacco in a mirthless grin.

"So we meet again, Señorita." He made no attempt to remove his hat. "It will be more nice, I zink, wizout ze boy friend. Ze crowd took 'im, no? You 'ad spot of trouble, yes?"

He sat down on a flat stone and drew at his cigarette. Celia sat down, too, on another stone. It was better to do that before her knees gave way under her. She said nothing.

"It was foolish to run away from Pedro, so you turn a good friend into an enemy. Zat is always foolish. You promise ten pounds—and you no pay. I bring you down 'ere to vary safe place, superfine—'ow you say?—bolt 'ole until rains come, an treat you like a caballero. But no—you run like silly rabbits, and make me a double cross. An so the crowd get you, an' serve you damn well right." The venom with which he uttered those last words was extraordinary.

Celia sat very still. She felt cold and sick with fear. Pedro's eyes were black as jet beads. They were fixed on her while he spoke with a kind of cold, appraising stare. He was gloating over her misery, over the white face drawn with fatigue and framed by the clumsy bandages, over the torn and filthy dress and shoes cut on the sharp-edged rocks, with one sole flapping loose.

"Ze crowd knock ze stuffing out of you, no? You like a crushed grape-skin with the blasted English pride squeezed out. I thought they'd kill you both. You must be—'ow you say—vary tough." He laughed, and then in a more business-like manner he resumed. "You 'ave no money left? Hidden in your stocking, in the lining of your stays? Don't lie to me. I shall find out."

She shook her head.

"You are a cheat. You rob me of ten pounds; me, Pedro. You pay me, not in money, but in kind."

She watched him dumbly. In her tired brain the terrified thoughts fluttered and dashed themselves like birds against a net. She watched the lean, sallow face marked with the lines of dissipation, of the vice that had spoilt him for the arena, the bony, spatulate fingers stained brown with nicotine, rolling another cigarette. Some instinct aroused by her desperate need, warned her to be silent, to do nothing, to conserve every remaining atom of her strength.

Pedro was in no hurry. He was enjoying himself. He had a chance at last to avenge all the humiliations he had endured day after day on the quay when the passengers landed from liners for a few hours on shore.

"Come wiz me, sare. I show you sometin' vary nice, vary new—"

He had been thrust aside, told to get out, threatened with the police. The police of San Rinaldo.

"Your ship she 'as sailed, Señorita. She went at midnight one hour after time. Maybe they sent a boat's crew on shore under first officer to search in bad 'ouses for missing passengers. That 'appen sometime, but if they can't find they no wait. Everybody else rounded up early in the afternoon when the shooting began in the streets, and taken back to the ship damn' quick. You had all been warned not to go into private 'ouses to play cards or watch native dance, not to drive out on any road farther than the Snake Park. So now what?"

She moistened her lips before she could speak. "I'm hungry—" He laughed as he searched in his pockets and produced half a bar of chocolate wrapped in a crumpled bit of silver paper.

"Say thank you very much, dear Pedro."

She repeated the words after him. obediently. "Thank you very much, dear Pedro."

He threw the chocolate over to her. It fell short. She picked it up and ate it ravenously.

"I have some tinned stuff in the cave," he said carelessly. "I will fetch you a tin of beans. Soon you will love me vary much. I will keep you down 'ere wiz me for a few days, until ze rains. Zen I take you to someone I know in a street behind ze Opera, an' I say, Madame, here is a nice girl, young, not beautiful, but well trained. You only 'ave to show 'er ze whip an' she jomps, she jomps through ze paper hoop. An' she will give me ten pounds, an' my honour zat 'as been wounded will be satisfied. So." And he nodded to her with the same devilish smile, lazy and satisfied.

Celia said, "Can I have the beans now?"

He was pleased to find her so docile. He had never before had an English girl at his mercy. Girls of the Latin race were not so easy to manage, they scratched and bit and shrieked voluble abuse until a blow silenced them. This one had been terrified to the verge of imbecility. It was time to slacken the strain. And so—"Why not?" he said, and rose and turned and went into his den where he kept his stack of tinned foods under his camp bed. He still moved with some vestiges of the lithe grace that had made him for a while an idol of the bull-ring. He had stuck his half-smoked cigarette behind his ear and he was whistling a tango from a record that was often played in that house where so much was to be seen that was nice and new.

Celia, meanwhile, stood up. Her mouth hung open and her eyes were fixed. She looked almost idiotic, but she moved with the unswerving certainty of one who has summoned all her forces and concentrated them on one object. She slipped off her shoes, ran across the ledge and started across the bridge, clinging to the second strand that was slung at about the level of her shoulders to be used as a hand rail. The twisted lianas under her feet sagged and swayed sickeningly, and looking down, she was made dizzy by the dark water swirling over the stones. In the middle the bridge curving under her weight almost touched the surface of the stream which at this spot had widened into a pool.

She was just scrambling on to the opposite ledge where the two ropes were fastened to a tree rooted in a crevice of the rock when Pedro came out of the cave and saw her.

He shouted something, and his voice echoed from wall to wall of the ravine. Celia, turning to see what he would do, felt her heart sink as he swung himself out on to the bridge in pursuit. "I will teach you to play tricks—"

The rock walls echoed the threat.

Celia, crouching on her hands and knees at the foot of the tree that grew slanting outward over the water, made no answer, but she reached for a sharp edged stone and sawed away desperately at the upper rope. The twisted strands of lianas were rotten with age and broke easily. As the rope dropped Pedro made a violent effort to keep his balance, staggered, and fell into the pool.

He went under and came up at once, spluttering curses and dashing the water out of his eyes. Celia, in growing panic, saw that he was a strong swimmer and that he would easily reach a place where he could land and climb up to her. And then—something happened—the water of the pool boiled up all round him with a flashing of wet fins and gleaming, lightning-swift bodies hurling themselves on their living prey Pedro screamed once

and vanished while the whole surface of the river was churned
up into a crimson froth.

Celia shrank back, appalled, covering her face with her hands.
She heard a voice that she did not recognise as her own, whisper, "Piranha—"

Chapter VII
BEHIND THE SCENES

When Celia entered the city several hours later, order had been
restored. She had often read this phrase in newspapers and had
assumed too easily that it meant that life was going on as usual. In
San Rinaldo it connoted a state of suspended animation, a sinister hang-over after the dance of death. That was no traffic in the
streets except for the trams which were running empty, driven by
soldiers, with other soldiers lying on the roof with machine guns.
Houses and shops were closed and shuttered. In several places,
especially at street corners where hasty barricades of household
furniture and mattresses had been overthrown and set alight after
being drenched with petrol, there were reddish brown stains of
dried blood, and more than once she passed a scuffling mass of
vultures picking the bones of a dead horse or mule. Her senses
were by this time so numbed by the shocks she had sustained and
by sheer physical fatigue that nothing she saw made any great
impression. Her goal was the British Consulate. There she would
be safe and she would be told what to do.

But there were soldiers on guard at the end of the narrow street
that led to the Consulate, and they would not let her pass. She
tried in her halting Spanish to explain that she was an English
subject, but they only laughed at her and mimicked her efforts.
Very soon they lost patience and one of them threatened her with
his bayonet, and she was afraid and turned away. As she passed
a window that had not been covered with a shutter she saw her
own reflection in the glass, incredibly dirty and dishevelled, her
blue linen dress in tatters, her bare feet grimy with the red dust of
the roads, her eyes bloodshot and blinking myopically under the

bloodstained bandage that covered the fair hair that might perhaps have persuaded the soldiers that she really was a foreigner. They were hardly to be blamed for taking her for one of the half-witted beggars who thronged the Cathedral steps on feast days.

She leant against one of the stone pillars of the arcade that surrounded the Plaza Grande, a place which usually at this hour was thronged with people eating ices at little tables outside the cafés. The Plaza was deserted. She stared vacantly at one of the posters advertising the touring Italian Opera Company which was giving nightly performances in the Opera House of San Rinaldo. A slip of paper announcing that that evening's show had been cancelled had been covered by another informing the public that the curtain would rise without fail at nine on the first act of *Faust*.

The names of the singers who were taking the principal parts were printed in large letters. Faust, Signor Ettore Masoni, Mefisofele, Signor Eduardo Cippi, Margherita, Signora Gemma Giannini.

Giannini. That was the name of the shy forlorn child who had cried herself to sleep every night when she first came to Toledene. Celia had befriended her, taken her out on half holidays. The unhappy little exile had no settled home. Her mother, a widow, was a singer, always on tour. She had paid one flying visit to the school and had embarrassed Celia by her extravagant gratitude and the gift of an immense box of chocolates tied with scarlet bows. "You have been an angel to my little girl. She has told me—"

Celia recollected her as large, exuberant, noisy, good humoured, swathed in furs and leaving behind her a trail of highly-scented, lace-edged handkerchiefs and suède gloves split down the back.

The staff, who, at Toledene, were excessively tweedy and averse to any displays of sentiment, had laughed about her afterwards, but Celia had secretly been rather touched by the evident sincerity of her gratitude.

It had been a day of alarms and excursions for the Masoni Cippi Company. They had been engaged by the Municipality and were at their orders. They had been told to remain in their hotel down by the docks, and that the Opera House would be closed until further notice. Some or the women were hysterical with fright, and the men smoked more than was good for their voices and told each other what il Duce would do with these people. La Giannini wrote a long, affectionate and very untruthful letter to her daughter, all about her personal triumphs and the enthusiasm of the South American audiences, and had her hair waved by the hotel barber. From him she learned that though no one knew exactly what the revolution was about it was generally understood that a part of the army at present stationed in the barracks of San Rinaldo had revolted under the leadership of Fernandez, who had returned from exile, against the government of General Peralta.

"And who is on top now?"

"Señora, that has not been made clear. But for some hours now there has been no shooting. It is finished—perhaps."

"Why perhaps?"

"Not all the army is here."

At eight o'clock the company was informed that there was no fear of further outbreaks and that they would be expected to give their performance. Anything was better than inaction. They set out gaily, and were only slightly dashed by the silence of the empty streets.

The power station was functioning and the arc lights hung overhead like a string of pallid moons while the sky signs flashed out their messages in red and white and green. The little group of singers huddled together rather like a flock of sheep, with the orchestra, shabby, hairy men hugging their instruments, trailing after them.

La Giannina heaved a loud sigh of relief as she sank on to the broken-springed, red-plush sofa in her dressing-room. The familiar smells of grease paints and cosmetics, garlic and defective drains, were reassuring. Assunta, her old dresser, a lean and withered little woman, brittle and dry as a cricket, had put out Marguerite's blue dress, and her golden wig with its two hanging plaits struck the authentic note of vacuous innocence on the littered make-up table.

La Giannina, settling down cosily into the familiar routine, hummed the jewel song as she stooped to unbutton the straps of her shoes. Her feet were apt to swell in hot weather and it was only during the spinning song that she got a chance to sit down, except, of course, at the end, when she was dying in prison. Assunta, who had gone out to see if she could get an ice for her mistress, came back empty handed.,

"The café won't open to-night. They say if they do the soldiers will come in, and they don't pay. Signora, there is a beggar woman outside the door, asking to see you. She won't go away. She gave me this piece of paper."

La Giannina took the crumpled scrap of paper and smoothed it out on her knee. The few words scrawled in pencil were not very legible.

"*I am Celia Holland who taught your Carmela music at Toledene. Will you please help me.*"

"Santa Madonna! Is it possible! A beggar woman, did you say? No doubt she was sent with this message. Bring her in, Assunta—"

"She is very dirty," objected the dresser.

"What of it? This piece of paper tells me nothing—"

Assunta went reluctantly, grumbling to herself. She spent a great part of her life getting rid of the undesirable hangers-on attracted by la Giannini's child-like credulity. The signora was too generous, it was so easy to work upon her feelings. With tears streaming down her plump, powdered cheeks she would empty her purse into outstretched hands. "Take it, take it. I shall earn more next week—" Assunta shuffling down the last flight of cement stairs to the stage door, shook her head. "And when you lose your voice, cara?"

Signora Giannini was still on the sofa resting and polishing her nails when her dresser returned with the bearer of the message.

She gazed in horrified surprise at the torn and mud-smeared frock, the dusty bare feet, the white face framed in blood-stained bandages. This was no Indian or half-breed girl. The eyes that met hers were blue.

Signora Giannini's jaw dropped, she flung up her hands in a dramatic gesture. She might be growing too stout to be convincing in the roles of Butterfly or Mimi but she was still a magnificent Tosca. She could act, and she loved acting both on the stage and off it.

"Madonna mia santissima! It is Miss Holland 'erself. Quick, Assunta, she is fainting. She, who was so good to my Carmela. What have these wretches, these mascalzoni, done to her—"

Celia began to cry, sobbing loudly and unrestrainedly like a child. The relief was so enormous, like a child she allowed herself to be stripped and placed in a bath. She revelled in the almost forgotten luxuries of hot water and soap while large tears still lolled down her cheeks. Assunta had accepted her as worthy of the Signora's confidence and her bony little hands were skilled and gentle as they unwound the bandages and worked with sponge and scissors on the clotted mass of hair.

"See where the poverina was struck down, the broken skin and the bruise. Who did that to you, cara?"

"I don't know. It was dark, on the beach. We were going to launch a boat, Roger and I and the girl. May I stay here?"

She was lying on the sofa, wrapped in one of la Giannina's rather gaudy satin kimonos. She had been given biscuits, and coffee from a thermos, with a dash of brandy in it. She felt much better though she was still trembling violently, and Assunta, standing behind her, was combing out the tangles in her hair. Time was passing and the Signora had been obliged to get ready for her call. She had slipped on her blue dress slashed with white and was sitting before her mirror giving some final touches to her make-up while she talked.

"Sicuro," she said, "but I want to hear all about it."

"It was through you that I got the post of governess to Señor Romero's little girls. At least—you recommended Toledene and mentioned me. They came to see the school and I showed them round. When they heard I was leaving next term they asked me if I would come here."

The Signora nodded. "I remember. They were staying at my hotel in Paris—or was it Cannes? Per carita! Were you at the estancia Romero then yesterday?"

Celia embarked on her narrative. La Giannina listened with rapt attention. Assunta, who only knew a few words of English, stood by the door, prepared to keep any chance intruder at bay.

The Signora was ready to go on the stage. Her large dark face plastered with the pink and white of Nordic maidenhood and framed by the absurd yellow plaits, betrayed some anxiety, but her manner was as warm and as friendly as ever.

"It is as well you came away when you did, cara mia. We weren't allowed to leave our hotel, but we heard that the estancia Romero was wrecked and burned down by the followers of General Fernandez. It seems that the Señora Romero is a niece of President Peralta. And there was another house burnt down in the hills they say, with two women in it, but that was not because of politics. I don't know the English word—" she turned to Assunta and said something rapidly in Italian, after which they both crossed themselves and Assunta fingered the little hand carved in coral that hung with some medallions of saints on a steel chain about her withered neck.

Celia was still feeling very ill and confused but she knew that there was more she had to say.

"Has General Peralta put down the insurrection?" she asked. "Because something ought to be done about the children. They must be found—"

La Giannina added a final touch of incongruity to her appearance by lighting a cigarette.

"That's just the trouble, piccina. Somebody has won, but we don't know if we are to shout Viva Peralta! or Viva Fernandez! It is a position of some delicacy. We have been told to proceed as usual. That means that the curtain should rise about twenty minutes after the advertised time on our tenor, Ettore Masoni, sweltering in a white beard and a dressing-gown. Per Bacco! Why must we have this silly affair in our repertoire? Verdi, Mascagni, Leoncavallo, Rossini. There is music. Ah, you should have heard me in the mad scene of Lucia di Lammermoor. Marguerite is not my favourite part, but I throw myself into it. I am an artist. I cannot help feeling."

"Couldn't I telephone from here to the English consul?" said Celia faintly.

"The lines have been cut. I have never been in a revolution before," said la Giannina, "it is even more unpleasant than I imagined. Lasci fare. Lie back and rest. And you, Assunta, lock the door and come over here."

La Giannina and her dresser whispered together for some minutes. La Giannina had a plan. Assunta protested, found fault and finally yielded.

"Signora mia, you are mad to risk so much for this girl. Not one of us, a foreigner——"

"Basta. She was kind to my Carmela. If you stand there arguing much longer I shall throw something at you."

Assunta, with a final eloquent shrug of her bony shoulders, left the room, and la Giannina came back to the sofa where Celia was lying back with closed eyes, wishing her head would stop aching.

"Poverina, how pale you look. We shall put you to bed soon—but first you must listen—"

She explained that Celia was to take the place and assume the name of a minor member of the company, a rather foolish and flighty young woman named Norina Benci who had disappeared under rather mysterious circumstances when they left Paris ten days previously.

"The boat left after midnight and it is possible that in the darkness and confusion she fell or was pushed overboard. She had admirers you understand, and there had been a supper. It is easy to lose one's balance. On the other hand she may never have come on board at all if one of those men asked her to marry him. They come riding into the towns with their pockets full of money," said la Giannina, with an evident effort to look on the bright side. "In any case her luggage was brought on ship and her papers were in her suit case. She shared my cabin—she was the niece of an old friend of mine and I had tried to look after her though it was not very easy—"

There was a discreet knock at the door. The singer went to open it. A fat and very swarthy little man, wearing a soiled white suit and perspiring freely, edged his way in.

"A message from the general. The performance is countermanded. He has sent an escort of soldiers to see us safely back to our hotel."

"He might have let us know sooner," said the Marguerite sourly. "Have you seen Assunta? Do you agree?"

Signor Masoni glanced in worried way past his stout prima donna at the girl lying on the sofa. "You'll get us all lined up against a wall and shot," he said in an agitated whisper. "Who is she?"

"She escaped from the estancia Romero that was burned last night by the rebels. She was the English governess to the two great nieces of General Peralta."

He flung up his hands. "Gemma, you are terrible. Why get mixed up in these things?"

"You do not understand. She is my friend. She was kind to my daughter, Carmela. It is only for a few hours. No one in the company would betray us and no one out of it knows that Norina did not come with us from Paris."

"The landlord of the hotel will know. We all signed our names in his register—"

"If he asks questions tell him she spent last night with friends and only joined us this evening."

Signor Masoni groaned. "You will involve us in a network of falsehoods for the sake of this benedetta Inglese—"

But he followed her when she went back to the sofa and bent over her protégée. "Miss Holland—poverina, see, she has lost consciousness—"

Celia's white face, sharpened by fatigue and suffering, appealed to Signor Masoni's fundamental good nature. He yielded.

"Bene. Give her some clothes from the company's wardrobe. We'll get her along to the hotel somehow."

La Giannina kissed him on both cheeks.

"Domeniddio will reward you, Ettore. You spoke of a General just now. What General? If Peralta still holds the city we have nothing to fear."

Signor Masoni extracted a rather dingy screw of paper from his coat pocket and took a pinch of snuff. When he had sneezed twice he said, "Unfortunately, the soldier who brought the message did not refer to the General by name, so we are still in the dark—"

Chapter VIII
CELIA FORGETS

THE nun who had glided like a cool grey shadow through the heat and confusion of Celia's feverish dreams turned out to be a real person sitting beside her bed. There had been other people, kind and well meaning, but intolerably noisy, with loud excited voices that pierced her head like knives; she had a vague recollection of swinging yellow plaits, and of a tall man in a red and blue uniform with a black spade beard, and another younger man whose face was familiar. Beyond these memories there were others which she did not try to recall. After a long time her lips formed words. "Have I been ill?"

"Yes. You are better now."

"How long?"

"Nearly six weeks."

"So long? The children—please—Maria and Pilar—"

The nun rose quickly and bent over her. "Don't move. Don't excite yourself. They are both safe. Their Indian nurse took care of them."

"Thank God—"

She fell asleep, and this time it was a healing sleep without dreams. Time passed. She was stronger, able to sit up, propped with pillows. Suora Maria degli Angeli told her she was to have a visitor. The young man whom she dimly remembered came in and sat down in the chair usually occupied by the nun. She knew him now. Señor Romero, her employer, the father of her pupils. He took her hand and pressed it.

"I hope you are going to forgive me, Miss Holland."

"Forgive you? For what?"

"For leaving you alone and unprotected, but for Metcalfe, at the estancia. My children, too. It you had all been killed by the crowd that sacked and burned the house that night I should have blamed myself for being too ready to believe that what has happened once cannot happen again."

"You weren't to know," she murmured.

"When I heard of the outbreak I chartered a 'plane and got Rambaut for my pilot. We landed here three days after Fernandez was shot. I saw my wife's uncle, the President. General Peralta. My children had been brought to the place the night before by their nurse. She saved their lives—but I was very angry with her. She told me that she hidden them in one of the native villages in the jungle and that all her fellow servants had scattered. When I asked her what had happened to Metcalfe and to you I discovered that you had not even been warned of your danger."

"Poor Catarina. She was always jealous, I think, because the children liked me."

"It was abominable. If it had not been for Signora Giannina who was singing at the Opera here that week—but they were leaving the next day. I had you moved to the Grand Hotel with Suora Maria degli Angeli. They told me that you had come on foot from the estancia—" he looked at her doubtfully, wondering if he ought to say more. No one knew exactly what had happened to her or how she had received the injury to her head. The doctors thought it probable that she would remember little or nothing and had advised him to be careful how he questioned her. "It is not as if her assailants could be brought to book, señor—"

So he changed the subject rather hastily. "In a day or two when you are stronger I will bring Maria and Pilar to see you. They sent their love and these flowers—"

"How kind you are," she said. "I hope the Señora wasn't too dreadfully worried."

He smiled. "I left her in Paris. She spends a great deal of money on cables. We have decided to have the children with us. We shall give up the flat and take a villa at Versailles. We are only waiting for you to be strong enough to travel."

"You want me to come, too?"

"Of course. You are willing?"

"It will be lovely."

Suora Maria degli Angeli came into the room, noiseless in her list slippers, to say that her patient had been sitting up long enough.

Don Juan came again two days later and this time he brought his two little girls with him. Maria and Pilar climbed on to the bed to kiss Celia, and sat staring at her with their huge dark eyes bright with satisfaction.

"Will you tell us stories on the boat?"

"Yes."

Pilar snuggled a little closer to her. "Catarina said you were dead. She said the faction of Fernandez would roast you at a slow fire. I kicked her," she said.

"That will do, Pilar," said her father repressively.

Later he told Celia that the Indian nurse was not to come to Europe with them. "She is faithful, but too possessive. I realize now that I exposed you to some danger with her," he said. "I am providing for her, naturally, but she is heart-broken. It can't be helped." He said no more. He had realised with some discomfort how easy it would have been for Catarina to get rid of the English girl as soon as she understood her to be a rival by putting one of the vegetable poisons known to the Indians in her food. He wondered if Celia knew that Catarina was staying in the hotel, in charge of the children. He had thought it best to keep her on until the English girl was well enough to take over her duties. There was, he hoped, no real danger now, but he had warned the nun not to allow Catarina access to Miss Holland's room, and the servant whose duty it was to carry up trays from the kitchen to the sick room had been told to be careful. In San Rinaldo these precautions aroused no surprise and no expressions of horror, and nobody seemed to find it strange that Don Juan Romero should leave his little girls in the care of a woman whom he evidently thought capable of committing a murder. Don Juan, who was a shrewd young man and who understood his own people, knew that Catarina would have died on the rack for Maria and Pilar and that she had, in fact, saved their lives during the twenty-four hours that the estancia Romero had been undefended, at the mercy of the rebels; but the fact remained that if the children were left any longer in her hands they would grow up little savages. He had hoped that he might keep her on as their maid, but he had seen that she was working all the time against Celia's influence and that it was better to make a break. He liked and trusted the English girl, and he thought she had done wonders with Maria and Pilar.

"You will stay on with us in Paris for a while I hope," he said. "I have written myself, to your father to tell him that you have been ill and that you are now much better. The doctor does not want you to tire your head by writing letters just yet."

"You are so kind to me," she said gratefully. "And you must have a lot to think about and to worry you. Is it true that the estancia was burned that night?"

"Yes."

He had been to see the blackened ruin of the great house on which his grandfather had spent millions. Nothing was left. Even the statues in the garden had been hurled to the ground and shattered. The magnificent furniture, the brocade hangings, the priceless Chinese carpets, the pictures, had gone to feed the flames. But as he climbed over the heaps of rubble he felt very little regret. A streak of obstinacy in his nature, combined with his Spanish pride, had made him reluctant to admit that he would never settle down there as his grandparents had done, but he had always disliked the place. His wife had hated and feared it— yes, Alma would be glad—and he cared more for Alma than for anything in the world. That locked room with its ugly secret, like a canker at the core of a fruit, had gone with the rest. The room, where his grandparents and his aunt had been struck down, and though it was by his orders that it had been preserved with its blood-splashed walls and blood-encrusted floor it was a relief to know that it had vanished from the earth.

And so he was able to answer Celia's faltered enquiry with unabated cheerfulness. "It is gone, yes. But nobody was hurt. And you must admit, Señorita, that as a pied à terre for a young couple with two children it was fantastic. For King Solomon, perhaps. There would have been room for most if not all of those surely superfluous concubines but I am very modern, I would find them embarrassing, and without them such a palace may be a little dull."

Celia laughed. She found Señor Romero's Latin common sense very bracing. "I suppose you have been happier in Paris—"

He nodded. "Yes, indeed," and then, to her surprise, his dark expressive face clouded. "It is a pity, it should not be. That is a dying civilization, it lives on the past alone. And this is a comparatively new country. But perhaps what we call civilization is dying everywhere. Something else comes—something better we must hope for the sake of Maria and Pilar—"

There was one other question she had to ask. "About the butler Metcalfe," she said. "Is he all right? Did he—get away?"

Don Juan took out his cigarette case, and, remembering that he was visiting the sick, replaced it in his pocket. He was curious to know what had actually happened at the estancia after the Indian servants had left, but the doctor had warned him to refrain from any attempt to recall the incidents that had apparently left little or no trace in the girl's memory. All the same he wondered very much if the middle-aged butler and the young governess left, as they had been, alone in that great house, had left it together, and where and why they had parted company.

"I have made enquiries," he said, "of course, I gathered that he reached an English liner that was in the harbour and was taken on board. He should be in England by now."

"I'm glad."

"You liked him?"

"He always stood by me. He helped me a lot."

"He was an excellent servant," Don Juan agreed. "Unfortunately, he was dishonest. Since I arrived bills have been coming in, bills he should have paid. He was—how do you say—feathering his nest. But Maria and Pilar were fond of him. They often talk about him. He allowed them to assist him in cleaning the silver. So I shall take no steps-even if any steps were possible. Let him go. And now—I think we have talked enough for to-day. You must rest—"

When he had left her Celia lay for a while thinking over what he had told her. She was sorry but not really very much surprised to hear that Metcalfe had been cheating his employer. She knew that his plan to buy that inn of his dreams, with the garden going down to the river, was becoming an obsession. Had they escaped from the estancia together? How queer it was that she should not be able to remember. The doctor and Don Juan had both warned her not to try. It might all come back later on. It was all there, at the back of her mind bundled away and covered up, a vague and confused impression of heat and darkness and pain and terror, with hurried glimpses, swift as sword thrusts, of eddying water alive with fish.

Suora Maria degli Angeli came in then, and took her temperature.

"Aie. This will not do. The Señor stayed too long and talked too much. Drink this—"

Señor Romero, meanwhile, had taken Maria and Pilar to the National Park to see the snake farm. The two little girls were unusually silent and subdued as they stood clutching their father's hands and staring at the writhing mass of reptiles in the pit below.

Pilar leaned across him to speak to her sister. "Maria, I wonder which kind Catarina would have put in Miss Holland's bed?"

"I wonder," said Maria pensively.

"What are you saying, Pilar?"

"Only that Catarina says she would have put a snake in Miss Holland's bed long ago if she'd known we would be taken from her. It is not so easy in the hotel, but she has made a little doll of clay and stuck it full of thorns," explained Pilar.

"We have seen enough of the snakes," said their father firmly. "We will go and eat ices."

The children were too young to know what they were saying. He should have got rid of Catarina before. Had she, his children's nurse, been mixed up in that dark cult of which he had heard rumours? It was just as well, he thought, that he and the children and the young English governess were sailing for Europe on the next boat. There should be no more delay.

CHAPTER IX
DEATH IN THE FOREST

MAJOR Enderby had walked into the village to post a letter and give his dog a run and on the way home he had dropped in, as he very often did, at the vicarage. Since the major, a lonely man, who had spent most of his life in India, had settled down at the White Cottage he and the vicar had become fast friends. As Mr. Holland had told Celia in one of his letters, the Major had come into the neighbourhood just in time to fill the gap left in his life by the death of Mr. Frere of Frere Court. They were both fond of chess, and when the game was finished, or the board set on one side for a while, they would sit together in companionable silence. The Major never talked much, but he was a good listener and the vicar, who was not himself a very observant man, had sometimes been struck by the knowledge the Major had acquired in a few months of village life and village ways.

This evening Mr. Holland had some news for him. His daughter, who, since her return from South America, had been living with her employers on the outskirts of Paris, was coming home for a holiday.

"She will be here probably some time next week," he said, rubbing his hands with satisfaction. "You and she will get on, I think, Enderby. I'm very proud of my girl. If you come to think of it she showed pluck in taking a post in a country like San Rinaldo. Very wild still, I understand, when you go inland. She never said much about that in her letters. Her employers are very wealthy people and they value her. They value her, I will say that for them. She met with an accident not long before they returned to Europe. I never heard the details though they were most kind in keeping me informed of her progress. I think it was some kind of fall. She hurt her head and apparently suffered a partial loss of memory. When I went over to see her last month Señor Romero warned me not to question her. They seem to think it may all come back to her one of these days. I must say she seemed perfectly normal."

Enderby listened patiently. His dog, a big Airedale, lay between them on the shabby hearthrug. It was natural, of course, that her father should look forward to the young woman's homecoming, but he very much feared that her arrival would mean a cooling off of a friendship. It was not likely, he thought, that Miss Holland would care to have him and Jock much about the place, dropping tobacco ash, leaving muddy foot and paw marks. He looked up after a while at the clock on the mantelpiece. "I had better be getting on, I suppose."

"You have your torch and a stout stick, I hope. You don't go by the short cut through the forest after dark," said the vicar anxiously as he followed him out into the hall.

"I keep to the road," said Enderby, "with Jock on his lead."

"Dear me. Then you think there is something in this scare? Mrs. Bond was telling me this morning after that the village children are all being kept indoors after nightfall."

"I don't know," said the Major slowly. "I heard that one of the Forest ponies was found in a swamp near Emery Down. It was in such a state that it had to be destroyed. Tomsett called yesterday to ask me if I had my dog under proper control. Fortunately I was able to assure him that he's never out of my sight. The idea seems to be that some large dog, or more than one, roam about at night. It may be so. There's a place over by Haven's Hill where they breed Alsatians and run boarding kennels. Tomsett told me he'd been there and they swore no dog could get out without their knowledge. There's another theory that some animal escaped from a travelling menagerie that passed through the Forest last August. That wouldn't surprise me."

"Why do you say that?"

"Well, I go by Jock. He's been very unlike himself lately. He's not easy in his mind. For one thing he used to sleep in his kennel in the garden, but he took to howling and dragging at his chain. I had to go down to him. Dogs don't sweat, you know, but he was trembling like a leaf. It would have been sheer cruelty to leave him there. For the last fortnight he's been sleeping outside my bedroom door. Good-night, Vicar."

"Oh, dear," said Mr. Holland. He peered nervously into the misty darkness of the laurel shrubberies. "Take care of yourself," he called after his departing visitor. "I can't see you even now. Why don't you switch on your torch?"

"I'm all right."

The vicar waited to hear the gate creak as Enderby passed out before he shut the hall door and hurried back to the warmth and comfort of his study fire.

The Major meanwhile walked as fast as a slight limp, a legacy of the Great War, would allow, down the road away from the village and past one of the entrances to Frere Court, on his way home. The woman who came in to cook and clean during the day always left during the afternoon. She came in the morning on her bicycle in time to prepare his breakfast. The White Cottage was a small, solidly-built, Georgian house, double-fronted, and with pillared portico over the front door. A former owner had surrounded the small garden with a high brick wall and for many years peaches and nectarines ripened there more quickly than at Frere Court, to the envy of a succession of head gardeners. Enderby had thought himself lucky to find a place so much to his taste and within his means on the market. He liked to be alone and the White Cottage was so small and so compact that he could run it efficiently without any servants living in.

But he was not thinking of his luck to-night. He had to give all his attention to Jock. The dog was behaving very strangely. Sometimes he rushed forward, dragging on his lead as if trying to persuade his master to break into a run, and then, when he was spoken to, he would cower back and creep along beside him, rubbing against his legs as if seeking protection and whimpering under his breath. They were on a by-road and there was no traffic and no sound at all but an occasional creak of a branch of the trees on either side, and once the thin shriek of a rabbit caught by one of the predatory creatures of the night, or perhaps in a poacher's snare. The mist that had come drifting in from the Solent earlier in the evening had thickened, and Enderby, who felt the raw chill of an English autumn after India, turned up the collar of his overcoat and wished he had worn a scarf. He was glad when they reached the wrought-iron gate in the high brick wall. He did not always trouble to lock it but to-night he was careful to turn the key and take it into the house with him. Mrs. Binns had another and could let herself in when she came in the morning. Quite unreasonable, of course. Whatever it was abroad in the forest at night it was certainly nothing human. The gate would keep it out, and it need not be locked.

He went into the dining-room and mixed himself a stiff whisky and soda before he went upstairs to bed, with Jock following close at his heels to curl up on the mat outside his door. The Major was Spartan in his habits. He was up at seven and taking a cold bath. The mist had cleared off during the night and it was a fine sunny morning with a touch of frost in the air. Jock had recovered his spirits and was scuffing and whinnicking in the passage downstairs, waiting to be taken for his usual run before breakfast.

Enderby, strolling along the road while Jock burrowed in the drift of fallen leaves in the ditch, looked about him contentedly, admiring the gleaming bark of the silver birches, the copper and gold of the beeches and of the bracken against the dark green of holly and yew. The sky overhead was a pale clear blue. There was nothing sinister about these woods by daylight. Whistling to his dog to follow he turned off the road by a path that led through a rather dense patch of undergrowth called Boar's Spinney. After a while he stopped to light a cigarette while Jock ran on, his nose to the ground, on the scent of a rabbit. He disappeared for a moment behind a briar bush and then came back to his master, cringing and cowering at his feet.

Enderby's lean weather-beaten face darkened but his voice was gentle as he spoke to the dog.

"What's the matter, old chap?" He wondered if the dog had been bitten by an adder. "Something behind that bush, eh? Come along, let's go and have a look—"

He went forward, Jock following reluctantly.

Behind the bush, lying face downwards with arm outspread, was the body of a man.

Enderby stooped to touch one of his hands. It was cold. Quite dead, he thought. Better not move him.

Jock growled. His master looked round and saw the village postman coming along the path on he bicycle. He stepped forward and hailed him.

The postman dismounted. He was a young man with a rosy cherubic face which paled somewhat as he caught sight of the body.

"Good lord! What's happened here, sir? Who is it?"

"I've no idea. I've only just found him, or rather my dog did."

"Is he—dead?"

"Very dead, I should say."

"Oughtn't we to turn him over and see who it is?"

"On the whole I think not. We can't help him. and the police would rather we didn't."

"The police, sir?"

The postman seemed startled.

"Of course," said Enderby with a touch of impatience. "Tomsett must be told and he'll get in touch with his superiors. You have to carry on with your round. Where are you going next?"

"On through the spinney to the main road to deliver a letter to old Beale."

"He's the old chap who lives in a sort of wigwam, isn't he? There's an A.A. box a little farther on. Take my key and ring up Tomsett from there. If he's out call Lyminghurst. Tell them I'm standing by until they send their people along."

"Very good, sir."

The postman remounted his bicycle and rode off, bending over his handlebars.

The Major called to Jock, but the dog had sat down on the path some thirty feet away and he would not come any nearer. Enderby, after standing for a few minutes gazing meditatively at the body and memorising every detail of its appearance, went over to a fallen tree-trunk on the other side of the path. It was a favourite trysting place for village lovers on a Sunday afternoon and the ground all about it was littered with cigarette cartons and silver foil, but the body lay in a swampy patch, and only a stranger to the forest would go off the path in that direction.

Jock had joined him and was resting his rough muzzle on his knees. He was silent now but his eyes appealed to his master to come away from that place. He was trembling.

Enderby rose as Tomsett came down the path on his bicycle.

"There you are, Major. Moore rang me up and said you were standing by. Been an accident or summat in Boar's Spinney, he said. I passed the word to Lyminghurst before I started. They'll be coming along with the ambulance. Coo!" his voice changed as he caught sight of the motionless figure in the frieze overcoat lying half buried in the bracken. "Was he like that when you found him, sir?"

"Yes. Moore came along just afterwards."

"Looks like he was running and tripped up over these briars. There's a footprint here in the soft ground with all the weight on the toe and the heel hardly showing. Oldish man too, and fattish," said Tomsett thoughtfully.

"Not the right build for violent exercise," agreed the Major.

Their eyes met. "Your don't think—"

"I go by my dog," said Enderby. "Look at him now. He won't come off the path. He knows more than we do."

"It's a pity he can't speak. It's queer. I heard last night that they've been having trouble with the hounds at the kennels over by New Park. Some nights they can't stop them howling. You think maybe this chap saw something or might even have been chased by something?" He hesitated. "What about turning him over?"

Enderby was about to suggest that he should await the arrival of his superiors, but he checked himself. Tomsett gripped the dead man's shoulder and shifted him, not without difficulty. "Gosh, he's heavy!" he grumbled, and then, on a sudden high note, "Oh, my God!"

They both stared at the distorted face. "His eyes," muttered Tomsett. "Looks as if he died of fright. Poor devil."

"Yes." The Major sounded curt. "Not nice to see. Here, take my handkerchief and cover it. Is he a local man?"

"I don't recognise him.".

"Well"—Enderby looked at his watch—"I'll be getting back. You know where to find me if I'm wanted."

"There's bound to be an inquest, sir. You'll be called to give evidence, no doubt."

"That's what I meant. They'll be along any time now, I expect, with the ambulance, and the doings. Have a cigarette?"

"Thank you, sir, but I'd better not be found smoking."

Tomsett looked rather wistfully after the Major as he walked away with his dog following close at his heels. A nice, friendly sort of gentleman, he thought, easy to get on with in spite of all that had been said in the village about his keeping himself to himself.

As he told his wife afterwards, "Policeman I may be, but being left alone with stiffs isn't my cup of tea, specially not a stiff that looked as if he'd died in a nightmare."

The inquest was held in the Parish Hall two days later. The coroner sat with a jury of local farmers and tradesmen and there were a few villagers in the small space set aside for the public. Three reporters from provincial papers were seated at the press table. After the usual preliminaries the jury filed out to view the body, which was lying in an outhouse. They returned perceptibly subdued, with two of them looking white and sick, and the coroner, Doctor Lucas, opened the enquiry with a brief statement.

"We are here, gentlemen, to find out how the deceased came by his end. He was found in Boar's Spinney soon after eight o'clock on Tuesday morning, lying face downwards on a patch of swampy land just off the path. The police were informed, and were on the spot within the hour. Doctor Reed, the police surgeon, arrived a few minutes later and was able to say definitely that death had taken place some time previously. Doctor Reed is present and as he is a very busy man we will not keep him longer than is necessary. I will take his evidence now. Call Doctor Reed."

The medical evidence was brief and to the point. The deceased was round about sixty and in poor physical condition.

"Undernourished?"

"No. I wouldn't say that. The indications were that the digestive system had been weakened by too much food and too little exercise. There was no trace of chronic alcoholism. The cause of death was heart failure due to over exertion, possibly accompanied by shock."

"A natural death?"

"Oh, quite."

The foreman of the jury asked leave to put a question.

"We got a shock ourselves, Doctor, just now when we saw the poor chap's face. Can you explain that, please?"

"The rictus and the starting eyes? In some cases, admittedly rare, traces of the final pang seem to be stamped on the features after death. That seems to have occurred in this instance."

"There's been talk of something abroad after dark—"

The coroner intervened. "That is hardly in the province of this witness. You are satisfied as to the cause of death, Doctor Reed? You found no traces of either an irritant or a narcotic poison?"

"None whatever."

"One other point. Would you say the deceased was a manual worker?"

"No. His hands were noticeably well kept."

"Thank you. That is all, I think."

Major Enderby was the next witness. He described how he had found the body, and his account was corroborated by the postman who came after him.

"Major Enderby was standing by and called to you as you rode up?"

"Yes, sir."

"Would you have noticed the body if your attention had not been called to it?"

"I think so. Indeed, I'm sure. It was in full view from the path."

"Did you come that way the evening before on your second round?"

"Yes, sir. Round about half-past five. It's getting dark but I'd have seen him right enough if he'd been there."

"Do you often see people walking through the spinney?"

"Hardly ever. The young ones go there sweet-hearting on fine Sundays, but it don't lead anywhere."

The coroner looked up from his notes. "How do you mean? You pass that way twice a day."

"It's the shortest way to the main Southampton road for me leaving Frere Court by the south lodge gate. I go in by the other entrance near the village and out by the Spinney to finish my round."

"I see."

Enderby glanced towards the press table. The three young reporters were scribbling busily. One, a pimply lad, was chewing gum. They were all very young. No doubt they had been sent to learn their job and did not expect to see their efforts in print.

The coroner was explaining that he had reversed the usual process and was taking the evidence of the police last. He called Police Constable Tomsett to describe how, in answer to a telephone call from an A.A. box, he had cycled to Boar's Spinney where he found a previous witness, Major Enderby, standing by the body of the deceased. The dead man's foot was caught in a briar, which showed that he had tripped and fallen heavily.

"You did not suspect foul play?"

"No, sir. I examined the ground within a radius of thirty feet. I found three prints which appeared to have been made by the deceased. The toe was clearly marked in the soft earth and the heel scarcely at all. There were no other footprints and no signs of a struggle."

"Did you move the body?"

Poor Tomsett turned very red. "I'm afraid I did, sir. The Inspector told me off about it. I realise now that I should have waited for him—"

"It is difficult sometimes to know what to do the best," said the coroner. "In this case, apparently no great harm was done."

Chief Inspector Lacy was the next witness.

"Have you established the identity of the deceased?"

"No, sir. His underclothing was new and of the quality obtainable in chain stores. His dark grey tweed suit was of good material and so was his overcoat, but they, too, came from a ready-made tailor with branches all over England. He had two pounds in ten shilling notes and seven shillings and fourpence halfpenny in silver and coppers in his pockets, a handkerchief, unmarked, a packet of Woodbines, a box of matches, and the return half of a bus ticket from Southampton to Sapcote cross roads."

"Have you been able to establish when the ticket was used?"

"Yes, sir. He must have left the bus at the cross roads at 5.45 the evening before. But the conductor does not remember him. That bus is always crowded with country people who've been into Southampton for shopping or the matinées at the Pictures. There was a lot of mist about too, and the conductor as well as the driver were keeping a sharp look out for cattle and ponies straying on the road. The mist got worse later. Our theory is that the deceased lost his way and got wandering about and then started running in what he imagined to be the direction of the road in a panic in case he should miss the last bus back to Southampton."

"He was wearing a watch?"

"Yes, sir. A cheap affair. More chain store stuff. But it goes all right, only gaining about five minutes a day."

"Are you asking for an adjournment while you continue your enquiries?"

"No, sir. There is no suggestion of foul play. We shall carry on, of course, trying to trace him, and we are circulating a full description and hoping that relatives may come forward, but a good many men of his age are without ties or any close friends."

"He was hardly of the tramp class?"

"No, sir. we may find out who he is quite soon. We haven't had much time—"

"Quite." The coroner was bland. "I fully appreciate that."

He summed up briefly and the jury lost no time in bringing in a verdict of death from natural causes.

Major Enderby, who was seated near the door, was one of the first to get out. He was out of the village and walking down the road that led to the White Cottage when the driver of a disreputable old Ford car came up behind him and stopped to offer him a lift.

Enderby recognised one of the reporters. It was the pale and pimply youth, but seen at close quarters he had some advantages to offset these drawbacks. The Major had to admit that his smile was disarming. He answered, however, with some brusqueness.

"No, thanks. I have to take a certain amount of exercise to keep down my weight."

The young man climbed briskly out of his car and fell into step beside him. "O.K.," he said cheerfully. "I'll walk with you if I may. Nobody'll pinch my bus. They're honest in these parts. I'd like to get your angle on this case for my paper, Major Enderby."

"You heard my evidence. I was not keeping anything back," said Enderby stiffly.

"Now don't get sore," pleaded the young man.

Enderby turned on him. "You see too many films. For God's sake stop talking bogus American. You're English, I suppose?"

"It's just a habit," the other admitted. "This natural causes stuff is no good to me. The editor won't use it. I'm not actually on the staff yet, but, oh boy, am I trying? And a good story would help a lot." He gazed at Enderby hopefully, like a dog that is expecting to have a stick thrown for him to retrieve.

Enderby shook his head. "Nothing doing, I'm afraid."

The boy looked disappointed but he bore up gamely. "I don't want to bother you, sir, but here's my card. Tom Smith—my friends call me Crackers. I've a sort of feeling that there's more in this case than meets the eye. If anything breaks, would you ring me up? You'd be doing me a tremendous favour. I'd be eternally grateful."

His persistence had its reward. The major was decidedly less grim than he appeared at first. The corners of his lips twitched as he glanced at the card that had been thrust into his hand.

"Very well," he said unexpectedly. "You may be right. If anything happens here I'll remember you."

He walked on, leaving young Mr. Smith to clamber back into the driving seat of his car.

CHAPTER X
HOMECOMING

CELIA, glancing out of her bedroom window in the intervals of unpacking, noticed that a favourite bronze red chrysanthemum in the middle border was still flourishing. In nearly three years there had been little outward change at the vicarage. Her father was perhaps a little greyer and Mrs. Bond a little harder of hearing, but tea by the study fire was as cosy as ever, there was the usual litter of papers and magazines, and the chessmen were set out as of old on the little table by the window. Celia, wandering round the room after tea was over, had picked up a red knight and set it back gently on its square. "You must miss him a good deal," she said.

"Who, my dear?"

"Mr. Frere."

"I do indeed. But I think I told you about Major Enderby. He and I play. I daresay he'll come round to-night."

"What is he like?"

"Well—he always reminds me rather of the Don in an illustrated edition I once saw of Don Quixote. Very tall and thin and a trifle haggard. He spent a good many years in the Far East, I believe, and was wounded in the War. I should say that he's had a hard life, but he doesn't talk about it. He's rather a silent sort of fellow, I suppose."

And then he had looked at his watch and exclaimed. "It's choir practice night. I must run—" and bustled away.

The Major arrived soon after supper. He shook hands with Celia and, after hoping that she had a good crossing, appeared gravelled for lack of matter. Celia, realising that he was merely extremely shy, exerted herself to talk about Paris and her pupils until he had got over the first shock of her appearance. The Airedale, who had followed him into the room, after eyeing her suspiciously from a distance for some time, walked over to her, sniffed at her hands and lay down at her feet.

"I hope you feel flattered," said Enderby. "That means a good deal from Jock."

"Does he mind being touched?"

"By the right people, no."

She bent over to stroke his head, and Enderby, watching her, noticed the primrose lights on her sleek hair and the clear clean lines of her cheek and throat. It was odd, he thought, that the vicar, who was proud of his daughter, had not told him that she was beautiful.

Jock was not only allowing himself to be stroked but actually wagging his tail. The vicar, who had been looking on rather uneasily, was satisfied.

"I just wondered," he said, "he's not been himself lately, has he? But you connect that with the existence of this—whatever it is—you think he gets the scent—"

"He knows something—and he's not at all happy about it," agreed the Major.

Celia, busy with a pile of unmended socks turned over to her by Mrs. Bond, glanced from one to the other. "You are being very mysterious," she complained.

"There have been tales going about for some weeks past of some animal that prowls about the Forest at night and scares the cattle and the ponies. The body of a foal that had dashed itself against a tree was found near Burley and there have been other cases of death or injury that might have been caused by the animals being hunted. Some think there is an Alsatian at large that has reverted to the habits of its wolfish ancestry. The alternative theory is that some predatory animal escaped from a travelling show."

"There is a third," said Enderby. "That it escaped from a ship bringing a cargo of animals for various zoos just before she docked at Southampton."

"It could jump overboard in the Solent and swim ashore? Yes, that's a possibility," said the vicar thoughtfully.

"Couldn't they use bloodhounds to track it?" asked Celia.

She noticed that both men were taking the story very seriously.

"I suppose so," said her father, "but bloodhounds are news. I know there's a general feeling that we ought to keep the thing out of the papers if possible."

"It was touch and go the other day after the inquest," said Enderby. "One of the reporters followed me down the road and tried to pump me. Quite a decent young fellow really. I managed to get rid of him for the time being."

The vicar paused in the act of filling his pipe. "Don't you agree with the verdict, Enderby?"

"Natural causes? Oh yes. The man's heart was dicky. It couldn't stand a shock. The question is—what shock?"

"You think he saw—"

"You should have seen Jock that same night going down the road to my place. I could hardly get him along. The poor brute was terrified."

"What is all this?" asked Celia. "What inquest? Was it somebody I knew in the village?"

The vicar explained that the body of an elderly man had been found in Boar's Spinney and that the medical evidence had shown that he died of heart failure.

Celia rolled up a pair of mended socks. "Was it a tramp?"

Enderby answered, "No. His clothes were nearly new and he had about two pounds on him, but nothing by which he could be identified."

"What would he be doing in Boar's Spinney?"

"Nobody knows. He got off the bus for Southampton at the Sapcote cross roads. The return ticket was in his waistcoat pocket. The serial number proves that he was travelling on the bus that is due at the cross roads at 5.45. I found his body the following morning when I was taking Jock for a run. The postman arrived a few minutes later. It seems that he takes the short cut across Frere Park and comes out by the door in the park wall beyond the lodge gates. As I expect you know the gates are kept closed now that there is nobody living in that lodge. I used to use that short cut myself sometimes last summer when the Freres asked me over to play tennis."

"I know the path across the park," said Celia. "I know every inch of these woods. Johnnie and I used to play Indians when we were children. I suppose it would save the postman about a mile, and it would be all right if you knew the way and where to turn aside to avoid the swampy bits. But on a dark night—and this man was a stranger—it's rather queer, I think."

"Your father saw him, Miss Celia, at the request of the police."

"Yes," said the vicar. "It was rather an ordeal I must confess. An unpleasant duty. Poor fellow. It might have been someone who lived here formerly, but not since I have been here. I never saw him before."

She looked from one to the other thoughtfully. "You are both worried about it all. I can see that. It must have been a shock for you, Major, finding him like that."

"It's not the first dead man I've seen, I'm sorry to say, Miss Celia, but perhaps I have got rather out of the way of it since I retired. I was in the Indian police, you know—or perhaps you don't."

"Well, I hope they'll find his relations," said Celia, and changed the subject. "Do you see much of the Freres, Major Enderby?"

He answered rather stiffly, "Not very much."

The vicar, who had been lighting his pipe, threw away the match.

"What about our game of chess?"

"I'm ready."

Celia jumped up. "I'll go and make the coffee. Mrs. Bond is a dear, but coffee isn't her strong point. Señor Romero's cook taught me."

They were still playing when she went up to bed soon after ten. She was tired after her journey and she allowed Mrs. Bond to bring her breakfast in bed. Her father had just come back from the church when she came down to the study.

"Well, darling, did you address the empty pews?"

"I had a congregation of one. Old Mrs. Parr. What are your plans for the day, Celia?"

"I must make a round of the village."

"Yes, yes, of course. They've been looking forward to your return. And you might reassure Miss Massey at the school. She fancies you may want to wrest the organ from her. Poor little soul, she's so conscientious."

"All right." She was standing by the window looking out on the dripping shrubberies and she did not turn her head as she went on. "About Frere Court—what sort of terms are you on there? In the old days I would be going over the first thing, and you and I would be dining there to-night—"

"Yes. It's different now. They don't attend church or take any interest in the parish. Roger Frere keeps up his subscriptions and is always pleasant if we happen to meet. There was a tragedy soon after they arrived. I may have mentioned it in my letters. His young half-sister was killed in a road accident. She was driving a car he had given her as a birthday present. His stepmother blamed him, unjustly I believe. He went abroad for a time and when he came home he brought a foreign wife."

The vicar was turning over the papers on his desk, hunting for the notes he had begun to make for next Sunday's sermon. Celia, glancing round at him, remembered that he liked to be left undisturbed on Friday mornings, and did not pursue the subject. The mention of Roger Frere had brought back that confused feeling. There had been something in which he had been concerned—or had she dreamed it?

She went up to her room to get her hat and coat. The coat, of olive green cloth, with a big fur collar, had been given to her by Señora Romero. How lucky she was, she thought, to have employers who were genuinely fond other. They were both of them extraordinarily kind. This coat—she would never have felt justified in spending so much on herself. The señora had chosen it for her at one of the fashion parades of a famous house in the Rue de la Paix. "Zat would suit you, chérie. Try it on. Never mind what it costs. Zat is my affair." It was, in fact, very becoming, and Celia felt that she had it to thank for the outspoken comments on her improved appearance of some of the women in the cottages that she visited in the course of the morning. They all seemed glad to see her, and sooner or later, when she had been told all about the bad legs and the rheumatism, and the children's tonsils, they would refer regretfully to the old days.

"Old Mr. Frere, he was a kind gentleman. There isn't a body here he didn't know by name, and soup and blankets and all. The new lot—well, they're Londoners. Always rushing about in cars. Miss Jupp's niece, young Doris, is between-maid there and she says Mrs. Frere spends her days playing bridge. Twice a week her friends come to play with her up at the house, and the other five she's off to her club in Bournemouth. And the young one is either laying about on sofas, yawning, or rushing off to dance at roadhouses—and not with her husband, mind you—with that half-brother of his."

Celia could only listen and condole with them. She was sorry. Her spirits sank a little lower at each recital. She decided to avoid all human contacts after lunch and go for a good long tramp through the Forest. She told her father she might go as far as Minsted.

"I'll try not to be late for tea."

He was deep in a book. It was his unsocial habit to read at meals, and he answered absently, "Whenever you like, my dear—" and then, rousing himself, "But don't forget, Celia. I warned you and so did Enderby. I don't quite like your going off the road alone even in broad daylight. Be home before dusk. Don't go too far. These November afternoons are very short."

"All right," she said. She hoped the thing, whatever it was, would soon be caught. Something ought to be done, she thought vaguely. She had always loved the Forest and especially in the autumn. To her it had always seemed a friendly place of happy memories. There were the trees she and John Frere had climbed, the streams where they fished for minnows and scooped up frog's spawn in jam jars, the pond on which they learned to skate one hard winter. Poor John. Too much of water hast thou—Oh, why did he have to be drowned when his life was so important!

She stopped to look about her and was struck by the silence. A dense plantation of firs, an unwelcome reminder of the activities of the Forestry Commissioners, blocked the view on her left, but on her right she could see past the shining trunks of silver birches to the rusty brown of the heather on the open moor and the misty blue distance. She looked at her watch. She should have started earlier if she meant to get as far as Minsted. It was time to turn back if she was to keep her promise to the vicar, and she had no wish to break it.

A man was coming towards her through the bracken from the more open part of the wood. He hailed her as he came nearer and she waited for him. If she had believed in ghosts she might have thought it was John Frere, but this man was thinner, less solidly built. It was, of course, Roger, John's cousin who had taken his place. When she dined at the Court once they had talked together on the drawbridge, while they watched the white shapes of the sleeping swans in the moat—and then again—somewhere—

To her surprise he seemed to be in the grip of some emotion. He gripped her hand hard and his dark eyes were eager.

"Miss Holland—Celia—I thought it must be you. I heard you were coming home on a visit. Coming back to England I dreaded what I should have to tell your father. And then, when we arrived, I learned that you were safe, and that I need not say anything at all."

She withdrew her hand, uncomfortably aware of the thudding of her heart. There was something here that must be faced.

"Then—it wasn't a dream," she said.

His face had fallen. Apparently he had expected a warmer welcome.

"A dream? I don't understand—" he said.

She explained. "You knew I was out in San Rinaldo? There was a revolution and the house where I was living was attacked and burned down. I escaped, but I was struck on the head—there's a scar here under my hair—and I have not been able to remember what happened. It faded just as dreams do, but I had a sort of feeling that you were mixed up in it, and it seems I was right. Perhaps if you tell me what happened I shall remember my part in it."

He looked down at her doubtfully. "If it isn't going to do you any harm. All right. There's a fallen tree just here. Shall we sit down?"

Chapter XI
CELIA REMEMBERS

When the vicar came in from visiting a sick woman at a distant farm he found Celia still lingering over a belated tea in the study.

"You came home early? Good girl," he said as he took his cup from her hand.

"I didn't actually, but Roger Frere came with me as far as the gate. We met in the Forest and got talking—"

The vicar was not a very observant person but something in her tone struck him. He looked up quickly. "My dear—is there anything wrong?"

"Not exactly, but it upset me rather. The Romeros told you I had an accident, hurt my head, didn't they?"

"Yes."

"Well—they didn't want to worry you, but there was more to it than that. There was a sort of revolution, which was suppressed after a few hours, but meanwhile there was some street fighting and—and lawlessness. Don't look so horrified, Father. It's all over, and I'm never going back to San Rinaldo. Let me go on. Roger Frere was on a cruise, and he came to see me that very day. You had asked him to, hadn't you?"

"I certainly did. But I never thought—and he has never said a word—"

"I know. He told me. He heard I was safe and I suppose he gathered that you hadn't been told all the details. I expect he thought the less said the better. It was all rather ghastly. It came back to me while he was talking, and I want to forget it again if I can. He and I and the English butler escaped together from the estancia. Metcalfe wanted to get on board the English ship in the harbour, but I felt I couldn't leave until I knew what had happened to the two little girls—my pupils. And Roger stayed with me. It got dark and we could hear men shouting. Eventually we met a Spanish girl who was hiding from the rebels too and she guided us across the fields to the shore. Then—I don't really know what happened, but there was some sort of struggle and I was knocked on the head and I must have lain there on the beach all night. I— got back to the town after a bit, and then I was ill for weeks, and I didn't remember what had happened."

"I should never have let you go," said the vicar.

"Roger told me that he was knocked on the head too, but the girl managed to drag him into a boat and push off, and they drifted out to sea. They must have got into a current that carried them far out, for they were picked up next day by a tramp steamer. When Roger recovered consciousness the captain told him he was going to signal the next boat he saw making for the coast to take the girl off because he was homeward bound to Cardiff, and she wouldn't be allowed to land without a passport. The captain had told her this and she was in a fearful state and threatening to jump overboard to the sharks rather than go back, and would Roger speak to her. Then he said that from what he could make out she had saved Roger's life and that might weigh with him. Roger said, 'What can I do about it?' The captain grinned and said 'Marry her.' Roger was petrified, but the captain explained that would give her British nationality and he could marry them then and there. Well, he went up on deck and had a talk with her and she told him she would be put in prison or shot if she went back because she was mixed up in politics, and if he wouldn't marry her she meant to drown herself. So he agreed. I'm telling you this, Father, but it mustn't go any further."

"No. No. Of course not. What an extraordinary—"

"Her name is Nina. She never told us her name that night. You have seen her. What is she like?"

The vicar hesitated. "Very dark. Beautiful, I suppose. I've only caught a glimpse of her passing in Cedric Frere's sports car. They don't attend church, you know, or come into the village."

Celia sighed. "I'm terribly sorry about it. She saved my life too, I suppose. But I didn't like her. Don't let's talk about it any more."

Celia was walking in the Forest a few days later when she met Major Enderby and Jock. The dog ran up to her and Enderby stopped to speak to her and after they had exchanged the usual remarks about the weather asked if he might walk back with her.

"You aren't finding it dull here after Paris?"

"I'm only here while my people are in Cannes for a holiday. The children are darlings and their father and mother are very kind to me. I shall go back to them soon."

"Your father looked forward to your coming home," he said gently.

"I know. But he doesn't really need me. I can't stay here. I think he understands. I'm restless. I must have lots to do."

She pulled off her beret with an impatient gesture and shook back her hair, moving forward with her face lifted to the sky.

"All these branches overhead, like a net. I want to fly, and I'm rooted to the ground," she said bitterly.

"I know."

She looked at him. "Do you?"

"Yes. I've been young too."

"It hurts."

"Yes."

They walked on silently. After a while she said, "You go to Frere Court sometimes?"

"Yes. I used to play tennis last summer, but lately I've had to give that up as I've gone lame. They ask me to lunch now and then."

"You always go?"

"Yes. As a family they're interesting."

"I was very fond of old Mr. Frere," she said. "Johnny Frere and I were always together in the holidays. Mr. Frere had quarrelled with his brother when he married again. He wouldn't have any of them here, except Roger, during his lifetime."

"The elder Mrs. Frere is a great bridge player."

"Father said that. And the younger—Roger's wife?"

She tried hard to speak casually, to keep the painful interest out of her voice, and hoped that she had succeeded, though Enderby, she felt, was the sort of person who would often be a recipient of confidences.

"I gathered that she doesn't care for cards, though actually I have hardly exchanged a word with her. She does not talk much. Whenever I have been there she has seemed to be half asleep. I'm used to that," he added with a half smile, "modern young women haven't much use for an old fogy like me. I hear that she is a remarkably good dancer and that she and her brother-in-law are regular frequenters of various roadhouses within a thirty-mile radius."

"She is very good looking?"

"Very, if you admire that type. I've spent a good many years in the East. One becomes inured out there to immense dark eyes."

"Is Roger's half-brother anything like him?"

"The blond, exquisite and languid Cedric? Not in the least. I hope I'm not intolerant, but I never meet that young man without longing to present him with an order, the order of the boot. His mother, of course, adores him."

"They sound pretty awful," she said.

"They are."

They had reached the place where their paths diverged. She held out her hand and said impulsively, "Thank you. You're the most understanding person I've ever met. You'll be coming along this evening? Father is expecting you—"

"I shall come."

But when he arrived a little before nine o'clock he found Celia alone. A man who ran a little poultry farm a mile out of the village on the Boldre Road was very ill with double pneumonia and had asked for the vicar. The doctor had fetched him in his car and was to bring him back.

"Is it a man called Lasseter?"

"Yes."

"I heard about him. He caught a chill getting up in the night to rescue his horse that had jumped a hedge and gone into a pond where it was slowly sinking in the mud."

Celia nodded. "He thought the horse had been scared by boys throwing a squib into his field."

"Yes. He's one of the people who have always laughed at the rumours that have been going about. He breeds Alsatians himself as a sideline and he resented Tomsett calling on him to ask if they could possibly get out unknown to him."

Celia had poured out the coffee. Enderby lit her cigarette and sat back with a sigh of content. It was odd now to remember that he had dreaded this girl's coming, fearing that she would spoil his friendship with her father. What was the secret of her charm, he wondered. Was it her complete lack of self-consciousness?

"I'd like to talk to you," she said, "about a letter that came by the afternoon post. In fact I'd like you to read it if you don't mind."

"Of course." He took it from her. "It seems to have followed you about."

"Yes. It was sent to San Rinaldo and redirected to Señor Romero's bank in Paris. They sent it on to the hotel in Cannes where the Romeros are staying, and Señora Romero enclosed it in a letter she wrote me. It's from Metcalfe, the English butler who was formerly in their service. Will you read it aloud?" Enderby complied.

"DEAR MISS HOLLAND,

"I was so thankful to learn, by means of a short paragraph in a newspaper, that you survived the dangers of the late revolution. You may have heard that I was taken on board the *Cerne Abbey* and allowed to return on it—or I should say *her*—tourist class to England. I regret that, owing to my necessarily abrupt departure, I'm not able to set right certain financial transactions in which I had become involved. I should be grateful if you could see your way to saying a word on my behalf to Señor Romero. I am well aware that he must look on me with a jaundiced eye.

Money is the root of all evil. But where you and the little girls were concerned my conscience is clear. I always tried to do my duty. I am staying at present at the above address, the Angler's Arms, at Teame. This is the inn I told you about. It is still in the market. My savings unfortunately do not suffice, but since a certain item of news has come to my knowledge I have great hopes of obtaining a loan. I am letting my pen run on, Miss Holland, but I always enjoyed a chat with you, if I may say so. The present owner is willing to wait, but not, of course, for an indefinite period, and I foresee that I may have to use all my persuasive powers. Meanwhile I wonder if you would be so kind as to advance me a trifling sum to pay my present expenses? Twenty pounds would be very welcome and will be repaid with the usual rate of interest. Hoping that you are none the worse for your very disagreeable experiences last May, I remain,

"Yours respectfully,

"JAMES METCALFE."

Enderby glanced at the date at the head of the letter. "This was written more than six weeks ago. He seems a cool customer. Why should he expect you to help keep him in clover at a country hotel. Why doesn't he try for another job if he hasn't enough money to retire?"

"I'm afraid he wouldn't get a character from Señor Romero. You saw what he said about financial transactions."

"I see. Then this begging letter is just a piece of colossal impudence?"

Celia hesitated. "Not quite that. Apart from these speculations which I didn't know about at the time he really was most reliable. Maria and Pilar were very fond of him, and he was most kind and helpful to me. You must remember that all the other servants were Indians or half-breeds. I could not have stayed there as I did for over two years if I had not trusted him. This letter doesn't do him justice. He's quite human really. You know how it is. Half-educated people are apt to adopt a stilted style and use very long words. I want to lend him the twenty pounds, but I think I ought to write first and make sure he is still there."

"Well, you know him and I don't, but I must say there's something about this letter I don't much care about. A slightly threatening tone."

"Oh no—" she cried.

"I don't quite understand—"

"I told you I had been a policeman. In my job one becomes used to reading between the lines of this sort of appeal. You'd be surprised how many upper servants provide for their declining years by doing a little blackmailing on the side."

Celia reddened. "Are you suggesting that I should be a likely victim, Major Enderby?"

"No. No. Please don't misunderstand me," he said hurriedly. "That was clumsily put. I did not mean that this man was threatening you. He's obviously merely trading on your kindness. No. To my mind, the operative phrase in this letter is—'Since a certain item of news has come to my knowledge I have great hopes of obtaining a loan.' This may mean that he has learnt something about his late employers, the Romero family, or it may date farther back to the people he was with before. In any case I advise you not to lend him any money without finding out a little more about his present circumstances."

"But how can I find out?"

"I know Teame. It isn't far on the other side of Salisbury. I'll drive out that way to-morrow and stop at the Angler's Arms for lunch. If Metcalfe is still staying there I daresay I can get into conversation with him—that is, if you will trust me to act as your agent? I'm afraid I offended you just now—" he said awkwardly.

"No, you didn't, and it's very kind of you to offer. I'd be very glad if you would go. I can't just leave it—"

"Very well. I think I hear the vicar—"

Celia jumped up and went into the hall and Enderby, after a momentary hesitation, followed.

Mr. Holland was struggling out of his coat and unwinding his scarf. His grey hair was ruffled and he looked chilled after his drive in an open car.

"Hallo, Enderby. I hope you've got a good fire, Celia—"

"Yes, dear. Come and warm yourself. I'll fetch your slippers. How is Lasseter?"

"He was conscious when I arrived and managed to say a few words. Afterwards he relapsed and the end came about half an hour ago. I'm sorry for young Dick Peel, his partner. The two young men were great friends, and they have worked so hard to make their little farm a success. I don't know if he'll be able to carry on alone. He blames himself for having been away the night their horse got into the pond. It was unfortunate, of course. If he had been there they might have got him out more easily between them. He's very bitter about it."

"Does he think the village boys threw a squib into the field?"

"He did at first, but he doesn't now. He talked of coming to see you, Enderby. He's certain it couldn't have been one of their own Alsatians. They are shut in their kennels at night. They've got an open run but it's wired over."

"Boys throwing a squib was Lasseter's own theory. After all, it was the night of the Fifth."

"I know. And all the young people busy with their bonfire in the Glebe meadow. I can't imagine any of them leaving it and walking or cycling three miles to do a wanton piece of cruel mischief. It's not as if Lasseter or Peel were unpopular. They are well liked in the village. I am afraid it can never be cleared up now."

The vicar sat down heavily in his chair by the study fire. Celia had gone to make fresh coffee. Enderby was watching the old man's troubled face.

"What did Lasseter say to you, sir."

"He said-it didn't make sense—'I saw them green'."

CHAPTER XII
THE ANGLER'S ARMS

THE Angler's Arms proved to be a long, rambling, two-storeyed house with a front flush on the village street and a long garden at the back sloping down to the river where there was a boathouse and mooring place. It seemed to be an old-fashioned place and not too well run. There was nobody in the dining-room when Enderby walked in after leaving his car in the yard and he had some time to wait before a rather untidy waitress who had remembered her lip-stick but forgotten to comb her hair, came in and approached him languidly.

He asked for the table d'hôte lunch and was told that there was nothing but cold beef or ham.

"No hot dishes?"

"You could have fried ham and eggs—and boiled potatoes."

"Very well. And a bottle of Bass." She was turning away when he said, "Have you a Mr. Metcalfe staying here?"

"We had. He's left." She went out to give his order in the kitchen, leaving Enderby to watch a fly, a survivor from the summer, crawling over the stained tablecloth. Obviously the Angler's Arms could do with a new broom. He was still waiting for his meal when a stout elderly man in his shirt sleeves came into the room.

"Good morning, sir."

"Good morning."

"Nice weather for the time of year."

"Yes. But a bit late for visitors, I suppose."

"Well, we haven't had any, and that's a fact. The girl told me you were enquiring after Mr. Metcalfe?"

"Yes. She said he had left. Perhaps you can give me his present address?"

"Are you a friend of his?"

"No. But I want to get in touch with him."

"You're not the only one," said the landlord sourly. "He went off for the day, taking a packet of sandwiches as he had done many a time before, and never come back. He owes me five weeks' board and lodging, and the stuff he left behind wouldn't fetch a ten shilling note. Properly done I've been, with him pretending he wanted to take over this place if only he could scrape together enough capital. Oh, I've been had for a sucker by Mr. Metcalfe and no mistake. That's right, Gladys, my girl. Set the dish down here."

"He just walked out on you?"

"That's right, sir. Owing me five weeks. There's not many I'd have trusted to that extent, but he had a way with him. He's been in good service same as I was, but I was a coachman in the good old days before motors, and he was indoors. He was younger than me by twenty years, and I do believe if he'd taken over this house he'd have made a do of it. Full of ideas, he was, and he'd have got more work out of the kitchen staff than I ever could. These girls put the wind up me," he added, glancing towards the door. "That Gladys now. If I was her father I'd give her a good hiding. A painted hussy."

"Rather strange that he should have disappeared like that," reflected Enderby.

"It may seem so to you, sir," said the landlord, "but it's not the first time I've been had that way. I should have known better than let his bill run on after seeing the cheap imitation leather suitcase he brought with him."

"Has it ever occurred to you that he might have met with an accident?"

The landlord scratched his head "Can't say it had. He wasn't the sort to get in the way of a speeding car. Cautious bloke. Heavily built, but quick his feet, too."

"He dyed his hair black, didn't he?" said Enderby casually.

"That's right. I noticed that. Grey at the roots. Well, there's no harm in a man trying to keep young and I said to him more than once, 'If you take over this place you'll need a wife,' I said. Fact is, I did very well here until I had the misfortune to lose mine. But I thought you said you hadn't met him, sir?"

"I believe I did see him once," said Enderby. "Did he tell you anything about his past life, where he had been in service and so on?"

"He's lived abroad, and in a warm country. That's all I know. He was very close about his affairs. He said he had a few hundreds saved and he hoped to get the rest as a loan on easy terms from someone he knew over here."

"Yes. Well, I'm afraid you're right, and that he's not likely to turn up again," said Enderby.

"I suppose you don't feel like settling his bill?" suggested the landlord.

Enderby smiled as he shook his head. "No. I can't accept any responsibility. I'm paying for my lunch though. How much? I must be getting along—"

"By the way," he said as he pocketed his change, "when exactly did he leave?"

"I don't have to consult a calendar for that. It was the fifth of November. Guy Fawkes' day. I'm not likely to forget it because we were joking about it when I gave him his parcel of sandwiches. He was going to walk to the corner as he usually did to catch the Southampton bus, and I said, "Lewes is the place. They have a proper do there. Bonfires and guys and a tar barrel.' Always pleasant, he was. I miss him about the house. Well, good afternoon to you, sir. Be careful driving, the roads are slippery with all these fallen leaves—"

Enderby drove straight home and walked into the village after tea with Jock. The vicar, he knew, would be taking a confirmation class, and he wanted to see Celia alone.

He found her sitting by the fire in the study reading a book which she laid aside as he was shown in.

"Have you found out anything?"

"I think I have." He narrated the substance of his conversation with the landlord of the Angler's Arms.

Celia looked worried. "Oh dear. It sounds as if he was really in very low water. I don't quite understand, though—"

"I'm afraid you're going to get a shock," said Enderby reluctantly. "Mind you—I've no proof—but I'm pretty sure in my own mind that the man whose body I found in the spinney a few days before you came over from Paris was Metcalfe. The description tallies. The heavy build, the dyed hair, grey at the roots. And then the dates. He left the Angler's Arms in the morning of the fifth of November. I found the body in Boar's Spinney the following day. He could have gone in to Southampton by bus and taken another bus into the Forest."

"Yes," she said, "it might be. But what would he be doing? He couldn't be coming to see me. He thought I was still in San Rinaldo."

"Isn't it more likely that he was hoping to touch Roger Frere for a fiver, or even perhaps this loan he talked about? The southern entrance into Frere Park isn't used, but he might not have known that. On the other hand, when he fell he was not going in that direction. He was coming away."

"If Roger had known anything about him he would have told the police," said Celia quickly, perhaps rather too quickly.

"Yes, of course," said Enderby, but his tone lacked conviction.

After a pause she said, "What are we to do?"

"Do?" he said. "Nothing. You know the verdict at the inquest. He died of over-exertion, a natural death. His heart was dicky. He was hurrying to catch the last bus after having lost his way in the mist. He stumbled over a tree root. We think we know who he was. But Metcalfe was a man without friends or near relations, and he had nothing to leave—"

"He had saved quite a lot," she said. "He told me, nearly a thousand pounds. What about that?"

"Did he tell you where he banked?"

"He didn't trust banks. He carried it about on him, in a belt, I believe. But that was in South America. He may have put it in the post office over here, or—or anything."

"I see," said Enderby. "I'm not pretending that the whole business has been cleared up by the fact that we've identified the unknown. But there's nothing actually that we can do at the moment. It wants thinking over. And meanwhile will you say nothing about it to anyone, not even to your father?"

"Very well."

The vicar came in from the choir practice before he could say more and, on the whole, Enderby was not sorry for it. There were aspects of the case that he did not wont to discuss with Celia until he had given them further consideration. It was obvious to him that Metcalfe had been confident of obtaining a considerable sum by means of blackmail either from Roger Frere or from some other member of the household at Frere Court. What possible hold could he have over Roger? Enderby had now heard from Celia. A brief account of their flight from the estancia Romero. Metcalfe had come with them in the car and had left them to make for the coast when the car broke down. He had received Roger when he arrived at the villa and had waited on him and Celia at lunch. No opening there for a blackmailer.

Enderby, walking home after a game of chess which he had lost, envisaged another possibility, but refused to build on it. The night was windless and very dark, with a fine falling rain. Now and again a falling leaf brushed his check like a moth's wing. There was a bitter tang of dead bracken and earth in the moist, cold air. Jock, on his lead, kept close to his master's side, and Enderby knew that he was trembling. There were lighted windows in the village street and the sound of voices and dance music from a loud speaker in the bar of the Rose and Crown, but there was nobody about. The terror by night, thought Enderby as he switched on his torch and walked steadily on along the lonely road to the White Cottage. He had nearly reached his gate when he was startled by a sudden sharp clatter of hooves on the tarmac behind him. He moved aside quickly and was only just in time to escape being knocked down and trampled by a herd of forest ponies. They tore past, apparently half mad with fear and vanished into the darkness.

CHAPTER XIII
NINA

"Is that you, Cedric, darling? Come in—"

Rhoda Frere had pushed aside her breakfast tray and was examining her face in a hand mirror. It was still a beautiful face in spite of the betraying lines at the corners of the thin red lips, and since her stepson had inherited Frere Court and his uncle's money she had spent a good many hours and run up a number of bills in beauty salons. She enjoyed the massage, the mud packs, the warm and heavily scented atmosphere, the flattering voices of the white-robed ministrants.

"Madame's skin is so fine—"

"Madame has such long lashes. Just a touch of the darkening lotion—"

And Rhoda, taut as a spring at the bridge table and at home, would relax with a sigh of content.

Some of those special treatments were terribly expensive but if she had spent her allowance, the ample allowance made to her by her stepson, she never hesitated to run up bills.

"Roger daren't complain," she told Cedric. "He owes me more than he can ever pay. A life. He killed Sybyl."

Sometimes Cedric was moved to protest. "That's darned unfair, and you know it. The thing was an accident, and poor old Sybyl's own fault. She was driving."

"That's what he says. I know better," she persisted.

It was no use reasoning with her. Cedric, knowing her as he did, had expected an uncontrollable outburst of fury when Roger came home from his cruise with a wife. A telegram from Cardiff had broken the news only a few hours before they arrived. To his surprise she had been very quiet and had received Nina quite civilly. Cedric, when he had time to reflect, realised that his mother had been wise. If Nina chose she could make their position untenable. But apparently she had no objection to their presence and no desire to assert herself as the mistress of the house. She was very young and very pretty in her dark, foreign fashion. She spoke little, but she was not at all shy. Cedric, watching her sometimes as she lay curled up on a sofa, thought he had never seen anyone so self-possessed, and so completely indifferent to any impression she might be making on others. She spoke English fluently. She told him once that she had spent a year in a boarding school at Eastbourne.

"Until you were expelled," he said teasingly.

"How did you know?"

He laughed a little uneasily, not sure if she was serious. He admired her very much. What could she have seen in an old stick like Roger?

It was a queer sort of affair altogether, thought Cedric. Nina, admitting a nervous dread of fire, would only sleep on the ground floor, and the little morning-room had been turned into a bedroom for her while Roger kept to his own old room on the first floor. Roger, presumably, had been in love with her once, but either his passion had been very short-lived or he was a very good actor. He was never uncivil, but he very seldom either looked at or spoke to his wife, and he seemed quite willing that she should go out in Cedric's sports car and dance with him at road-houses or be his partner when they played tennis on the hard court.

Nina was a tireless dancer and a fine tennis player when she was in the right mood. In these matters she seemed incapable of moderation. She must be either in swift and violent movement or curled up on a sofa or lying full length on the grass doing absolutely nothing. She never opened a book or picked up a newspaper and she never did any needlework. If her stockings or any other garments needed mending she threw them away. Roger had asked her if she would like to have a maid, but she declined. She was, as Cedric began to realise after a time, essentially unsociable. She needed him to drive the car to places where there was a dance orchestra and a good floor, and as a partner when they arrived, but she barely answered when he spoke to her and never initiated a conversation. Cedric, himself an unashamed egoist, had to confess that in Nina he had met his match. Beautiful as she undoubtedly was, she began to have a curiously chilling and depressing effect on him. After all the hours they had spent together in the pursuit of pleasure she was totally uninterested in him.

"I'm not a human being to her," he thought resentfully, "just a carnival doll."

There was no question of a heartache. Cedric was a hard-boiled young man, well aware of the commercial and social value of his own good looks, and always prepared to cash in, in his own crude language, on his sex appeal. Since the death of his uncle he had lived on Roger's bounty. Before that he had haunted the offices of theatrical and film agents, and his charming smile and the clear-cut profile he had inherited from his mother had secured him an occasional small part with one or other of the British film companies.

Now, after several months of idleness, he was remembering his former ambition to try his luck in Hollywood. He was finding his mother's possessive affection increasingly irksome, and there was another reason, connected with Nina, which he did not care to formulate even to himself, why he wanted to get away.

The only opposition he was likely to encounter would come from Rhoda Frere. He had never yet pitted his will against hers for the simple reason that so far they had wanted the same things.

He smiled at her as he sat down on the foot of her bed and lighted a cigarette. "My sweet, you look about eighteen in that pink velvet arrangement."

"Don't be absurd, Cedric," she said, but she looked pleased.

"What are you doing with yourself to-day?"

"I thought of running up to Town to get my hair cut and do a show."

"Alone?"

"Yes." He hesitated. "I've been thinking—I can't help fancying that Roger and Nina would settle down together, the Darby and Joan touch and all that—if I went away for a bit."

She raised her eyebrows. "My dear boy, how very altruistic. Do you really want them to settle down together as you call it? Try to use your brains, my precious, just this once."

"I don't know what you're getting at."

"Never mind," she said. "I won't labour the point. You've been doing very well, and I'm not cross with you, darling. If you're so bored why don't you go to Cannes or Monte Carlo for a few weeks and have a good time? Roger will supply the necessary funds."

"He might, and then again he might not," said Cedric slowly. "I agree that he's been soft so far, but I'm beginning to think there may be a hard core and that if we dig much further we shall get to it. Hasn't that occurred to you, Mother?"

"Do you mean that he is trying to keep you here?"

Cedric grinned. "Oh no. He isn't so fond of me as all that. We had a heart to heart talk yesterday evening, as a matter of fact. The wide world is calling, and the third son of the wood cutter scored in the end, and all that. And, after all, thanks to you, my lovely mother, I have a face that is camera proof. There's Hollywood. He seemed to think it was a good idea."

"No," she said.

He felt his anger rising but he still tried to placate her. "My sweet, do try to be reasonable. I shall come back. Mobs of my admirers will be waiting for me as I come down the gangway or step out of the plane, to beg for my autograph. I shall have pots of money, and everybody will be pleased. Hang it all, Mother, there's no point in upsetting Roger more than we have to. The poor devil always gets a raw deal."

Mrs. Frere's face had hardened as it always did at any reference to the stepson to whom she was indebted for all the luxuries she so much enjoyed. "Are you trying to tell me that Roger has dared to ask you to go away?"

Cedric, who was bored and irritated by his mother's tendency to make scenes, answered curtly. "Certainly not. The suggestion came from me. You didn't really expect me to be satisfied to dance attendance on my sister-in-law for the rest of my natural life, did you?"

"I think you might be patient a little longer," she said, reddening with anger under her mask of powder.

"What do you mean by a little longer? Until she gets tired of me and finds some other fellow with nothing better to do than run round with her? I want to try my luck in Hollywood. Roger's willing to pay my fare out and give me enough to keep me there for a while. He's not a bad old stick really."

"Yes, and if you fail and come back to find that he and Nina have settled down, as you call it, and produced a baby, you'll have lost your foothold here."

"I can't help that," he said, "You—you don't understand."

She looked up at him quickly. "You're not in love with her, I hope."

"I am not."

"You mean—it's all on her side? She's being troublesome?"

"Not that either. She doesn't care two hoots for me. She's too bone lazy to drive herself, and she needs a dancing partner. That's all there is to it."

"In that case, Cedric, I really must ask you to stay on here. Just a little longer, darling. You and I will go on a world cruise together one of these days, and we might visit California. I suppose there are hotels I could stay in while you make the round of the studios. Leave things to me, dear. You'll spoil everything by being over-hasty."

"Oh hell," he said sulkily. "I've heard all this before, wait and see, don't be in a hurry, every time I try to get away from you and do something for myself."

"You are all I have in the world since Sybyl was killed, Cedric. I've done my best for you."

"I don't say you haven't. What I do say is that I'm fed up. You won't talk me over this time, Mother. I'm going. Not this minute, but in a week or two, so you may as well get used to the idea. Try to look on the bright side. You'll be able to swank at your bridge clubs about your son the famous film star."

"Cedric—"

"It's no use, Mother," he said with unusual firmness.

He bent over her and his lips brushed her cheek. "Try to be sensible for once."

"You are keeping something from me."

He did not answer that. He only repeated, "I've got to get away—"

"But, my dear boy, why? There must be a reason. After all it can't be so very distasteful to go about with a girl like Nina, and the life you lead here is pleasant enough, surely."

"Don't keep on, Mother. Don't harry me—" suddenly there was a note in his voice, ragged and shrill, that betrayed nerves strained to breaking point. "I must be off now. One can't drive fast in this weather—"

After he had left her, Rhoda Frere got up and dressed. She was going into Bournemouth to play bridge at her club, driving herself as usual in her Austin Seven. But first she went to find Roger. In spite of everything Cedric had said she still held her stepson responsible for what, from her point of view, would be a major defeat. Cedric was her only child, the one person in the world for whom she felt any affection, and she did not intend to part with him without a struggle.

Roger was in the room which in his uncle's time had been called the study. He interviewed his tenants there and transacted the business of the estate. When Mrs. Frere went in he was standing at the french window which, like all the other ground floor windows, opened on the terrace looking out on a lawn white with rime and trees that in the last few days had lost their few remaining leaves.

"I want to speak to you, Roger."

He turned away from the window. "Very well. Won't you sit down?" When he spoke he reminded her of Cedric. Their voices were the one thing they had in common. He looked worn and anxious, but Mrs. Frere did not notice that. She had never looked at him if she could help it.

"I am going to be quite frank," she began.

He smiled faintly. "You generally are, I think."

"You are trying to bribe Cedric to leave the Court."

"Is that his version of the conversation we had last night?"

"He said it was his own idea, but I can read between the lines. You want to get rid of him. Not satisfied with having killed my daughter you want to deprive me of my son."

Roger had turned very white. It was some time now since she had last turned the knife in the wound. She knew, she must know, that he had loved Sybyl. He was amazed by her cruelty. He said: "You have always been abominably unjust to me over that. I put up with a good deal at the time, I made allowances, but I warn you now that if you reopen the subject you will have to leave this house."

Rhoda Frere loosened her fur coat at the neck and leaned back in her chair. "You would turn me out of doors? That would be quite in character with what I know of you," she said acidly, but she was conscious of a slight tremor of fear. He had never stood up to her like tins before. Had she gone a little too far? Like most people who get a subtle satisfaction from the indulgence of bad temper she usually said far more than she really meant and was completely reckless of the effect she produced on her victims. Roger had been so long-suffering that she had never attempted to restrain her flow of invective where he was concerned. Was it possible that she had reached his limit?

She resumed, after a perceptible pause, in a much calmer tone.

"Very good. We won't bandy words. Cedric has just told me that you were willing to pay his fare out to California and give him enough money to keep him there while he tries to get a part at one of the film studios."

"Yes. That has always been his ambition, as you know. He told me last night that he wanted to go and I agreed to help him. He may not succeed, but almost anything would be better for him than hanging about here at Nina's beck and call."

"Are you suggesting that there is any harm in their going about together?"

He was silent for a moment, apparently choosing his words, before he answered. "No. But I don't think it is doing either of them any good. For one thing people talk even in these days. I've let her do as she likes—but she's very young, and a foreigner. She doesn't understand our way. She has a very difficult temperament with queer reactions. I don't think anyone here understands her."

"Do you?" she asked sharply.

"No. But she is my wife. I must try to learn if we are to spend the remainder of our lives together."

"And you think it will be easier with Cedric out of the way?"

"It may be. It's worth trying."

"It hasn't occurred to you that he is all I have and that I shall be utterly wretched without him?"

"My dear Mother," he said more gently, responding to her quieter manner, "you can't expect to keep him always with you; besides, he will be coming back. Or, if he is successful you could go out to him."

She smoothed her gloves out over her knee and said, without raising her eyes, "then you won't change your mind? You could stop him. He can't go without money."

"No. He wants to go. I shall give him his chance."

She stood up. "Very well. Then that is that."

When she had gone he sat on for a while gazing into the fire. He shrank from his coming interview with Nina, but he did not see how it could be avoided. She had always been on her guard with him, cool and self-contained, except that once in the cabin of the tramp steamer that had brought them to England when she had knelt at his feet, clasping his knees, imploring him to marry her, her great dark eyes dilated with fear, her trembling lips almost as white as her cheeks as she stammered,

"You don't know—you don't know what they would do to me—"

He had been horribly embarrassed and a good deal shocked by the quandary in which he had been placed. When they were picked up drifting in a small open boat Nina was still steering and she had previously rigged up some kind of a native sail while he lay unconscious. Her story was that they had been attacked by stragglers from the crowd who had followed them from the road down to the shore. Roger had been struck on the head. Nina had managed to hide, and when their assailants were gone she had crept out from among the bushes where she had been lying and had contrived to launch the boat which had already been dragged down to the water's edge, and to lift Roger into it.

"What about Celia Holland?" he had asked her.

"She hid too, but she would not come with us. She said that when it was light she would make her way to the town. She was in no danger. In San Rinaldo they like the English," she assured him.

He could only hope she was right, but her indifference to Celia's fate contrasted rather oddly with her fears for herself.

"They wouldn't really hurt you either, would they?" he said. "No one is safe from a drunken mob running amok in the middle of the night, but surely in cold blood and broad daylight—"

She had clutched him more tightly. "Roger—you don't under-stand. It is not the same thing——-"

"You mean that you're mixed up in their politics, a girl of your age?" He was still incredulous.

"Yes. Yes. That is it. Don't ask me any more. I can never go back. Never. If you will not marry me I will jump into the sea."

He had yielded, though not with a very good grace. She was beautiful, but she was not his type, and he was far from sure that he liked her. Still he supposed that if they did not get on together they could get a divorce later on. The captain, a Welshman and a strict Wesleyan, insisted on performing the marriage service that same day. She was legally his wife. But the marriage was not consummated. Nina, having gained her point, was not encouraging, and Roger, still suffering from the effects of slight concussion and secretly exasperated at having been saddled with a woman he did not want, was in no mood for love making.

If, either during the voyage or after they had landed in England, she had appealed to his chivalrous instincts their relations might have improved but she had seemed very sure of herself and in no need of his help or guidance. He saw very little of her while they were on the boat. Her meals were served in her cabin and she slept a great deal and seldom came on deck, to the unconcealed relief of the captain.

"I don't hold with women on board ship," he told Roger.

"All very well in their place on shore, but at sea they're trouble makers, especially if they're good looking."

They spent two days at Cardiff after landing. Nina had to buy some clothes. She had been living in a pair of slacks and a woollen pullover borrowed from the second mate. She spent a morning shopping while Roger bought a car. When they met at lunch in the hotel dining-room she was wearing a brown silk frock and a thick blanket cloth coat. He asked her if she had got everything she wanted and she answered indifferently that she had. He realised for the first time that she was that strange anomaly, a pretty woman who is genuinely careless of her appearance. Well, he thought, that was a virtue, if a negative one. She was not vain. Nevertheless she attracted more attention than he cared about wherever she went. Her frock might be dowdy and ill-chosen, the men who passed their table or edged their chairs round to get a better view, saw the lovely olive-skinned face framed by the blue-black, wavy mass of hair, the brilliant dark eyes, the full red lips. She ate on unconcernedly. Roger had already discovered that she had a very hearty appetite. He suggested a visit to a cinema, but she declined the invitation, saying that she had never gone to the pictures in San Rinaldo. She hated crowds and the feeling of being shut in.

"Well, is there anything else?" asked Roger, dreading the prospect of an evening spent in the hotel lounge where Nina would go to sleep and he would be bored stiff.

She yawned. "We might go somewhere, and dance."

He agreed rather doubtfully. He was not a very good dancer. His doubts had been justified. The experiment had not been a success and it had never been repeated. Nina complained that he was clumsy and trod on her feet.

Roger, who was well aware of his deficiencies, could only say he was sorry. "You'll find my young brother Cedric more adequate. He's supposed to be very good."

He had suggested that she might like to spend a week or two in London before they went down to the Court. "If you have not been there before you might like a little sightseeing, and we could go to some theatres."

But Nina said abruptly that she hated towns. Cardiff was bad enough, and if London was bigger and more full of people she would dislike it even more.

"All right," Roger said equably. "Then we'll go home to-morrow."

He sent a telegram to his stepmother announcing their arrival. He had already cabled to the British consul at San Rinaldo to ask if Miss Holland was safe and had received an affirmative reply. That was a weight off his mind. He had never felt so sure as Nina professed to be that Celia had been in no danger when she was left to shift for herself. He could not take any share of the blame for that since he had been unconscious, but he had been none the less worried and unhappy. He told Nina that he had cabled. She merely shrugged her shoulders. He had already discovered that it was a waste of energy to try to make conversation with her or try to arouse her interest in what went on around her.

When they arrived at the Court he had the unexpected pleasure of seeing his stepmother disconcerted by Nina's complete indifference. It was like watching a wasp trying to sting a steel plate. After the first encounter they settled down to live under the same roof more easily than he had anticipated. They were both egoists, but they did not want the same things. Nina's requirements proved to be remarkably few and simple. Tennis on the hard court, Cedric to drive her out and dance with her at roadhouses when she was in the mood for that form of exercise, plenty to eat, sofas with lots of cushions on which she could curl up and sleep. She had, it seemed, no social ambitions, and refused to return any calls or accept invitations. These, in any case, were not numerous as the Freres were not popular in the neighbourhood.

Roger, who, except during the few months he had spent at the Court with his uncle, had never known peace or happiness in his home life, had become an expert in keeping out of the way of his family, and by his unexacting standard they were getting on well if they avoided open quarrels. He had been grateful to Cedric for taking Nina off his hands. Well, that was over. He wondered rather uneasily why the young man was in such a hurry to leave the Court. He had always seemed quite satisfied to idle about at his step-brother's expense. Cedric would not admit to being in any kind of trouble, but he was obviously very nervy and at times he had a hunted look. It was strange, Roger thought, that his mother, who adored him, had not noticed how much he had changed of late, but, like most very selfish people, she was not observant even where those she loved were concerned.

Roger knocked the ashes out of his pipe and went in search of his wife.

He found her dozing on a sofa by a roaring fire in the drawing-room.

She blinked at him sleepily without speaking. It was some time since they had been alone together. He saw less than ever of her since she had taken to having her meals in her own room.

"It's dark in here," he said. "Shall I draw back that curtain?"

"No. The light hurts my eyes."

"It shouldn't. Would you like me to take you to an occulist?"

"No."

"I'm afraid you'll miss Cedric if he goes to Hollywood," he said rather awkwardly.

"Miss him? Why?"

"Well—you like dancing, and I'm no use for that."

She answered languidly. "It will not matter. I do not have to dance. Lately I have not liked it so very much. They have too much light. One can dance alone, you know." She had turned her head and was gazing past him through the window at the lead figure of Pan on his pedestal glimmering against the dark green of the clipped yews. Roger watched her uneasily. What was she thinking of? Neither of him nor of Cedric he felt sure.

"Your handsome young brother is a baby. His mother spoils him. All Englishmen are babies, so simple and kind and foolish. Such nice boys. Nice. Nice. Nice." She had picked up a silk cushion and with every repetition of the word she struck it lightly with the flat of her hand.

Roger flinched a little under the lash of her amused contempt. It was the first time she had said so much and he was not sure that he did not prefer her silence.

"I suppose you want he-man stuff," he said. "You won't get it from me, I'm afraid. I'm sorry. We haven't made a success of our marriage, have we. Do you want a divorce? I dare say it could be arranged—"

She shook her head. "No. I am not complaining. You do not understand. I like it here. I only ask to be left alone."

He checked a sigh. "Well, we're both young. We've got our lives before us. Can't we—" he held out his hand and then as she did not seem to notice it he quickly drew it back again. It was strange, he thought, that he should feel this reluctance to touch her. How was he to fight against that instinctive aversion? He set his teeth and waited a moment before he struggled on.

"We ought to try to settle down together like—like other people, Nina. You—you'd like children, wouldn't you?"

She shook her head. "No. You don't understand. It is impossible. The women in my family never marry—" she broke off biting her lip as if she had said more than she intended.

Roger had come prepared to be patient with her, and besides she was talking sheer nonsense. "You married me."

"That was different. I had to. I had to get away." She shuddered, huddling down among her cushions. "You are cruel to remind me of it—"

"You are safe here," he said gently. "Nina, I don't think you have realised that Celia Holland, the English girl who was with me that night, is here in this village now."

She lifted her head to look at him. "But—wasn't she killed on the beach? She was struck on the head—"

"Yes. In the darkness and the confusion you could not find her. You dragged me into the boat when our assailants had gone, but you had to leave her. No one can blame you for that, Nina. You had saved her life already once when you took us into the leper woman's hut. One of the first things I did when we landed in England was to cable to San Rinaldo for news of her. I learned that she was safe."

"You never told me."

"Yes, I did, but you didn't pay much attention. You often don't seem to be listening—"

"Well, I am listening now," she said in a hard voice. "Why is she here? What has she come for?"

"This happens to be her home. Her father is the vicar of this parish, as you would have discovered weeks if not months ago if you took a normal interest in your surroundings."

"Has she been here long?"

"Two or three weeks. She is governess to the children of Don Juan Romero. They are living in the south of France at present. I don't know if she has come home for good or only on a holiday—"

"What does she say about me?"

"My dear Nina—what should she say? You never even saw each other. She told me her adventures after she came to herself alone on the beach at sunrise while we were drifting out to sea in that boat. I told her we were married—"

"You have seen her then?"

"Naturally. I have met her out walking in the Forest. Nina— she's just an ordinary sort of girl, not particularly clever or anything, but as straight as a die and extraordinarily understanding and kind. I'd like you two to be friends. I'm sure she could help you to—to get used to things over here. Won't you write her a little note and ask her to tea? I won't butt in. Just you two. I'm sure she'd be pleased—"

"I'll think it over," she said. "I can't be hurried. You know I don't like meeting strangers."

"Celia is hardly a stranger. You did save her life, Nina. She's not the sort of person to forget."

Nina sat up, hugging her knees and laughing softly to herself.

"That is funny," she murmured, "you nice, stupid Roger, you will never know how funny that is."

He got up to leave her. He had been led into saying rather more than he had meant to say. He could only hope that he had not done more harm than good.

"It's not raining now. Oughtn't you to go for a walk or something?"

She yawned. "No. I shall sleep."

He stood for a moment hesitating, looking down at the tumbled mass of dark curls, the lovely curves of olive-skinned cheek and throat, the lithe strength of the bare arms and the clasped hands. What was the force that operated like an invisible ray to prevent him from touching her? Something that welled up from beneath the surface of his consciousness and flowed between them like a cold stream to keep them asunder. She did not raise her head to look at him, and he went away without another word.

Chapter XIV
NIGHT FEARS

ENDERBY had settled down for the evening by his sitting-room fire when the bell rang. Jock growled. He had been restless all the evening, listening to the south-west wind moaning in the chimney and rattling the window panes. Enderby told him to lie down while he went to the door. He peered out into the darkness and the driving rain.

"Oh, is that you, Peel? Come in."

Peel was still in his working clothes, a shabby raincoat over still shabbier breeches and leggings, and a faded pullover. His boyish face was drawn and weary. He began to apologise for coming at such an hour. "I'm single-handed now, as you know. Doing poor Lasseter's jobs as well as my own."

"I know. Sit down and warm yourself. There are cigarettes in that box. Have a whisky and soda—"

"Thanks."

"I'm sorry about Lasseter," said Enderby. "Hard luck. Shall you find another partner?"

"I might. But I don't fancy it. He left his share of the doings to me, you know. We both made wills to that effect. But our stuff doesn't amount to much. We've been hanging on by our eyelids and hoping for better times. If only I'd been home that night to help him get the pony out of the pond he might not have got so chilled. He always had to be careful of his chest. You don't believe one of our own dogs was to blame, do you, Major? Some people are saying that."

"I think it most unlikely. What is your theory, Peel? or haven't you got one?"

"I think it's some beast escaped from a travelling menagerie. The show people won't admit losing it because they're afraid of trouble with the police. If it isn't caught soon owners will be afraid to leave their ponies in the Forest. I heard to-day that Dale's mare was found lying dead outside his gate."

"Savaged?"

"No. But Dale says she must have been driven hard for miles. I suppose this brute, whatever it is, lives on rabbits and so forth, and hunts the ponies for sport."

"It could be."

"Can't anything be done, sir, to trap it? The police are no use."

Enderby drew at his pipe. "They need more evidence before they can move, I fancy. They've done their best so far. Peel. The owners of every dog within twenty miles has been warned. No tracks, no traces of a lair. I'm told that the head verderer is sceptical about the whole thing. He says it doesn't take much to frighten a pony, and that's true, of course."

"Just a series of coincidences and old wives tales, I suppose," said Peel bitterly. "I don't think. I tell you, sir, the people in the village are scared stiff. The women won't let the children out after nightfall. I was in the Rose and Crown bar last night and some of the chaps who were on the jury at that inquest on the old man who was found in Boar's Spinney were talking. The general idea is that he died of fright."

Enderby glanced at the younger man's strained face.

"I found him, you know. It certainly looked as if he had been running away from something. You realise that it was the night your pony got into the pond?"

"Was it? Good Lord! That looks as if—I say, sir, you agree with me, don't you, that it's real?"

Enderby nodded. "Yes. But the evidence that has convinced me wouldn't weigh with the police. I have had my dog since he was a puppy and I've always thought him completely fearless, but he has changed a great deal in the last few weeks. Look at him now listening for some sound outside the house. He's never at rest. A mass of nerves. And more than once when we've been in the Forest he has stopped dead and come crawling back to me for protection, whimpering under his breath in sheer terror. I thought it might be some form of hysteria and I took him to a vet at Southampton, but he couldn't find anything amiss. Now—well, there it is. I believe he knows more than we do."

"My Alsatians aren't any too happy," said Peel, "I've kept them shut up in their kennels more than usual, of course. If this isn't cleared up soon I shall have to sell them and give up breeding. I hate the thought of parting with them. Ada of Boldre has won lots of prizes and she's had some lovely puppies. I've been specially careful because Alsatians can jump a fairly high wall."

"Yes," said Enderby, "take every precaution, and try not to worry. I'm glad you came to see me about this. I'll think it over. Something will have to be done."

"Couldn't it be tracked with bloodhounds?" hazarded Peel.

"It might be possible," said Enderby doubtfully, "but where and how are they to pick up a scent? It could have been tried in the Boar's Spinney affair, but it was assumed at the time that the victim died of shock from a fall following on over-exertion. His heart was weak, you know. There was no evidence of any outside agency. And I fancy, judging from Jock's reaction that the hounds might refuse to follow the scent if they picked it up. Still, it's an idea. I'll get in touch with a man I know who breeds them. I agree with you, Peel, that we ought to take some action before it's too late."

Peel looked at him curiously, puzzled by his tone. "What do you mean by too late, sir? Do you think that the thing, whatever it is, may start actually attacking ponies and cattle and perhaps human beings?"

"Made bold by immunity. Something like that. I confess I'm not cosy in my mind, not at all," said Enderby gravely. "But don't repeat this to anyone. Peel. We don't want to start a worse panic than there is already. These things are largely psychological, drawing their strength from forces we can only guess at."

Peel seemed puzzled but obedient. He promised that he would be careful. "Another question is how do we deal with the brute if we come face to face with it. I've a gun licence and I shoot rabbits on our own bit of ground, but I don't know what the police or the verderers would say if I carried it about."

"If you take my advice," said Enderby, "you'll keep indoors after dark for the present. We'll see what the bloodhounds can do. Did you come here on foot?"

"I came on my bicycle."

"Then I'll run you home in my car. We can strap your machine on to the luggage grid."

"Thanks awfully, but there's really no need—"

"I think there may be. Anyway, it's a rotten night—"

Enderby felt sorry for young Peel. He seemed a decent fellow struggling to make a livelihood. It was clear that he had been very much depressed by the death of his friend and partner. Enderby offered to lend him books and so far overcame his unsocial habits as to ask him to drop in any time for a chat. He was touched by the boy's gratitude. He drove him back to the roadside cottage where he lived in the utmost discomfort, preparing scratch meals for himself in a frying pan in the intervals of looking after his poultry and his Alsatians. They were greeted as he pulled up at the gate by loud barking and excited yelps from the kennels.

"Come in and see them now if you like," said Peel.

"Another time. Remember what I said, Peel. Take care of yourself. Good night."

He let in the clutch.

Peel called back quite cheerfully. "Good night, sir, and thank you."

The headlights cast a little patch of light on the wet road. The screenwiper swung to and fro clearing away the mist of rain on the glass.

Enderby, glancing at the clock on the dashboard was surprised to see that it was past one o'clock. They had sat talking by the fire longer than he had realised at the time. He blamed himself for not having taken the boy home earlier. He had looked very tired, and he would have to be up at six to feed his chickens. No wonder that at such an hour and on such a night there was no traffic on the roads.

He was within fifty yards of his own gate when something emerged from the darkness and fell just in front of his car. He braked hard just in time to avoid running over it, and got out to bend over the body of a man sprawling face downward on the road. He was dressed only in pyjamas and a dark, camel-hair bathrobe fastened about the waist by a cord. He was partly conscious and struggling feebly to his knees.

Enderby helped him up and recognised him. It was Roger Frere. The older man, staring at that white distraught face in the glare of the car's headlights, saw that he was in no state to answer questions. He half-dragged, half-carried him into the back of his car and drove it straight into his garage. Then, when he had locked and bolted the gates he went back to where Roger sat huddled on the seat with his elbows on his knees and his face in his hands.

"Shall I bring you a nip of brandy here, or can you walk into the house."

"I'll—I'll come," said Roger huskily.

Jock, shut up in the sitting-room, was barking frantically and jumping up at the door.

Enderby, switching on the lights for the passage and the staircase as they came in, saw that Frere's dressing-gown and pyjamas were not only sodden with rain but caked with mud and torn in several places by briars.

"We're about the same height," he said casually. "I can fit you out, but you'd better have a bath first, as hot as you can bear it, while I make some tea. I could do with a cup myself. Come down when you are ready."

The stiff, white lips strove to utter. "You're very—good."

"Not a bit. Take it easy—"

All the same Enderby wondered, as he moved about downstairs, filling the kettle and setting it on the gas ring, and making up the sitting-room fire, if he had been wise to leave the other alone even for a few minutes, and he went more than once to listen anxiously at the foot of the stairs. He had silenced Jock with a word, but the dog was still obviously uneasy, going first to the front and then to the back door, and coming back to gaze up into his master's face as if there was something he wanted to say.

Enderby waited to hear the bath water running out before he made the tea. He was just pouring out the first cup for himself when Roger came into the room. He looked rather less ghastly, but still like a man recovering from an illness, bloodless, sunken and shrunken, and Enderby noticed that his hands shook as he lifted his cup to sip the scalding hot tea. But a little colour came into his face as he drank, and he spoke in something not too unlike his usual rather diffident manner as he set the cup down.

"Just after two. But don't worry. We'll turn in presently. You'll spend the rest of the night here, I hope? I have a spare room."

There was a perceptible pause before Roger answered, and the older man fancied he needed time to assimilate the meaning of what was said to him. It was a symptom, an occasional after-effect of shock.

"Thank you. I—that might be the best thing. I seem to be rather—done in."

He took a cigarette from Enderby's proffered case and succeeded in lighting it with his third match.

The fire had blazed up and they both sat silently enjoying the warmth. Jock, after padding to and fro several times between his master's chair and the door had gone back to his basket. After a while Enderby said quietly, "would it help you to talk things over? Just as you like."

Again there was an interval before Roger replied. "No. I have nothing to say. Nothing. Thanks all the same."

"Very well, Frere."

"You're not offended?" said Roger anxiously.

"Not a bit. It's up to you. Sometimes an older man can help. That's all."

"Very decent of you. Don't think me ungrateful. You must have thought it very odd; me wandering about in pyjamas in this weather. Very absurd. Quite mad." Roger moistened his lips and struggled on. "The fact is I used to walk in my sleep when I was a kid. I hadn't done it for years, but it seems to have come on again."

"Do you mean that you woke up after going to bed in the usual way and found yourself outside in the rain and the darkness?"

"Yes."

"I see. And was to-night the first time after a long interval?"

"Yes."

"I see. It's a good thing I picked you out with the headlights of my car. If you had not found shelter you might have pegged out before morning," said Enderby gravely. He felt fairly certain that Roger was lying. "Would you like to turn in now? I'll give you something to make you sleep. Some quite harmless tablets. Shall you want a message sent to the Court in the morning? Will they be alarmed when they find you are not in your room?"

"I shouldn't think so," said Roger uncertainly. "I often went out early during the summer but I haven't lately—"

"My housekeeper arrives from the village on her bicycle soon after seven. I'll write a note now and get her to take it if you like."

Roger thought a moment and then shook his head. "Better not. Very likely my absence won't be noticed. We don't live in each other's pocket. If you'll lend me some clothes to go back in, I can probably slip in through the library window without any fuss or bother. I—I don't suppose it will happen again."

"I hope not," said Enderby. "You don't look very fit, Frere, if you don't mind my saying so. Perhaps you need a change. I don't think sleep-walking in the Forest is very safe just now. I expect you've heard the rumours that have been going about of some predatory beast at large frightening the cattle and the ponies—"

Roger threw the end of his cigarette into the fire. "Yes. But it's just a yarn, isn't it? Like the Loch Ness monster, but even less authentic. No one has seen it?"

Enderby answered deliberately. "I think the stories have some foundation in fact."

"I doubt it," said Roger. "My uncle used to say that the country people are great romancers. They dramatise the most ordinary events at times. Their actual lives are rather drab. What was I saying?"

Enderby took his arm. "I'll take you up to your room," he said firmly.

Though he very seldom had visitors he always had the spare room ready and the bed made up. He administered the tablets he had prescribed and saw Roger safely into bed before he switched off the light.

"Sleep well—"

"Thanks. I hope to. I feel very drowsy and comfortable. I say, it really is frightfully good of you—"

"Never mind that. Goodnight."

Twenty minutes later he went back, opened the door very gently and listened. Deep even breathing from the bed assured him that the tablets had taken effect. He transferred the key to the outside of the door and turned it in the lock before he went back to his own room. His face was very grave. He was troubled in his mind. The events of the last few hours had been far from reassuring. The thing he had feared was taking a threatening shape. He lay long awake, conscious of the black encircling woods, tormented and moaning under the lash of the gale.

CHAPTER XV
DORIS JUPP'S FORTUNE

"Come along, Jessie," said Mrs. Bligh genially. "If you've finished out in the scullery you've earned a rest and a slice of bread and dripping." She filled a cup from a saucepan full of a bubbling brown liquid on the kitchen stove and pushed it across the table.

The little between-maid, who was a newcomer and still stood in awe of the stout bustling capable woman who ruled over the kitchen, took it gratefully and held it between her cold red hands coarsened by much dish washing.

"Coo! What a day!"

Mrs. Bligh, who was sitting close to the roaring fire in the stove, with her skirt folded back over her vast knees, glanced towards the window. The lower panes were of frosted glass but through the upper ones, she could see wind-tormented trees against a leaden sky. "You're right. Give me the town this time of year. All these woods give me the horrors, and the ground's like a sponge. I can't think why I stay."

Amy Mostyn, the parlourmaid, stirred her cocoa with a faint smile of contempt for the rustic Jessie who was blowing on hers to cool it.

"I can," she said. "You get good wages, and half the time you've nothing to do. Look at to-day. All of them out one place or another, and only our lunch and dinner to think about."

"That's where you're wrong," said Mrs. Bligh vigorously. "I'd rather they stayed home and enjoyed my good cooking. All this running about to bridge clubs and road-houses and living on sandwiches and meringues and what not'll be the end of the upper middle classes, and let me tell you, my girl, that they used to be the backbone of England. A good solid five-course dinner eaten at home, and boiled mutton and rice pudding for the nursery, that's what we ought to be preparing in a house like this. The lady at my first place when I was a couple of years younger than you, Jessie, weighed fourteen stone, but what of it? Her children and her grandchildren thought the world of her. I'll bet she was happier, even if she had lost her figure, than the one upstairs here with her slimming exercises and her aspirin and cocktails and her everlasting bridge. And as for young Mrs. Frere, she's a foreigner and they're apt to be queer, but in the old days she'd be having a baby to settle her by this time. A drop more cocoa, Amy?"

"I don't mind if I do? Where's Doris? She's slower over her work every day."

The cook's broad good-humoured face clouded over. "She's poorly again. Poor kid, she does have these turns. She called down the stairs to me and I told her to go and lie down. You'll have to carry on with her work, Jessie. It doesn't matter as all the family's out. Did any of them say when they'd be back?"

The parlourmaid, who was superior, sourish, and verging on middle-age, looked down her long nose as she replied, "Mrs. Frere is lunching with friends in Bournemouth and will be playing bridge afterwards. She may be late, she said. Our golden-haired beauty drove his car back from London through all that rain last night. I didn't hear him come in, did you? He was late, as usual, for breakfast. Lucky for him there's a hot plate. He told me to ask Mrs. Roger if she'd come with him to a place where they have a new glass dancing floor. She said she would. They got off half an hour ago. If you ask me I'd say the sooner he's off to Hollywood the better for all concerned."

"Ah," said the cook weightily. "His brother gives way to him too much. A quiet life's a good thing, but you can buy peace at too dear a price as he may find out before he's done. A syphon in his own house."

"Cypher is what you mean, cook."

Mrs. Bligh replied with dignity. "I mean what I say. He's gone off by himself, I suppose?"

"To Southampton, he said. I was in the hall, dusting. He may be late, too. He looked queer, I thought."

Mrs. Mostyn shook her head. "One of these days he'll break out, and then you'll see. It isn't natural for a man to bear so much so quiet."

"Coo!" said Jessie.

Mrs. Mostyn, who had forgotten her, turned majestically. "You get on with those bedrooms, my girl, and no messing about with madam's powders and stuff or I'll wash your face myself at the sink." Jessie went reluctantly. She liked listening to the gossip of the older servants. On the other hand, it would be fun to try on some of Mrs. Frere's hats and admire herself in her long mirror.

Poor Mr. Roger, she thought. It seemed hard that he should be the odd man out. He was kinder and more considerate, more of a real gentleman than Cedric, but you couldn't expect a foreign person to know that.

When she had gone Mrs. Bligh resumed. "I know madam's sort. I was once a temporary cook in a private hotel not far from Prince's gate. Chock a block it was with Colonels' widows playing bridge and quarrelling. But the young one's got me guessing. She never sets foot in my kitchen. What do you think of her, Amy, just between you and me?"

"It's hard to say," said the parlourmaid thoughtfully. "I suppose her queerness comes of her being foreign. She's different. She's got funny ways. For instance, she uses a lot of scent, proper reeks of it, but no make-up. Not that she needs it, she's got lovely skin and you never saw such lashes, as thick and as long as those they stick on in the films. And, mind you, cook, she's a real lady. What I mean is, she's used to being waited on, and more of it than she gets here. One can always tell. But being always half asleep is so strange. She never says a word at meals, just eats her food and stares out of the window with her eyes half shut, and when I take the coffee into the drawing-room afterwards there she is on the sofa curled up, and I know better now than to disturb her. She don't drink coffee anyway, nothing but water. Well, there it is. You can make a long list of the things she does different or leaves undone, and at the end you don't know her any better."

"Not the kind to make a man happy," said the cook.

Miss Mostyn answered primly. "I wouldn't know about that. Well, I must be getting on if I'm to get my silver cleaned before lunch."

She had gone up to her pantry and was setting out her brushes and saucer of jeweller's rouge when Jessie came clattering down the service stairs, calling as she came.

"Mrs. Bligh—Miss Mostyn—"

The parlourmaid went out to her. "What's happened? Have you broken something?" she asked sharply.

Jessie's cap had slipped to one side, her plump cheeks were pale and her childish blue eyes dilated with fright.

"Please—while I was doing the bedrooms I heard Doris overhead carrying on something awful."

"What do you mean?"

"I mean moaning and crying out, and then being sick—"

Miss Mostyn's thin lips tightened in disapproval. "She's over-eaten herself again or taken something to disagree with her. Always stuffing herself with sweets." She hesitated. "I'd better go up to her, I suppose."

She went briskly up the stairs to the top floor. Jessie followed and lingered in the passage while the older woman went into the room shutting the door after her. Doris seemed to be quiet now, but somehow Jessie was not reassured. Miss Mostyn came out again rather quickly. She still seemed annoyed. "She doesn't think of all the trouble she gives other people when she makes a pig of herself," she said. "Run down now, Jessie. Fill one of the rubber bottles and bring up a jug of hot water and a cloth. I'm coming down to tell Mrs. Bligh. I think she ought to have a drop of brandy—"

The parlourmaid was unsympathetic but she was brisk and capable. Within half an hour the patient had been made comfortable with fresh sheets and a clean nightdress and a hot bottle at her feet. Miss Mostyn, noticing that she had traces of a rash on her face and neck, thought she might be sickening for measles and kept Jessie out of the room as much as possible. Doris had swallowed the brandy though she complained that it burnt her inside.

"I feel better," she said faintly, "and thank you for all you've done—"

"Let it be a lesson to you. Greed's one of the seven deadly sins, young Doris. Try to get off to sleep now. I'm going down to my dinner."

Mrs. Bligh was just dishing up the steak and onions when she came into the kitchen, and her interest was perfunctory. "Better? That's all right. Draw up your chairs, both of you. I've got a lovely apricot tart in the oven—"

It was cosy in the firelit kitchen and they lingered over their meal. Afterwards Mrs. Bligh made tea while Jessie took the dishes out to the scullery.

"I daresay that poor kid upstairs could do with a nice cup well sweetened. Will you take it up to her, Amy?"

"Oh, all right," said the parlourmaid ungraciously. "I little thought when I got up this morning that I was to be run off my feet."

But when she came down again her manner had changed.

"She's been sick again. I'd like you to come up and have a look at her."

Mrs. Bligh, who had taken a greasy pack out of the table drawer and was dealing out the cards, laid them down quickly and heaved herself out of her chair. The back stairs creaked under her weight as she went panting up to the top floor, closely followed by Miss Mostyn.

The red patches on the sick girl's face and neck had faded but her eyes were very much inflamed. She was afraid of the sharp-tongued parlourmaid but she was rather fond of the stout good-natured cook and she tried to smile at her.

She murmured something. Mrs. Bligh nodded reassuringly. "I daresay. But don't you worry. Whatever it was upset you, has been got rid of and no mistake. You keep quiet, that's a good girl. Maybe you'll fancy a milk jelly for your supper. Best thing you can do now is to get a bit of sleep."

"I feel—awful—"

"You'll be better soon."

Miss Mostyn joined her in the passage and they conferred in whispers.

"What do you think of her?"

"Not so good. It's more than a bilious attack. I'm going down-stairs now to ring up the doctor."

Doctor Quin was out on his round. His wife answered the call. "I'll tell him as soon as he comes in."

"When will that be?"

"I can't say exactly. Some time between two and five if he has not been detained. Is it urgent?"

"It's Doris Jupp, the housemaid at Frere Court, Ma'am. She's having a bad sick turn."

"Oh—that doesn't sound very serious."

"Maybe not, but she looks like death."

"What did you say? I didn't quite catch. Is it Mrs. Frere speaking?"

"No. Mrs. Bligh. The cook."

"Oh. I see," the voice sounded more distant. "I'll tell the doctor—"

She made a note on the pad left on the hall table for that purpose and rang off. The doctor came in at ten minutes to five.

"What's this?" He sounded weary and impatient. His wife answered him from the drawing-room. "The Freres' cook rang up. One of the maids has a bilious attack or something. Come and have tea first, darling. You must be worn out and I'm sure it can't be urgent—"

He came in and took the cup she poured out for him but he would not sit down. "I'd better get over there before the evening surgery." He sighed. He was not looking forward to a five-mile drive through the forest in the streaming rain. His wife looked at him anxiously. "Why not ring them up before you start?"

"No. I'd better go—"

There was mist drifting in with the rain from the Solent and he had to drive slowly. It was nearly six and had been dark for some time when he reached Frere Court. There were lights in the hall and in one of the upper windows.

The little maid who admitted him was pale and dishevelled and looked as if she had been crying. "Where is my patient?"

"Upstairs, sir. Cook and Miss Mostyn are both with her. This way, if you please—"

He found the two women bending over the bed, their shadows cast by a candle on a chair flickering gigantic over the wall. Frere Court had been renovated from time to time, but it had never been thought necessary to take gas or electric light up to the servants' rooms. Quin picked up the candle and waved to them to move aside while he made his examination. After a moment he muttered "Good God!" He was feeling for the girl's pulse. They all waited in a silence so profound that the ticking of the cheap alarm clock on the chest of drawers sounded unnaturally loud.

Mrs. Bligh moistened her lips. "Is she—is she gone, sir?"

"I'm afraid so," he said harshly. "What have you been doing to her?"

"Me, sir? Nothing. We've been waiting for you all the afternoon."

I know. I know. I was out. I came as soon as I could. What was it?"

Mrs. Bligh described the symptoms. "She's a hearty feeder and over fond of sweets and such-like and I thought it was just a bilious attack—"

"When did it start?"

"Soon after ten. She was doing the bedrooms. She told the other girl and left her work to lie down."

"Did you inform Mrs. Frere?"

"None of the family are at home, sir."

"Do you mean that you are on board wages?"

Oh, no. Mrs. Frere drove over to Bournemouth as she generally does. I rang up her club just now, but she wasn't there. She might be playing bridge with friends. The others are all out but I couldn't say where, only that they're not expected back to dinner."

"I see. Well, I shall have to use the telephone now. The body must be removed for a post-mortem."

Mrs. Bligh looked startled. "Oh, dearie me! Is that necessary?"

"Unless she has been seen by some other doctor within twenty-four hours," he said grimly. "She hasn't? I thought not. But first I want two jampots and some paper and string. You can leave me here for the present. Send the girl up with them."

He got both women out of the room and shut the door. The cook was shaking with anger and mortification. "Well, I never in all my born days. Anyone'd think—"

Mostyn took her arm. "Come along down to the kitchen. We can't do no good up here. What we both want is a nice cup of tea."

Jessie, returning from her errand, reported that the doctor had opened the door a few inches to take the jampots and the paper and string from her and that she had heard the key turned in the lock as she moved away.

"What does he want them for?"

"Never you mind," said the cook, darkly.

Very soon they heard the doctor's voice speaking at the telephone. They were still drinking their tea when he came down to the kitchen. He seemed to realise that he had antagonised them by his abruptness and to be anxious to be on a better footing. "This is pleasant," he said as he looked round the warm lamplit kitchen and sniffed the aroma of hot cake. "Nothing like tea, eh? I bet you needed it."

Mrs. Bligh, who was never one to nurse a grievance, relaxed at once. "Won't you have a cup yourself, Doctor, and a slice of my raisin cake."

He thanked her and Jessie got another cup and saucer from the dresser and brought a chair nearer to the fire.

"You seem very comfortable here," he said. "All quite happy, eh?"

"All places have their drawbacks," said Mrs. Bligh, "but we're satisfied. I think I can speak for you two girls as well as myself?"

"If I wasn't," said the parlourmaid, "I shouldn't be here."

"And you could have said the same of that poor girl upstairs? No troubles that you know of?" he said, casually.

But the casual tone could not deceive the two older women. They exchanged glances before the cook said, "None that I ever heard of. What do you say, Amy?"

Miss Mostyn looked down her nose. "I couldn't say, I'm sure. She's a local girl, like Jessie here. Brought up by an aunt, I believe. She never told me anything about her affairs."

He turned to Jessie. "Had she a boy?"

"Well—there was Bert Moore. They used to go about together, but they haven't lately. She never said nothing to me. You see, I'm four years younger than her. She sort of looked down on me."

"You shared her room here?"

"Until about a month ago. She said I snored though I'm sure I never, and Mrs. Frere said, very well, I could go to the little room at the end of the passage."

The doctor set down his cup. "And you heard or saw anything to suggest that she was unhappy? Be careful how you answer."

They all stared at him, Mrs. Bligh with a dawning horror, but Jessie seemed merely puzzled. "No. She was all right. Just as usual. But I wouldn't have known if she had been. She wasn't one to talk about herself ever. Always a bit of a dark horse like."

"I see." He got up as the front door bell rang. "That will be the ambulance. You had better all stay down here while I see to things—"

He hurried out. Jessie began to cry. The other two ignored her.

"What did he mean?" whispered the parlourmaid.

Mrs. Bligh shook her head. "When I laid out the cards before going up to her there was death in the pack. The ace of spades on the queen. It's a sure sign. I remember when my mother's brother—"

"Hark," said Mostyn. "They're bringing her down—"

They crowded together at the foot of the kitchen stairs listening to the murmur of voices above and the heavy tread of men carrying a burden. Jessie, choking, clutched the cook's arm. "Oh, Mrs. Bligh, you don't think she—took something—"

Chapter XVI
A BOX OF DATES

THE inquest on Doris Jupp was opened two days after her death and formal evidence of identity was given by the aunt who had brought her up. The enquiry was then adjourned for a few days.

"I expected more of a crowd," Enderby told Celia. He had called at the vicarage on his way home and found her alone. "I said as much to Tomsett, and he told me there were rival attractions, market day at Ringwood and some film star or other due to land at Southampton."

The church bell had begun to toll as he spoke. He looked at Celia and she nodded. "The funeral is this afternoon. I went to see poor old Miss Jupp yesterday. She's quite bewildered. It was so sudden. But she says the Freres have been very kind. The elder Mrs. Frere sent her five pounds to buy her mourning and Roger is paying the funeral expenses. They both sent flowers and the other maids clubbed together for a wreath, so she was quite overflowing with gratitude to everybody at the Court. But you don't want to hear all this—"

"On the contrary," said Enderby.

Celia, who was darning her father's old cassock, paused in the act of threading her needle to look at him.

"You say that as if—there can't have been anything wrong. Miss Jupp was so angry about that. She said a man whom she supposed to be the insurance agent and who afterwards turned out to be a policeman in plain clothes had been asking her all sorts of questions about Doris and if she had many admirers and—and that sort of thing. Her aunt said she used to go out with Bert Moore at the forge, but that was broken off some time ago, and so far as she knew there wasn't anybody else, and that Doris was never one to run after boys."

"I think I saw her once or twice during the summer when I was at the Court playing tennis," said Enderby. "She helped the parlourmaid bring tea into the garden. Cedric jumped up to do something for her, and I heard him call her Doris. The parlourmaid is middle-aged and rather grim, but I remember thinking that her *aide-de-camp* was a pretty fluffy little thing."

"Oh, dear," said Celia, "I do hope you're wrong. That is, if you mean what I think you mean."

"I know no more than you do," he said, "a little more about procedure perhaps. The inquest has been adjourned, and the police are making enquiries. I'm afraid that means that the verdict is not likely to be death from natural causes."

He broke off as Mrs. Bond came in with the tea trolley and a plate of new-made scones. Celia laid aside her work and poured out the tea. The tolling of the bell had ceased.

"Father won't be back yet. He has to go a round of visits. He was saying that he thought she might have had a duodenal ulcer."

"It sounded like that," Enderby agreed. "I heard a good many details from my housekeeper who had them from the milkman who got them straight from the horse's—or rather the cook's mouth. But I gathered that the doctor was not satisfied and that he rang up the police and had the body removed for a post mortem without even waiting for the return of the family."

"It must have been a shock for them," said Celia.

"No doubt," said Enderby drily. He stirred his tea. "Two inquests in less than two months. Sooner or later these things become noticeable."

Celia gazed at him. "You think there might be some connection? If poor Doris killed herself because of an unhappy love affair—that's what you've been hinting at, isn't it? The young man might have been Lasseter. She would have been fearfully upset at his dying like that. That may be it, if she did—did take something—"

"An irritant poison? Possible," said Enderby, "but not probable. Flaubert's Madame Bovary took arsenic, but in my experience people who are tired of life prefer something from the barbituric group. Look here, Celia, all this is guesswork. I know I can talk freely to you and that what I say will go no further. There's something very queer going on. If it's what I half suspect it is the local police will soon be hopelessly out of their depth. I can't tell at present whether the death of Doris Jupp fits into the pattern or is something extraneous dropped in by Fate to make it a bit more difficult."

"Oughtn't you to go to the police and tell them what you suspect?" she asked anxiously.

He shook his head. "They would laugh at me. They might even send for a couple of doctors and have me certified. I must have some proof. At present I have none." He set down his cup and struck a match to light her cigarette. It crossed his mind, not for the first time, how strange it was that he who during all his years in the east had so little to do with women, should be confiding so freely in a girl he had only known for a few weeks and depending so much on her sympathy and her understanding.

"Have you seen Roger Frere lately?"

"Not since this happened. I met him a few days ago in the forest. He said he had been talking about me to Nina and that she hoped I would come to tea with her some day. Of course I said I would be very pleased, but that kind of general invitation doesn't mean anything. I rather gathered that she is not settling down as quickly as he had hoped and that he wants her to meet more people. He said his step-brother was going out to California next week."

"I don't suppose he will now," said Enderby.

"You mean—because of Doris?"

"If the girl took poison—or was poisoned," said Enderby bluntly, "everyone at Frere Court will be more or less under suspicion. Suppose Cedric had been making love to her and she threatened to complain to Mrs. Frere. His mother spoils him, but I daresay she bullies him, too. She's that sort of woman, possessive, overwhelming, the type that drives weaker natures to hole and corner dealings and deceit. I don't say that is what happened, but it's not impossible. Well, I must be getting along—"

"Don't forget to-morrow is the night for chess." Celia was going with him to the door. She picked up a long oval box from a side table. "Try one of these stuffed dates? It's my first Christmas present. Somebody who believes in posting early. I can't imagine who it can be. I haven't tried them yet, but they look good."

Enderby checked himself in the act of taking a date to look rather more closely at the neat rows of shining brown fruit, powdered with sugar and slightly distended by their stuffing of nuts. "They look very luscious, as you say. When did they come?"

"Yesterday. Oh—I never thought—" Celia flushed a little. "Did you send them?"

"No," he said. "No. I'm afraid I can't claim the credit. The handwriting on the parcel was not familiar?"

"I didn't recognise it at all. It might have been anybody. The ink had run."

"Did you keep the wrapping?"

"No. And I'm afraid it's no use looking for it. Mrs. Bond always burns the stuff in the waste-paper baskets in the copper fire. But it does not matter much. Sooner or later someone will say, 'Did you get those dates I sent you?' and I shall say, 'Thanks so much—'"

To her surprise Enderby persisted. "Did you notice the postmark?"

"No, I didn't. The stamps were English. I did notice that, because I had thought it might be from the Romeros in Cannes."

He was silent for so long and his face was so grave that she felt something like alarm. "What is it? What's the matter?"

"Nothing, I hope," he said. "I don't want to frighten you, Celia, but I have just realised that if there is anything in my theory you may be in some danger. Have you some relations or friends you could go to stay with at short notice?"

She shook her head. "I'm not going away."

"All right. I didn't really think you would," he said with a half smile, "but you've got to be careful."

"What does that mean exactly?"

"Don't go out alone at all after nightfall, or any distance off the main roads even in broad daylight. And don't eat sweets sent you by an unknown well-wisher."

He saw her eyes dilate and her fingers stole up to her lips. "Oh, dear," she whispered, "and if you hadn't come in I should have begun them. But I can't believe it. I—I'm quite harmless—"

He looked down at her thoughtfully. "I fancy some knowledge that might be fatal either to its possessor or to others may be within your reach. But if we take reasonable precautions you should be safe enough. May I have this box to take away with me? I have a friend who is an analyst."

"Yes. Yes, please do." She hesitated. "I don't pretend to understand. Is my father in danger, too? Would it be better for him if I went away?"

"I don't think so. In any case, from what I have seen of the vicar you wouldn't be able to move him."

"A pig-headed family," she said, trying to speak more lightly. "You don't take your own medicine. It's after dark and you're walking back alone to the White Cottage. You haven't even got your dog with you."

"I couldn't take him to the inquest. I shall be all right," he said, but she thought he looked about him rather sharply, trying to pierce the misty darkness, as he stood on the step winding his muffler about his throat.

"Good-night, Celia."

"Good-night."

She closed the door and went back to the sitting-room. She was wondering what her father would say if she repeated to him the substance of some of her recent conversations with Major Enderby. When he was with her she was convinced by his earnestness, but when he had gone a gnawing doubt was at work in her mind. He was always hinting at some dark mystery. Wasn't far more likely that there was a prosaic explanation for everything that had happened lately?

She remembered that when he first came to the White Cottage her father had written to her about him that, though he was reticent about himself it was understood that he had been in the Indian police and that he had had a severe nervous breakdown. Her heart sank as she reflected what this expression sometimes connoted. Wasn't it possible that on certain subjects he was not quite sane? And yet—this fear of some undefined menace that haunted the forest by night was no figment of Enderby's imagination. More than one of the village women had advised her not to go off the roads even during the day. It was only to-night, when he hinted that there was some sinister mystery about the death of poor Doris Jupp that Celia began to feel that her faith in his greater knowledge and experience might be mistaken.

When the vicar came in some time later and was smoking his pipe, in slippered ease, by the fire, she sounded him on the subject.

"The Major attended the inquest. He came in for a chat on his way home. Have you heard what was the cause of her death, Father?"

"That poor girl at Frere Court, you mean? I have not, but I had a word with her aunt after the funeral and she told me Gladys was always very fond of rich cakes and sweets, and that she often had severe bilious attacks as a result of over indulgence. The most probable cause would be a duodenal ulcer. The heart didn't stand the strain of the vomiting and the doctor was sent for too late. It was unfortunate that there was no responsible person in the house when she was taken ill."

"Major Enderby seemed to think there might be more in it than that," she said.

The vicar showed a trace of impatience. "I like Enderby," he said, "he's a good fellow, but I'm beginning to think he's a bit of a scaremonger. Queer things may happen in the East, but this is Hampshire, and we're a humdrum law abiding crowd. He'll realise that himself in time. Meanwhile, my dear, we must not take him too seriously. Are you going up to bed now? Good-night and don't you get fanciful."

CHAPTER XVII
CALLING IN THE YARD

ON HIS infrequent visits to London Enderby usually lunched at his club in Pall Mall. The head waiter, who had been in his battery twenty years earlier, always saw that he had his favourite table in the window.

He was eating his sole with the sauce for which the club chef was famous when another member, who had finished his lunch, came up to him. "Enderby, I'm delighted to see you. I had no idea you were back in England—" he said heartily.

Enderby's rather sombre face lighted up. "How are you, Sir James? You look fit," he said as they shook hands. "I've been home about a year now."

Sir James Welland drew up a chair and lit a cigarette.

"Why didn't you look me up?"

"I had an illness," said Enderby briefly, "the doctors advised a long rest. I took a cottage in the country and have been living a hermit existence."

"Better now, I hope?" said Welland.

"Yes. And I was thinking of coming round to the Yard on the strength of our old friendship this very afternoon. I nearly wrote to you in the spring when I saw in the paper that you had been appointed Assistant Commissioner. It's not too late, I hope, to offer my congratulations."

"Well—it's not altogether a bed of roses, you know," said Welland ruefully. "I'm not at all sure that if I had realised all the worry—we've had several foreign potentates over here since I took on, and looking after them is no picnic. I envy you the peace of the country. Whereabouts is your cottage, by the way?"

"Hampshire. The New Forest. Swain Green is the nearest village." He attacked the omelette au Rhum set before him by the waiter.

"Swain Green. Where have I heard that name quite lately?" Welland dropped his half-smoked cigarette in the ash tray, and leaned forward. "I remember. It was this very morning. Enderby, do you know any people named Frere in your part of the world?"

"I do."

"And you were coming to see me. Was that a coincidence? I mean—was it to be just a friendly visit or were you going to talk shop?"

Enderby smiled. "I'd rather not be pinned down. Are the local police calling in the Yard over the Jupp case?"

"They are. But how did you know? We were told that she was generally supposed to have died a natural death and that the inquest was a mere formality."

Enderby hesitated. "Perhaps I had no valid reason for suspecting anything else. But it's a strange household. I've been anticipating trouble, but I don't know how the housemaid became involved. I'm saying too much. I may be wronging the family. This girl's tragedy may be extraneous. You have evidence of foul play?"

Welland nodded. "And how. But this must go no further, Enderby. If it became known locally it might hamper the investigation. I am sending down one of our most promising men. He's still young, but he has several successes to his credit. May we rely on you to give him some help? He will be working with the local people, as usual, but it seems that several of their most experienced officers are down with 'flu. I doubt if they would have applied to us but for that."

Enderby took a card from his case. "This is my address. If he will come and see me I'll tell him all I can."

"If you'll come along to the Yard now I'll introduce you to him. He is going down to Hampshire to-day, but he won't have left yet. I'll ring up to make sure while you finish your coffee."

Enderby agreed, and within half an hour they were seated in the Assistant Commissioner's room at Scotland Yard.

Sir James sat down at his desk while Enderby went over to the window. The fog was thickening, slowing down the traffic, and the syrens of the boats on the river wailed like lost souls.

"This is Detective-Inspector Collier, Major Enderby." Enderby saw a youngish man with a lean active figure, brown hair turning grey at the temples, and very shrewd blue eyes. Not, he observed with a relief, a policeman of the narrow, hide-bound type.

Collier was less favourably impressed. In Enderby he saw a man who at some time had tried his physical and mental powers to the uttermost, and had never quite recovered from the strain, struggling gallantly but not quite successfully against the handicap of years and of bad health. He acquiesced civilly when Sir James explained that the Major might be of great assistance to him, but he was not enthusiastic.

Enderby, who was sensitive to atmospheres, said quickly, "I shall be on hand if you want me. I shan't butt in."

"I'll be glad of your help, sir," said Collier more cordially. He always tried to avoid hurting anybody's feelings. "May I ask if it is in connection with this case that you are here?"

"It may be," said Enderby. "There's something damnably wrong about the place and has been for several weeks past, but I have not been able to get any concrete evidence. Guesses and suspicions—wild guesses and wild suspicions—aren't good enough. I didn't want to be laughed at. But I've got something at last."

He took a long narrow brown paper parcel from his overcoat pocket, unwrapped it and laid it on Sir James' desk. "Here you are." He removed the lid.

Collier came nearer and the Assistant Commissioner adjusted his glasses.

"Stuffed dates," he said. "My wife has a weakness for them. I must say they look good."

"I shall not offer these to Lady Welland," said Enderby. "I sent them to a friend of mine, an analyst, Quentin Laban, and I called at his laboratory this morning to collect them with his report. I have it here, signed and witnessed by his assistant. You notice the dusting of sugar? Well, there's some sugar but it's mostly powdered glass."

"Good Heavens." Sir James stared at the box as if he had seen a snake coiled under the neat row of shining brown fruit.

Collier said nothing, but he looked at Enderby with increased attention.

"This is serious, Enderby. How did you get hold of them? Who tampered with them?"

"I can't tell you that. I don't know. They were sent to the daughter of the vicar of Swain Green. know. She showed them to me and said she had no idea who the giver might be. They had come by post without any covering letter. Unfortunately, the wrappings had been destroyed. She was not suspicious, but she allowed me to take the box away. Those are the facts. Whether there is any connection with the death of Doris Jupp—"

Collier looked questioningly at the Assistant Commissioner who nodded. "We can take Enderby fully into our confidence, Collier."

"Yes, sir." He turned to Enderby. "There may be a connection, but powdered glass was not used in the case of Doris Jupp. Nearly two grains of arsenic were found in the organs, over one grain in the vomited matter. The doctors say they are not prepared to swear when the poison was taken. She began to be ill a little before eleven. It might have been at supper the night before or at breakfast that morning."

"I see," said Enderby slowly.

Sir James cleared his throat. "It's rather a pity you didn't send this box straight to us for examination, Enderby. There might be fingerprints—"

"I tried it for prints first of all before sending it on to Laban. There were several but all made by the same person, Celia Holland, the recipient. No doubt the person who tampered with the dates had been careful to wear gloves. The Bertillon system has had too much publicity," said Enderby. He added rather stiffly, "I'm sorry you think I took too much upon myself. My suspicions seemed so far-fetched. I didn't want to waste your time or become an object for ridicule."

"My dear fellow," said Welland, "you would be hearing from me if you had come without an atom of evidence. I happen to know something of your record in India."

Enderby smiled faintly. "Thanks. But I've no illusions. After my breakdown I lost confidence in my own judgment, and that's fatal. This case, for instance, I believe I hold some of the threads, but I wouldn't care to handle it alone. I should not have felt like that a few years ago. Well," he picked up his hat and gloves, "I only came up for the day and I want to catch the 3.40 down. Good-bye, Sir James." He shook hands first with the Assistant Commissioner and then with the Inspector.

"You'll be seeing me again before long, sir," said Collier. "I'll be glad of all the help I can get. By the way, you won't mention this date business to anyone, will you? The less said the better at present."

Enderby hesitated. "Miss Holland should be warned, I think. She should be on her guard."

"I agree, sir, but I shall be seeing her myself this evening or to-morrow morning at the latest."

"I see. Very well."

Sir James had touched a bell and a young constable had come to show him out. When he had gone Collier looked expectantly at his superior officer.

"You'll have that box of dates examined by our own people, sir?"

"Naturally. It's a good rule to take nothing for granted, Collier. But don't underrate Major Enderby. He had a great reputation among those in the know in India, and not only in India. He made a special study of eastern folk lore and of the secret rites of some ancient religions that are supposed to have been stamped out though actually they are still practised in some parts of the world. That illness he referred to broke what might have been a brilliant career."

"What sort of illness was it, sir?"

"Does it matter?" the Assistant Commissioner's raised eyebrows indicated that he thought his subordinate's curiosity misplaced. "I don't know the details. I believe he was given a couple of years leave to recuperate. At the end of that time the doctors wouldn't pass him fit for service so he resigned. You heard what he said himself. You are being put in charge of this case, Collier, and it's up to you to profit by the Major's first-hand knowledge of the people at Swain Green, or not, as you think best."

"You mean I'm to have a free hand as to that, sir?"

"Exactly. Well, I can't spare you any more time now, Inspector. You're going down at once, of course. Who will you take with you?"

"Sergeant Duffield if I can get him."

"You had better ask Superintendent Cardew about that." The A.C. had picked up his pen and was already busy with the pile of reports on his desk.

Collier saluted and went out, treading delicately. The Superintendent received him with his usual gruff good humour. "What have you done to deserve a kick in the pants?" he enquired.

Collier winced. "Is it as obvious as that? I got across the Old Man. Asking too many questions."

"Silly questions?"

"I don't think so. But the old school tie was involved. Perhaps it doesn't really matter. Can I have Duffield to hold my hand, Superintendent?"

Cardew grinned. "I knew you'd want him. He's ready."

"Thank you, sir."

Cardew waved his hand. "I hope it keeps fine for you."

Chapter XVIII
POLICE AT FRERE COURT

The Freres had dined and were having coffee in the drawing-room. Nina was curled up on the sofa as usual and apparently half asleep. She never took coffee. The elder Mrs. Frere, handsome and erect in her black velvet gown and bridge coat of dull silver edged with monkey fur, sat by the fire warming her hands.

"It's absurd, of course," she said, "did you tell them you had booked your passage and that it was important that you should be in Hollywood before that company began casting for their next picture?"

"Naturally I told them," said Cedric irritably. "They simply didn't listen. I rang them up just now and reminded them that my boat sails tomorrow from Southampton, and how much longer was I to be held up because one of the maids in a house where I happened to be staying had appendicitis, or whatever it was? Hell! It serves me right, I suppose, for allowing myself to be buried alive down here instead of standing up to Roger to make me an adequate allowance to live in Town."

As Roger was not present Mrs. Frere allowed herself to remark that Cedric's present allowance would have been sufficient if he had not been so extravagant.

Cedric opened his eyes very wide. "My dear Mother—fancy you standing up for him. Wonders will never cease."

"Don't be a fool," she said curtly. "The allowance was what I considered suitable. Roger would have given you much less. I insisted and he gave way as he usually docs if one is firm enough. But never mind that now. What did the police say?"

"It was that fellow Lacy. He said it was no longer in his hands. I asked him what that meant, and he said the Chief Constable had called in Scotland Yard, and that they were sending somebody along and that he was on his way now."

"It is really intolerable," began Mrs. Frere and broke off as the door opened and Mostyn, the parlourmaid, came in with a card on a salver.

"Somebody to see Mr. Frere, madam—"

"He is not here, Mostyn. He may be in the study. You had better tell him. Where have you left this person? In the hall?"

"No, madam. I put him in the morning-room."

"Oh, well, I suppose that will do."

When she had gone, mother and son looked at each other. Mrs. Frere was too well made up to show any change of colour but she made a nervous movement. "The little fool," she said.

"Who do you mean?"

"That girl, Doris."

Cedric shrugged his shoulders and said nothing. Meanwhile Inspector Collier had been shown into the study. Roger, who had been turning out a box full of stamps, got up and came forward to shake hands. Collier thought he looked ill and worried. His eyes were strained and restless and his manner was uneasy. He gave Collier the impression of a man with something to hide.

"I must apologise," Collier began, "for calling at such an hour. My excuse is that my time is limited. I have to ask a few questions of everybody. My colleague, Inspector Lacy of the local police, was here the other day, I know, taking statements which I have seen. I'm sorry to bother you again, but there may be just a point or two—it's only a matter of form—"

"I quite understand," said Roger, "you must do your duty. It's a most unfortunate business. Was it ptomaine poisoning? No one else here was affected."

Collier, who was turning over the pages of his notebook, ignored the question. "I have a transcription of your statement here. On the Monday evening you were at home. You dined alone. The elder Mrs. Frere had gone to Bournemouth and Mr. Cedric Frere was in London. Your wife had complained of a headache and gone to bed." Collier paused a moment. "I gather that you occupy separate rooms?"

"Yes."

Roger took a cigarette from his case. Collier, who was watching him closely without appearing to do so, noticed that his hand was shaking.

"And what happened then?"

"I read for a while, and then—I felt I needed exercise—I went for a walk."

"A dark night, wasn't it, and raining?

"Yes. What of it? You can't stop for rain in this country."

"I suppose not. What time did you get home?"

"I called on a friend who lives not far off. It was raining pretty hard then and he persuaded me to stay the night."

"So you did not come home until the following morning?"

"That is so."

"You weren't afraid that your absence would cause anxiety?"

"No. I don't suppose anyone noticed. I had breakfast with my friend, but I came over directly afterwards. Breakfast is served here at nine. There is a hot plate and we come down when we like. My half brother and I, that is. Mrs. Frere and my wife have trays taken to their rooms."

"There's nothing about this in your first statement, Mr. Frere."

"I wasn't asked. In any case it's hardly relevant, is it?"

"Probably not," said Collier pleasantly, "but it's too early to say one way or the other. I'm collecting facts, Mr. Frere. When I've got them all I shall sort them out as you were sorting those stamps."

"It was my uncle's collection. I'm sending it away to be valued," said Roger. His tone was dull and lifeless.

"I see. Well, about this friend. No doubt he will corroborate your account. Could you give me his name and address?"

"Certainly. His name is Enderby, Major Enderby, and he lives at the White Cottage. Turn right when you come out of the lodge gates. The house stands alone about half a mile along the road."

Enderby. Collier was startled, but he did not show it. "Thank you, Mr. Frere. We come now to the day of the girl's death. You have given an account of your movements—"

"Yes. I went into Southampton by bus. I had some lunch at a restaurant below Bar and afterwards I went to a cinema. After the show I had tea at the same restaurant and did some shopping."

"What sort of shopping, Mr. Frere?"

"Well I bought some socks and ties at an outfitters, and cigarettes."

"Did you buy any sweets?"

"No."

"You came home by bus?"

"Yes. I arrived about half-past seven and found a policeman in the hall. Doris died soon after five, the doctor had rung up for the ambulance and her body had been removed. Mrs. Bligh, the cook, told me all about it. She was very much upset, poor woman."

"It was a shock to you, too, wasn't it?"

"Of course. I didn't realise at first that she had had the entire responsibility. She had rung up my stepmother at her club in Bournemouth, but unfortunately she wasn't there."

"Yes. I shall be going into that presently with Mrs. Frere."

"I don't know what you're trying to get at," said Roger, "but I'm afraid I can't do much to help you."

"Who engages the staff here, Mr. Frere?"

"The indoor staff? My stepmother. I look after the men out of doors. But, as a matter of fact, I haven't had anything to do. They were all here in my uncle's time. I have made no changes."

"About Doris Jupp, Mr. Frere. She was a local girl?"

"Yes."

"How did she strike you?"

"I don't quite understand."

"Well, she had been here several months. She was the house-maid. She would lay out and put away your clothes, bring up your early tea and so on. You must have seen something of her and formed some impression surely?"

"I see. I'm afraid I didn't notice much about her. She was all right. I didn't dislike her. Not very efficient, perhaps. She was very young, of course."

"She was a pretty girl, wasn't she?"

"Yes, I think she was rather."

"Was she inclined to be forward, trying to attract attention?"

"I don't think so. Not mine, at any rate."

"Your stepbrother's perhaps?" said Collier quietly.

"I shouldn't know about that."

"You are on good terms with your stepbrother, Mr. Frere?"

"Fairly. We differ about money. I think he's extravagant, and he thinks I'm mean."

"You went into Southampton by bus. Don't you drive a car?"

"I have one, but I don't use it much. I'm not very fond of driving. I had a very bad smash. At least—my stepsister was driv-ing—she was killed—"

"Thanks. I think that will be all to-night. I think if I may be allowed the use of that room I was shown into when I arrived I could see people there. I'd like a few words with your stepmother before I question the servants."

"Yes, of course. Mostyn will tell her—" Roger rang the bell.

"Oh, by the way," said Collier casually. "I wanted to call at the post office in Southampton, but I couldn't find it. Could you direct me? I shall probably be there again to-morrow."

"I'm sorry," said Roger. "I've no idea."

"He did not fall into that trap," thought Collier, as he waited in the morning-room for Mrs. Frere. He could have sent the box of dates from there—if he sent them. Was he responsible for the death of Doris Jupp? Had he made love to the girl and then grown tired? The local police had hinted at some such motive. It was rumoured that the Freres did not get on together though they had only been married a few months. "She's a foreigner," Lacy had said. "A good looker, but more for show than for comfort, if you ask me. Always gallivanting off to road-houses with the young fellow, her brother-in-law."

Collier was standing when Mrs. Frere came in. She did not ask him to sit down but remained standing herself, resting one hand on the back of a chair.

"You wished to see me?"

"I shan't keep you long, Mrs. Frere. My name is Collier. Detective Inspector Collier of New Scotland Yard. I have been called in to assist the local police in the matter of Miss Jupp's death."

She looked at him with cold distaste. "All this police activity has been worrying me a good deal. I assumed—we all did—that the poor girl died as the result of the breaking of a duodenal ulcer. I knew of one such case years ago."

"I am sorry, Mrs. Frere. She died of arsenical poison. She had taken considerably more than a lethal dose."

"Good Heavens! This is terrible. I think we had better sit down—"

She sank into a chair and searched for a handkerchief in her black velvet evening bag. "What possessed her, Inspector? She seemed quite cheerful and contented. I believe the maids I have now get on very well together. I suppose it might be a love affair. You ought to be able to find out about that. She is a local girl. Was, I should say. I can't get used to the idea that she is gone."

"Would she be able to get hold of arsenic easily here, Mrs. Frere?"

"I don't know, I'm sure. I shouldn't think so. It's not like disinfectant that is used for cleaning."

"What about weed killer? Have you any on the premises?"

"Not in the house. The garden is not my department. My stepson looks after the outdoor staff and orders what may be needed."

"I see." Collier thought of another question, but decided not to ask it. Instead he said, "You had already gone out when she was first taken ill?"

"Yes. I have a little car which I drive myself. I spend a good deal of my time in Bournemouth. I am a member of a bridge club there. Unfortunately, I was not at the club but at a friend's house when the cook rang up. Living as I do with my stepson and his wife I think it advisable to efface myself as much as possible. Don't think I'm complaining. They are kindness itself to me, but I have a dread of being in the way. Young people like to be by themselves when they are settling down to the give and take of married life. It is always a trying time," said Mrs. Frere indulgently.

"Did you see Doris before you left the house that morning?" asked Collier, ignoring this dissertation.

"She brought up my early tea as usual. I was half asleep then. An hour later she brought my breakfast tray and letters. She asked me if she should run the water for my bath and I said she might. I told her I should want my car at half-past nine. We have no chauffeur but the undergardener cleans the cars and sees that the tanks are filled and so forth."

"She would have to go into the garden to find him and transmit your order?"

"She might, I suppose. He is generally somewhere about in the morning. He does odd jobs for the cook too. He's a sort of handy man really. I see what you mean. If there is any weed killer it would be in the potting shed. If she went there to find Harris and he wasn't there, and she saw it on the shelf she might—if she was unhappy—as one assumes she must have been—have yielded to an impulse."

"Yes," said Collier. "It might have happened like that. It's one of the possibilities to be borne in mind. You're very quick to see a point, Mrs. Frere."

"Am I?" she said faintly, apparently not ill pleased by the compliment. She had thawed considerably since the beginning of their interview and was being, for her, unusually gracious to a social inferior.

"Looking back can you remember if she seemed at all upset?

Mrs. Frere considered. "She was a well trained servant, Inspector. She would not show her feelings. She said, 'Good morning, madam.' Perhaps not quite so brightly as usual. I remember now I glanced at her and noticed that her eyes seemed inflamed. It occurred to me that she might have been crying, but then I thought it might be a cold. It seemed nothing much and I dismissed it from my mind."

"How long had she been in your service, Mrs. Frere?"

"Let me see. This is December. She came to us last April."

"She had a good character?"

"Quite good. She had been with Major and Mrs. Fairchild at Boldre. She left them because she didn't get on with their cook. Her weakness was greediness. She had a passion for sweets and pastries, and I gathered that she used to go into the pantry and help herself. Naturally the cook was annoyed. My cook, Mrs. Bligh, managed her better, and I believe the poor girl was trying to conquer her fault."

"Would you say she was an attractive girl?"

Mrs. Frere's carefully-plucked eyebrows went up a little. "You mean attractive to men? Not particularly I should imagine. She was quite ordinary in appearance. But she may have been for all I know."

"Thank you. I don't think I need trouble you any further. Might I see—" he consulted a list in his notebook—"Mr. Cedric Frere now for a few moments?"

Mrs. Frere smiled. "Of course, he'll be thrilled. But I'm afraid you'll be wasting your time. He is not likely to have noticed anything."

Collier opened the door for her and she acknowledged the courtesy graciously. "You are being very considerate. I can see you realise how terribly upset I have been over this."

Collier glanced over the notes he had made while he waited for Cedric. Terribly upset. Well, perhaps. The lady had struck him as being exceptionally well poised and of the hard modern type. As a witness she was, if anything, a shade too slick for his liking. She was giving nothing away. But he had to admit that the probability was that she had known very little about the dead girl. Collier remembered that his mother had considered herself responsible for her maids' moral welfare and that their young men were interviewed before they were allowed to come to tea in the kitchen. But times were changed. He looked up as Cedric lounged into the room. "Mr. Cedric Frere?"

"Yes. You're the policeman from Scotland Yard? We shall be getting into the papers. I wish I'd seen more crime films. I've always given them a miss. Fred Astaire is more my ticket, or costume stuff. I had a part in *The Forty-Five*. Did you see that?"

"I am Inspector Collier," said Collier repressively. He did not care for the kind of young actor who relies almost entirely on his good looks. He eyed Cedric's sleek golden head with distaste as he resumed. "I have the statement you made to Inspector Lacy. We'll just go through it if you don't mind—"

Cedric lay back in his chair with his legs dangling over one of its arms. They were long slim legs and he seemed as spineless as a cotillon doll that had been thrown aside. His eyes were half closed, and a cigarette hung precariously from his lower lip. "But I do mind," he said gently. "I told the other fellow I knew nothing about the girl. I was not in the house when she was taken ill, and when I came home it was all over."

"You had gone up to London the day before?"

"Yes. I'd talked things over with my brother and he had agreed that I should go over to Hollywood. More chance of getting a job if you're on the spot. I went up to book my passage on the next boat. She sails to-morrow morning. And I did some shopping. I had thought of spending the night in town but I decided to come home. I got in fairly early, between ten and eleven, garaged my car and went straight up to bed."

"Did you see anyone?"

"No. The family had turned in. Lights out everywhere. It was a foul night, raining cats and dogs, and a thick mist."

"And in the morning?"

"Jupp brought my tea as usual and drew the curtains. At least I suppose it was Jupp. I'm not very chatty at eight a.m. and I didn't look at her."

"Did you see her again?"

"I had breakfast alone. Roger wasn't down. Rather unusual for him. He's full of virtues and early rising is one of them. Afterwards I saw my sister-in-law and arranged a day's outing. I took her in my car to a road-house I had heard of on the London-Brighton road where they have a rather special band for their afternoon tea-dances. We didn't get back, as I said just now, until between eight and nine when it was all finished."

"Did Doris Jupp know that you were going to America?"

"She may have done. It wasn't a secret. I say—look here—" Cedric sat up and threw his half-smoked cigarette into the fire. "What are you hinting at? I've told you the girl was nothing to me."

"Quite," said Collier. "But girls can be very foolish. They can fall in love without receiving any encouragement. Just between ourselves, Mr. Frere, do you think that can have happened in this case? If it was so the idea that you were going away might supply the motive—"

"The motive? Oh, Lord! Then it was suicide? She had taken something?"

"That is an established fact, Mr. Frere. That is why I am here."

Cedric seemed to have forgotten his affectations. He had turned very pale and he sat hugging his knees in an attitude devoid of grace. "How perfectly ghastly. What was it? Did she drink metal polish or disinfectant? Poor little fool. What a horrible way to die."

"It was arsenic," said Collier briefly. "Can you suggest how she could have got hold of any?"

"Haven't the slightest. Wait a mo. I read a book of famous trials once. A chap called Seddon soaked fly papers, but I shouldn't think shops would stock fly papers in December. Or there's weed killer. I believe it's used here on some of the paths."

"Thanks. That might be helpful," said Collier, making a note of the fact that Cedric did not seem to be entirely devoid of ideas on the subject of poison. "What we have to get at now is a motive. She left no letter, you see, and made no admission to the other maids who were with her during her last hours."

He looked expectantly at Cedric. That young man had recovered from his first shock and was beginning to think along his usual lines. Would 'young girl kills herself for love of film actors' be good publicity or not? He decided that it would not.

"Don't run off with the idea that the poor kid was goofy about me," he said earnestly. "I'm sure she wasn't. Darn it, I'm not the only pebble on the beach. She probably had a boy in the village, or it might just as well have been Roger. Now I come to think of it I heard them talking once when I was passing his bedroom door. No harm in it. It was one morning when she would be about, sweeping and dusting, but it did just cross my mind that he might be glad of some girl who would give him a civil hearing. His own wife, Nina, hasn't much use for him. I don't want to give the show away, but you're bound to hear that sooner or later. Perhaps you have already."

"When did this conversation in Mr. Frere's room take place?" enquired Collier. There was nothing in his manner to indicate that Cedric had given him a line to follow. The little squirt, he thought, with increased distaste. But squirts can be useful.

"Oh, I really couldn't say about that. I didn't pay much attention. I just thought, poor old Roger. Good luck to him. Something like that."

"Was it quite recently? Last week, for instance?"

"No use trying to pin me down, Inspector. I'm hopeless about dates. Might have been a fortnight or so."

"I see. Well, as you've introduced this subject, Mr. Frere, perhaps you won't mind my asking if your half-brother objected to his wife going about with you?"

"No, of course not. Don't be absurd. As a matter of fact I've been trying to do him a good turn by keeping her amused. Our sort of life bores her stiff. His idea of exercise is taking the dog for a run, and of a jolly evening reading some book by the domestic hearth. Nina hates walking and she's afraid of dogs. And she never opens a book."

"Mr. Frere does his best to please her, doesn't he?"

"Does he?" Cedric seemed amused by the turn the conversation had taken. "What makes you say that?"

"Well, there don't seem to be any dogs here. Most people living in the country keep several."

"I suppose they do. But we aren't really country people, you know. We lived in a boarding-house off Redclyffe Square until a year ago when Roger came into this place. My mother was keen to come, but now she spends most of her time at her bridge club, which is probably as near as she can get spiritually to the atmosphere of Earl's Court."

Collier suppressed a smile. It occurred to him that this young man was not nearly such a fool as he chose to appear.

Cedric gazed at him blandly. "Haven't we wandered away from the point a bit? Quite an interesting little chat, but is it being very helpful?"

"Impossible to say at this stage in the enquiry what facts may be relevant," said Collier with equal blandness.

"Well, can I sail to-morrow?"

"I'm afraid not."

Cedric kicked a footstool. "Damn. But I expect you're right," he added unexpectedly. "*Les absents ont toujours tort.* If I wasn't here to say my say I'd be blamed for everything. I don't mind staying in England a bit longer, but I don't want to stay on in this house. Any objection to my running up to Town? You can have my address there."

Collier, watching him without appearing to do so, thought he betrayed genuine anxiety at last as he waited for his answer. "I'm sorry, Mr. Frere. I shall be down here and I'd like you to remain within reach for a few days longer. Of course I can't prevent you if you insist on going, but for your own sake I advise you to stay."

"Oh, hell," said Cedric fretfully. "The reason I want to get out of here has nothing whatever to do with Jupp. Can't you take my word for that?"

"Can you tell me the reason?"

Cedric moistened his lips. He seemed definitely uneasy now and he avoided Collier's eye. "No. I can't."

"Then I'm afraid I must ask you to wait a little longer."

"All right. Is the inquisition over?" Cedric's tone was now frankly insolent. He was used getting his own way. "Whose turn is it now? Or have you finished snooping for to-night?"

"Not quite," said Collier placidly. "I'm seeing the servants now." He got up and rang the bell.

"Go to blazes," replied Cedric.

Collier looked at his watch as he waited for the bell to be answered. He had arrived soon after eight and it was not yet ten. The servants could wait a little longer. When Mostyn came he asked her to inform Mrs. Roger Frere that he would be glad if she could spare him a few minutes.

"I don't think you can see her," said Mostyn. Her voice was expressionless but she omitted the "sir" as an indication of her opinion that a policeman could hardly be a gentleman. "She's gone to bed."

"Isn't it rather early?"

"Mrs. Roger is not one to sit up late unless she's out at a dance. And I believe to-night she has one of her headaches. She hardly ate any dinner."

"I see, then I must put that off until to-morrow. I'd like to ask you a few questions—" he consulted his list. "Miss Mostyn, isn't it?"

"That is my name."

"Won't you sit down?"

Mostyn sniffed. "I haven't finished my silver."

"I won't keep you long," he said pleasantly. He drew forward an easy chair. "May as well be comfortable." He settled the cushion at her back and smiled at her as he resumed his seat. He was rather proud of his technique for thawing cold and reluctant witnesses. "I can see from your previous statement—I have it here—that you are one of the people we like to deal with, intelligent, observant, keeping a cool head when others are flustered. It's not a common type, Miss Mostyn, I assure you, and I think I am lucky to have you here to help me."

"Well I do notice things," said Mostyn modestly.

"You and Mrs. Bligh between you looked after Doris when she was taken ill and you were with her when she died?"

"Yes."

"Did she talk much?"

"No. Only to say she did feel awful. When she was easier she was too exhausted to speak, and I think she was afraid to move or open her mouth then for fear of bringing on another attack."

"She did not say anything that would suggest that she knew what was the matter with her?"

Mostyn thought a minute. "When Mrs. Bligh first went up to see her she said, 'I know I'm a greedy pig, but don't say it serves me right.' She looked so bad even then that Mrs. Bligh couldn't be hard on her. She said, 'No, no, I won't. You'll be better soon.'"

"Did you know to what she referred?"

"Well, Mrs. Bligh was often on at her for eating too much and too fast, and stuffing herself with sweets between meals."

"Had she, to your knowledge, eaten anything from a private store either the night before or that morning?"

"She had some peppermint bullseyes in a paper bag. Doctor Quinn found the bag with two sweets left in it in her apron pocket and took it away with him."

"I know," said Collier. "They were quite harmless."

"I thought they would be," said Mostyn. "She handed the bag round the evening before and we all had one and felt none the worse."

Collier looked at his notes. "For supper that evening you all had cold boiled bacon, potato salad, and what was left of a treacle tart that had been sent up to the dining-room for lunch. Now cast your mind back. Was there anything Doris had which was not touched by the others? Pickles or sauce, or one of those portions of cheese wrapped up in silver paper?"

"No."

"And in the morning she took up the early tea. Do you have any in the kitchen?"

"Yes. Cook makes it in a big pot from which she fills the little pots on the trays for Mrs. Frere and Mr. Cedric."

"Only those two?"

"Mrs. Roger doesn't have any, and Mr. Frere has lemonade which is made the night before and left on the table by the bed."

"When do you have your breakfast in the kitchen?"

"Soon after the teas have been served. The dining-room breakfast is at nine. There's a hot plate and the gentlemen ring for their coffee when they come down. Mrs. Frere and her daughter-in-law have theirs in their rooms. The old one goes in for slimming and don't have anything but toast and orange or tomato juice. Mrs. Roger has hot water and rusks—"

Mostyn as she became more friendly was growing discursive. Collier brought her back to the point.

"Did Doris eat her breakfast as usual? She didn't complain of feeling unwell then?"

"She seemed all right. I didn't notice anything. I was listening for the bell. Mr. Cedric had come down, but Mr. Roger was late that morning."

"Is he often late?"

"No. Mr. Cedric is the one, but this time it was Mr. Roger. I waited and waited, watching the clock. It was twenty to ten when he rang and I took up his coffee. I could see then how it was. He must have had a bad night and overslept himself. He looked ill. But he went out just the same. He told me he was going to Southampton and wouldn't be home for lunch. They were all out that day. Just as well in a way as Mrs. Bligh and me had our hands full with poor Doris."

Collier paused a moment before he said, "Was Doris unhappy about anything? She might not have told you, but anyone as quick and intelligent as yourself would have an inkling. An unfortunate or unsuitable love affair, for instance."

Mostyn shook her head. "She used to go out with a boy called Bert Moore, but she broke that off. Said he was mean and expected her to pay her own bus fares and for going in to the pictures if they went to Southampton, and that he bored her stiff talking about football."

"There was nobody else?"

"I don't think so. She wasn't one for boys. There used to be a picture postcard of Clark Gable stuck in her looking-glass, but

I fancy that belonged to young Jessie when she shared a room with Doris. She wasn't one of the romantic ones—or, if she was, she kept it very dark."

"A good-natured sort of girl, wasn't she? Not one to make enemies?"

"Certainly not."

"Thank you very much. Miss Mostyn. I think I shall have just time to see Mrs. Bligh to-night."

Mrs. Bligh, flustered by the prospect of the coming interview, was reassured by the parlourmaid. "He's as nice as can be. Quite the gentleman."

CHAPTER XIX
CELIA IS WARNED

COLLIER had engaged a room at the Rose and Crown. It was far too late to call at the vicarage after he left Frere Court but obviously it was the first thing to be done the next morning. He had decided not to send in his official card, but Celia simplified matters by answering the door herself. He had been keeping an open mind where she was concerned. She was a friend of Major Enderby and an attempt had been made on her life. That alone would have ensured his interest, but he found himself favourably impressed. Without being exactly pretty she was definitely easy to look at, and Collier, who was one of those men who dislike the modern young women's lavish use of cosmetics, approved the absence of make-up on a naturally clear skin.

"Did you want to see the vicar? I'm afraid he has gone out."

"I wanted a few words with you, Miss Holland. You have not seen Major Enderby perhaps since he came back from London?"

"Then I must introduce myself. I met him yesterday. I am Detective Inspector Collier, of the C.I.D." He produced his warrant card.

Celia eyed it with lively interest. "Will you come in—" She led the way into the comfortable, shabby dining-room where the housekeeper had just finished clearing away the breakfast. "What have you come about exactly, Inspector? Or oughtn't I to ask?"

"The local police are very short-handed just now, Miss Holland, plenty of routine work without handling a major crime, so the Yard has been called in, and here I am."

"A major crime—" she repeated. "Does that mean that Doris—"

Looking at her he decided that there was no need to beat about the bush. "Doris Jupp died of arsenical poisoning, Miss Holland. She took—or was given—a very large dose within twelve hours of her death."

"How awful. Poor girl—" Celia had turned pale. "Could it have been an accident? I mean—it's a white powder, isn't it? Could she have mistaken it for sugar, or—or sherbet? When I was a little girl I used to buy a haporth of sherbet at the village shop. You licked it up and it fizzed."

Collier smiled involuntarily. "So did I. But arsenic in that form is not so easily come by, Miss Holland. If Doris was ever in service in the house of a doctor who did his own dispensing—but even then doctors keep their poisons under lock and key. And we have her aunt's statement. She was in two places before she went to Frere Court. Her first employer was a Colonel's widow at Lyndhurst, her second a retired clergyman at Boldre, neither of them situations in which arsenic would be easily obtainable. I am afraid we have to face the fact that she either committed suicide—or was murdered."

"I see," said Celia rather faintly. "But who would want to do such a thing. Poor Doris. She was a good-natured sort of girl. Quite harmless. I thought people generally committed murders to get money, and she hadn't any."

"You don't think it was suicide then?" he said.

"Only if—if she was in trouble."

"She wasn't. So far as we can discover she had no troubles at all. She was walking out with a young man named Bert Moore, but she broke that off herself some months ago. She wasn't a neurotic type. According to the cook at Frere Court she was a solid, stolid young woman with a weakness for rich food which, occasionally, brought on a bilious attack."

"That's what makes it so extraordinary," said Celia.

"Yes," said Collier, "but people aren't always what they seem on the surface. Did you know her well, Miss Holland?"

"I remember her as a little girl at the parish teas and school treats, but I've been away for some years and I've only been home a few weeks."

"And ever since your return unpleasant things have been happening."

"Well—yes—but how did you know?"

"Just a bit of gossip overheard in the bar of the Rose and Crown, something about two inquests in not much over six weeks."

"Yes. That's true. And Major Enderby thinks there is some connection. Did he tell you that?"

"Is he an old friend of yours, Miss Holland?"

"Hardly that. He came to live here about a year ago. He plays chess with my father."

"I see. You knew nothing of him before he came here. Well, he seems to have saved you something."

"What do you mean?"

"He took away that box of dates that was sent you to be analysed. It's just as well for you that you didn't eat them, Miss Holland."

She gazed at him horrified. "Not—not arsenic—"

"No," he said grimly, "it's not that sort of case. That would be too easy. The dates were treated with powdered glass."

"Oh—" she covered her face with her hands.

He moved uneasily, wondering if he had been too abrupt. "I'm sorry," he said, "you had to know."

"Of course." She dropped her hands on her lap and faced him again. She was white to the lips but her eyes met his steadily. "I hope I'm not a coward. But it's rather awful to realise that anybody can hate one—like that."

"In a case like this one is probably dealing with an abnormal mentality. My difficulty is to find any connection between the death of Doris and the attempt to injure you. I am hoping you can help me," he said. "Think. Is there any person whom you may have offended, or who might conceivably be jealous of you?"

"Jealous of me?" For the first time she showed a trace of bitterness. "I've earned my living as a governess ever since I left school. This isn't a rich living and my father has no private means. I can't imagine anyone envying me particularly. My life isn't insured. That's a motive sometimes, isn't it—"

"You have no idea who sent you the dates?"

"None. They came by post. I threw away the brown paper wrapping and I didn't notice the post marks."

"It might be as well to go away for a while," he suggested. She shook her head. "That was Major Enderby's idea. But I told him I wouldn't. Of course I shall be careful after this. If any more food comes by post I'll hand it over to you."

"Yes, please do."

"I shall not tell my father," she said. "I don't want him worried. He's not so young as he was, and his heart isn't strong. And I don't want a fuss. I'm not really afraid. I'm hard to kill. I went through quite a lot in South America." She went with him to the door. "I hope you'll find out something. A crime without a motive must be very difficult. I wish I could have helped you."

Collier's next call was at the White Cottage. A middle-aged woman opened the door and showed him into the front sitting-room. Enderby had just returned from a walk in the Forest and was changing his muddy boots before the fire while Jock stretched himself on the hearthrug. He began to growl as Collier was admitted but his master silenced him with a word. When a drink had been offered and declined and Collier had taken a cigarette from his host's proffered case and lighted it, Enderby said, "Have you seen Miss Holland?"

"I have just come from the vicarage."

"That's all right then," said Enderby with unconcealed relief. "Perhaps she'll listen to sense now, and go away. You warned her, of course, that she was in danger."

"Yes. But she said she wouldn't go."

Enderby groaned. "Did you tell her she might have died a sticky death? Powdered glass is no picnic. It was a damn near-run thing."

"So I gathered. But why? Two crimes, one carried out and one attempted, and each without any apparent motive."

"You are assuming that one person is responsible for both?" Jock had come over to his master and was resting his shaggy head on his knees. Enderby bent over him, fondling his ears.

"It is difficult not to," said Collier, "but I'm trying not to assume anything at this stage. I hoping you will be able to help me, Major."

"I will if I can, certainly. I think that in Miss Holland's case I can suggest the motive. Fear. I fancy Miss Holland may know too much to suit the person who sent that box of dates."

"But—Miss Holland told me she was quite in the dark. I must say that she struck me as an entirely honest and trustworthy witness. I understand that she was a friend of yours—"

"She has honoured me with her friendship," said Enderby quietly. "She is all that you say. I think she is in the position of one who unknowingly holds the key to a problem. As for Doris Jupp it is possible that she had seen what she should not and had therefore become a potential danger. But I confess I am puzzled by the difference in the method. Why not arsenic for both—or glass for both? You only came down yesterday. Have you seen the Freres yet?"

"I went there yesterday evening and saw everybody except the younger Mrs. Frere, who was unwell and had gone to bed early. By the way, Mr. Frere told me he came to see you the evening before Doris Jupp was taken ill and that as the weather was very bad you put him up for the night."

"Yes."

"It struck me as rather odd that he should be out walking after dark and in heavy rain, but he told me that since an accident he had had he drove himself about as little as possible."

"Yes. It happened just after I came to live here, and I've heard all about it. He had given his stepsister a car for a birthday present. They were in it together. He says she was driving and he told her to slow down but she wouldn't listen—or perhaps she didn't hear him—anyhow the car overturned at a sharp bend. He was seriously injured and she was killed. Mrs. Frere blamed her stepson and refused to believe that he was not driving at the time. He went abroad for some months when he was well enough and when he came back she had quieted down, but I don't think she has ever forgiven him."

"Rather hard on him if he wasn't really responsible," said Collier. "He met his wife while he was abroad, I suppose?"

"Yes. And that hasn't turned out well, either."

"So I gathered from his stepbrother."

Enderby nodded. "What did you think of Cedric?"

Collier was silent for a minute, then he said, "He ran true to type, casual, irresponsible, as insolent as he knew how to be. He's been here some time, hasn't he, living at the Court at his elder brother's expense."

"Yes. Roger was here with his uncle for a year before the old man died, I believe. Mr. Frere couldn't stick the second family, but as soon as he was gone they came down and they've been here ever since."

"But now young Cedric seems uncommonly anxious to get away. I gathered that he had had no offer from Hollywood so it couldn't really hurt him to miss the boat that sailed this morning, but he didn't like it at all. There's something amiss with that bright lad. He's got the jitters. I gained the impression that he's had a shock recently."

"That's interesting," said Enderby. "I haven't seen him for some time. Last summer they asked me over occasionally to play tennis, and once and only once for bridge. Mrs. Frere had a couple of women friends over from Bournemouth and I was to make a fourth. Wow!" Enderby laughed rather ruefully. "If ever a rabbit sat down with three tigresses. I still see Roger now and again but the rest of the family have dropped me and I can't say I'm sorry."

"Are you in Roger Frere's confidence, Major Enderby?"

"I am not."

"You have no objection to driving your car after dark?"

"None. My eyesight is pretty good. I try not to take needless risks—"

"I was wondering why you did not drive Frere home. Surely it would have been easier than putting him up for the night?"

"Perhaps. But he would probably have got pneumonia. He was wet through. He had a hot bath and went straight to bed in my spare room."

"Wasn't he wearing a mac?"

"No."

"It must have been raining when he set out—"

Enderby looked at him. "All right. You may as well have it. He was wearing a dressing-gown over his pyjamas. He was wandering across the road just by my house when the headlights of my car caught him. He was all in. He didn't tell me what was the matter. He went home after breakfast the next morning wearing one of my suits. So for as I know nobody had noticed his absence. But I wouldn't found a case against him on this if I were you."

Collier made no immediate reply. He was remembering that Cedric had overheard his brother talking to Doris Jupp in his room. There might be no harm in that. And Cedric might have been lying. On the other hand there was obviously something very wrong with Roger. He had given Collier the impression of a man who had nearly reached the limits of endurance. "They seem queer as a family," he said. "You're not suggesting that I'll find the solution of this affair elsewhere, are you, Major?"

"In a sense, yes. You'll have to go a long way both in space and time to find the solution. In any case I doubt if you'd believe it. That's why I'm not going to hand it to you on a plate."

"You know who murdered Doris Jupp?"

"I didn't say that. I'm not sure about her. But I haven't got to guess about the powdered glass. That's not an English trick."

"You're right there. And Miss Holland has been living in South America. She told me so this morning."

"The republic of San Rinaldo to be exact."

"You think the dates were sent to her from there?"

"They might have been. But I don't think they had so far to travel to reach their destination. When Roger went abroad he took a South American cruise. His boat touched at the port of San Rinaldo and he drove out to the estancia Romero where Celia Holland was living. They got mixed up in an abortive revolution. I don't know all the details. What I know I have heard from Celia herself. Frere eventually escaped with a señorita whom they met by chance and who saved their lives. I rather fancy they were married at sea and he brought her home to Frere Court."

"I see. So Miss Holland knew the younger Mrs. Frere before her marriage."

"In a sense. I gathered that they spent a part of one night together in the fields, hiding from the rebels. Frere and his future wife got away in an open boat which was picked up two days later by a tramp steamer, and Celia Holland remained on shore and reached safety after numerous adventures. She had a bad time, I'm afraid, and she doesn't care to talk about it. And so far as I know she has not tried to renew her acquaintance with the girl Frere married."

"Isn't that rather strange?"

"I don't think so. It is common knowledge that the marriage has not been a success. I fancy Celia's sympathies would be with Roger. He was often down at the vicarage in his uncle's lifetime and the vicar was very fond of him."

"Does she see anything of Frere?"

"She told me herself that she has met him now and then walking in the forest, and I heard from my housekeeper that some children gathering firewood had seen them, but that must have been close to the road for none of the village children have ventured far into the woods since the scare."

"What's that?"

"Well, for a good many weeks now there have been rumours of something that roams the forest at night and stampedes the herds of wild ponies. Some people think it's an animal that escaped from a travelling menagerie and others that it is an Alsatian whose owners won't admit that it sometimes gets out at night. Locally, it is held responsible for the death of the unknown man whose body was found not half a mile from here early in November."

"You mean he had been set upon? I don't remember the case. Was it reported?"

"Only in the local press. He hadn't a scratch. The verdict at the inquest was natural causes. His heart was dicky and he had been running, presumably to catch the last bus to Southampton. But I found him. I'm not likely to forget his face. He died of fright."

"That would be one of the inquests I heard a man refer to in the bar of the Rose and Crown. Two, he said, and he seemed to think that was too many."

"I'm inclined to agree with him," said Enderby drily.

Collier glanced at his watch. "I must be going. I made an appointment through the telephone with the younger Mrs. Frere, but she can't see me until this afternoon. She seems an elusive lady. One final question, Major Enderby. Would you say she might be jealous of her husband?"

"It's not impossible, but—" Enderby checked himself. "I'd rather not say anything more. I have a theory, but if I told you what it was you'd send for a couple of doctors to get me certified. I must have proof. I'm waiting for it and I hope to have it within a few days." He rose to see his visitor out. The dog followed them into the hall, close at his master's heels. "You warned Celia to be careful?" he said anxiously. "I shan't be easy about her until this business is cleared up."

"I warned her. She promised she would be. What breed is your dog? He looks like a thoroughbreed Airedale."

"He's an Airedale but I'm not sure that he's thoroughbreed. I've had him from a puppy but I haven't got his pedigree."

"You are very much attached to him I daresay."

"Yes."

"May I drop in again to talk over the case with you?"

"Please do."

Collier glanced back and waved his hand when he reached the garden gate. Enderby, a lean erect figure, was still standing on the threshold with his dog beside him. He had certainly been helpful, but Collier was still not quite sure whether he either liked or trusted him.

Chapter XX
JESSIE'S EVIDENCE

Inspector Collier had brought a colleague, Sergeant Duffield, down from Town with him. Normally, the sergeant would have accompanied him, but the local police were so short-handed, owing to an epidemic of influenza, that Duffield had been given a job that would otherwise have been undertaken by one of their men, and was organising a canvas of all the chemists in Bournemouth and Southampton and smaller towns in the county to check up on the sales of arsenic. There were enquiries to be made, too, of dealers stocking weedkiller and fly papers.

"Rather a forlorn hope," said Collier. He had driven over to Welchester, after leaving Major Enderby. The Chief Constable had come over and wanted to see him. Inspector Lacy, who had been in charge of the case until the Yard was called in, was also present.

"I think the girl poisoned herself," said the superintendent. "Lacy doesn't agree. Roger Frere's his prime suspect. I hope he's wrong. Old Mr. Frere was greatly liked and respected. We don't want a scandal like that. It seems far more likely to me that the poor little fool fell for him. She must have known—all the servants knew—that his marriage was a flop. She was romantic. We found a pile of paper novelettes in her room. Cinderella stuff. You know. If he turned her down she might get desperate. She was a respectable well-conducted girl, mind you—"

"It does sound likely the way you put it," Lacy admitted with a natural reluctance to contradict his superior officer. The Chief Constable looked at him approvingly. "It's the most likely explanation. You found an opened tin of weedkiller in the potting shed, didn't you? Two-thirds of it had been used on the paths since it was bought last spring. The girl could have got at that. I should work on those lines if I were you, Inspector."

"I am keeping an open mind at present, sir." Collier determined not to say anything at present about the box of dates. "It may have been suicide, but in that case I would have expected her to leave a letter. They generally do want to dramatise themselves at the last, poor little idiots. There is another point which has to be borne in mind. I have been studying the statements made by her fellow servants and I talked to two of them last night. She had plenty of time before she died to confess what she had done.

"It seems clear to me from what she did say to the cook and the parlourmaid that she had no idea what was really the matter with her. There is no evidence as yet how and when the poison was taken. At supper she ate what the others did and the same at breakfast. Even the sweets that were found in a paper bag in her apron pocket had been shared with the other girls."

He paused a moment. "There was some talk in the bar of the Rose and Crown about an inquest that was held there only a few weeks ago."

"An elderly man was found dead in the forest. He has not been identified, but he came from Southampton, and you know these port towns have a shifting population. There was no mystery about his death. Heart failure. He had walked too far and too fast."

"And this scare in the village about an animal that prowls after dark? Is there anything in it?"

The Chief Constable allowed himself to betray some impatience. It seemed to him that the man from the Yard might keep to the point. Their time was as valuable as his.

"Perhaps you haven't much experience of country folk, Inspector. They have a natural sense of drama, and their tales lose nothing in the telling. I thought that nonsense had blown over. We had complaints of herds of ponies stampeding and we sent out extra men to patrol the district at night, but they never had anything to report. No actual damage has been done. The Hunt gets the usual claims for hen-runs raided by foxes, and nothing more. That's right, isn't it, Superintendent?"

"Yes, sir. It was all hearsay."

"The villagers seem to take it seriously," said Collier. "The landlord of the Rose and Crown told me the women and children won't stir out alone after nightfall, and the maids at Frere Court get the lodgekeeper or the gardener to escort them through the park with a lanthorn on their evenings out."

"You mustn't believe all you hear, Inspector. Well—I must say that I hope the Superintendent's theory will be proved the right one. It's a pity, of course, that the girl didn't leave a confession. You see, Roger Frere's uncle was very well known locally."

There seemed nothing more to be said, and Collier took his leave after the Chief Constable had renewed his promise to give him all the help they could.

He was going back to Frere Court. Night had fallen when he drove again up the mile long double row of limes to the house. He got out of his car and walked about a little before ringing the bell. He found that the moat was only open on one side of the building. It then passed under a stone culvert and presumably flowed underground to reappear in the small lake a quarter of a mile away. Where there was no moat a row of french windows opened on to a stone-flagged terrace and a lawn enclosed by dense shrubberies of laurel and rhododendron. He met no one and the silence was profound. The rain-sodden earth squelched like a wet sponge under his feet. He shivered involuntarily in the clammy darkness that seemed to cling to him like a black shroud and, turning, made his way back to the main entrance.

The door was opened by the parlourmaid who told him that Mrs. Roger Frere was expecting him and showed him into the drawing-room.

"Inspector Collier, madam."

The long room was lit only by the fire burning on the hearth and a heavily-shaded reading lamp on a table by the sofa.

A voice, low pitched and rather husky, asked him to come nearer. "Sit down, please."

"Thank you."

Collier cleared his throat. He found it rather difficult to begin and Nina Frere did not help him. The light was so dim that he could only see her face as a pale oval blur as she turned her head in his direction. She sat up among the tumbled cushions with a movement that was unexpectedly easy and swift. He had stumbled over the edge of a rug as he moved towards the chair she had indicated. "I'm afraid I can't see very well in here. Could we have some more light?"

"I am sorry, but my eyes have been so weak lately. The light hurts them."

"In that case, of course—I just have to ask you a few questions, Mrs. Frere."

"Please do."

"You recall the evening before Doris Jupp was taken ill?"

"I think so. Yes."

"You were at home that evening?"

This time there was a perceptible pause before she answered. "Was I? Yes. Cedric had gone up to London to make preparations for his journey. Roger was giving him the money to go to Hollywood so he was glad, but his mother was very angry."

"Oh, why was that?"

"She wants to keep him always with her. Some mothers are like that. She was angry not with him but with Roger. So she would not sit down to dinner with us. She had a tray sent to her room. I often do that, too. I do not like eating with other people. After dinner I was sleepy so I went to bed. I do not know what Roger did. Perhaps he read in the library. He is fond of reading." She sounded contemptuous. He heard the silk of her dress rustle as she changed her position, and she yawned.

"You occupy separate rooms?"

"Yes."

"You say Mrs. Frere was angry. Was Mr. Frere a good deal upset about it all?"

"I do not understand."

"I'm afraid I expressed myself badly. I have reason to believe that your husband was seriously worried and distressed that evening. Can you suggest any reason for that apart from a disagreement with his stepmother?"

She yawned again "Was he? I am afraid I cannot help you at all. I was out all the following day. I went for a long drive with Cedric. We danced at a road-house. I did not see Roger again until we came home, and then it was all finished and the body had been taken away."

"You must have been greatly surprised as well as greatly shocked?" suggested Collier. He was beginning to think that the younger Mrs. Frere was what Americans would describe as a tough baby. Her matter-of-course dismissal of the tragedy was a little too much for him and he could not keep the note of irony out of his voice.

She seemed to feel that it might be advisable to justify her attitude. "I was very sorry, naturally, but I was not surprised. In my country girls often kill themselves for love. They go into a shop and order a cup of café and with it they drink sublimate, and then they fall down and scream and they are taken off to the hospital. It happens every day. One is accustomed to their foolishness."

"What country is that, Mrs. Frere?"

She was silent for a moment and he felt as if a door had been closed. It was clear that she regretted her sudden loquacity. She had said more than she meant.

"It does not matter," she said sulkily. "I am English now."

"Then you think Doris committed suicide on account of an unfortunate love affair?"

"Si. Si. She was in love with Roger, if you must know—"

"What makes you say that, Mrs. Frere? Have you any evidence?"

"The way she looked at him."

"Is that all?"

"Yes. I know, but I cannot tell you how or why."

"You speak very good English, Mrs. Frere. Where did you learn it?"

'I was at school in England for a year."

"Mrs. Frere, in your country are people ever killed with powdered glass?"

He cursed the dim light that made it impossible to see any change of expression. The fire, too, had died down. She was rather slow in answering.

"Powdered glass? I do not know. I cannot help you at all. Have you nearly finished, please? I am tired."

"I'm sorry," he said, "I won't bother you any more now. You need not ring. I can find my way out—"

Collier rather prided himself on being able to tell when a witness was speaking the truth. Though Nina Frere had been reticent on some points he could not help feeling that she really believed what she had said about Doris. He had come to the interview with a very strong suspicion that she was responsible for the girl's death and that the motive would be found to be jealousy of her husband or her brother-in-law. But after hearing her he could not believe that she was deeply involved. True, in his experience all poisoners were extraordinarily callous. He would not expect her, if she was guilty, to be regretting the sufferings and the death of her victim, but she would feel fear on her own account. Though she had betrayed uneasiness and had evaded answering some of his questions he had noticed that they had not been questions relating to the dead girl.

As he left the drawing-room, Mostyn, the parlourmaid, was crossing the hall with a tray of silver and glasses on her way to the dining-room. He followed her.

She set her tray down on the oak refectory table. Dinner was being laid, he noticed, for three.

"Who is going out to-night?"

"Nobody. Mrs. Roger will have something on a tray. She's getting very queer, if you ask me," said Mostyn. "Lately she hardly ever turns up at meals."

"Is she in bad health?"

Mostyn sniffed. "You can take it from me that she hasn't lost her appetite, not for meat anyway. You'd be surprised the amount she puts away. A whole steak, and she likes it rare."

"But there's something wrong with her eyes, isn't there?"

"That's true. She can't stand a strong light. She's taken to wearing dark glasses during the day. Well, I can't stop here talking. I'm busy. Do you want to see any of the others?"

"There is one more name on my list. Jessie Dowser. The between-maid, isn't she?"

"That's right. If you want to see her now you'd better come downstairs to the servants' hall. Cook won't want you about in the kitchen while she's dishing up."

"That will suit me."

She took him down to the sitting-room in the basement which had been furnished for the use of the staff with wicker armchairs, a bookcase filled with cheap reprints of standard novels, and a wireless set. The fire had been laid but not lit.

"We aren't in here much during the winter," Mostyn said. "The kitchen is more cheerful and cook's got her own portable."

The little tweenie came in shyly and sat in the chair Collier placed for her, rubbing her work-roughened hands together and staring at him in an awe-struck manner.

"Now, Jessie, there's nothing to be afraid of. I just want you to try to remember everything that happened the day Doris died. Did she seem all right at breakfast?"

"Yes. She'd been up as usual with the early morning teas. Two trays for Mrs. Frere and Mr. Cedric. The cook fills up their tea-pots from ours. Mrs. Frere just has tea, but Mr. Cedric likes bread and butter cut wafer thin. It's always the same. You take it in and draw the curtains. Mr. Roger has a glass of lemonade, but that's made overnight so there's no need to go in. You just knock at the door. And Mrs. Roger doesn't want to be disturbed so she's left to sleep as late as she chooses."

"That's quite clear. What happened that morning?"

"I got on with my work at the sink, and then cook called me into the kitchen round about eleven for a bit of bread and dripping and a cup of cocoa."

"Elevenses?"

Jessie nodded. "Then she said Doris was poorly and I must do her work, and after I'd been upstairs for a bit I heard her crying out. I ran up to her room and found her all doubled up. She said she felt awful, and I went down and told Miss Mostyn."

"She didn't tell you she had taken anything?"

"No. At least—she did say something about wishing she hadn't drunk the lemonade and that it wasn't half bitter."

Collier looked up quickly. "There's nothing about lemonade in the statement you made to Inspector Lacy."

"I'm sorry. I've only just remembered it. I don't know what she meant unless it was what Mr. Roger has. I wouldn't put it past her to drink that if he left it, but he never does. I've had to help with the bedrooms since Doris died and there's never anything left in the glass when I take it down to the kitchen."

"Who prepares the lemonade?"

"Sometimes its Mrs. Bligh and sometimes Miss Mostyn. Oh—you don't think—" she gazed at him, open mouthed, the picture of dismay, as the possible import of what she had been saying became clearer to her.

"No, no," he said hastily, "it's probably of no importance, but you were quite right to tell me. Only—see here—don't mention it to anyone else at present. You understand?"

"I—I think so."

"That's right. Not a word to a soul. You can keep your own counsel I'm sure. Now listen to me. You're to ask for an afternoon off to-morrow."

"It is my half day."

"Splendid. Then you can slip off without any fuss. I'll pick you up in my car outside the lodge gates at three."

Jessie shrank a little. "I—I'd rather not—"

He smiled down at her. "You're not afraid of me? I'm a policeman though I don't wear uniform, and old enough to be your father."

"I'd sooner not," she said stubbornly.

He had an inspiration. "Your home is in the village, isn't it?"

"Yes. I live along with my gran and my young sister 'Ilda."

"Will you come with me if I bring one of them along?"

She answered reluctantly. "Maybe I would then."

"Right. Then I shall expect you at three."

He left the house by the back door and walked through the stable yard and round to the drive where he had left his car. The drawing-room windows were still dark, but there were lights in the dining-room and he could see Mostyn's prim shadow on the blinds as she moved round the table putting the last touches to her array of silver and glass. There were lights, too, in the library, and someone had turned on the wireless. Collier's headlamps shone dimly through the mist. He drove carefully down the avenue and sounded his horn and halted before he turned into the road.

There had been no time for lunch and he was tired as well as hungry. He had dinner served in his own sitting-room at the Rose and Crown. Afterwards he sat by the fire scribbling notes for the report he would be sending to Superintendent Cardew at the

Yard. He was a good deal worried. Since his talk with Jessie he was seeing the case from another and more disturbing angle. If the arsenic had been in the glass of lemonade it seemed to follow that Roger Frere and not Doris had been the intended victim. If that was so all the efforts of the police to find a motive for the elimination of the girl had been a waste of energy. Roger had been saved by the fact that he spent that night at the White Cottage. Doris, doing the bedrooms after breakfast, and seeing the lemonade untouched, had yielded to the temptation to drink it herself. The pointing finger had shifted—but not far. The murderer must still be a member of that household. Or—no—it was too soon to say. Collier checked himself, knowing that he was going too fast. This clue, like others, might break in his hands.

The lemonade. Who would have the opportunity to shake in that pinch of the deadly powder, or the spoonful of water in which fly papers had been soaking? Cedric Frere was the only one with an alibi, and his was not perfect. He had arrived home some time before midnight. He could have entered his brother's bedroom while the latter was, as he would assume, asleep. Roger was not there. But would he have noticed that? He would have felt his way in the dark to the night table where the glass stood. Cedric could not be left out of the count.

Collier meant to take Jessie to Welchester to make a statement which could be signed before witnesses. But meanwhile would she have the sense to hold her tongue? He had warned her, but had she really understood the purport of what she had told him? He recalled her plump childish face, the round and rather vacant blue eyes. There she was—if he was not wildly wrong—under the same roof as the killer. If she talked—and he could not feel sure that she would have the sense to obey his injunction—if she talked some way might be found to silence her.

Collier got up and walked restlessly about the room. He could not have forced her to come away with him then and there. He could only hope for the best.

CHAPTER XXI
THE NIGHT OF THE SOUL

AFTER Jessie Dowser had appended a sprawling signature to the statement that had been read over to her she was sent to rejoin her little sister who had been waiting outside. They were to go to the pictures and have tea with the wife of one of the policemen.

"I'm inclined to agree with you, Mr. Collier, that she had better not go back to Frere Court under the circumstances," said the Superintendent. "She's brought us a bit of dynamite here, though she doesn't seem to realise it."

"If we can avoid putting the murderer on his guard—" said Collier, "I suggest ringing up the Court and saying that Jessie was taken ill while spending the afternoon with friends. A doctor thinks it may be appendicitis and she is being kept under observation for a few days."

The superintendent nodded. "That will do. See to it now, Lacy."

When the inspector returned he was grinning. "The cook answered the 'phone. She wants to know who's going to peel the vegetables. Quite a flow of language she has."

His superintendent looked worried. "I hope we're not exceeding our duty. I don't want any trouble. We haven't much to go upon really, Collier."

"I shouldn't have drunk that lemonade. It wasn't half bitter," quoted Collier.

"Yes if we can believe Jessie. But, man, no proof that the lemonade was poisoned. She may have been mistaken. As I see it we're no nearer making an arrest."

The Chief Constable, who had hardly spoken so far, intervened. "That's the worst of these poison cases. If the thing is planned with a reasonable amount of care it succeeds. But we've got to carry on and clear the thing up to our own satisfaction even if it ends in apparent failure. What will you do now, Collier?"

Collier was silent for a moment. Then he said, "Do you know Major Enderby, sir?"

The Chief Constable looked blank. Inspector Lacy answered, "He's only been here about a year, sir. He bought that house on the Boldre Road and lives alone there, with a woman from the village to come in and do the rough work. A very quiet sort of gentleman and hasn't made many friends. I fancy he was out in India before he left the Army. We've nothing against him."

"The name is familiar," said the Chief Constable.

"He was the one to find the body in Boar's Spinney last month, sir. He gave evidence at the inquest."

"Of course. I remember now. What of him? How does he come into this?"

"Well, sir, I met him at the Yard before I was sent down here. He's a friend of the Assistant Commissioner. It wasn't about this case. He's friendly with the vicar and his daughter, and Miss Holland had had a box of dates sent her from some unknown source. He was suspicious and had them analysed—"

Collier told the story of the dates as far as he knew it in some detail. He was listened to with close attention. When he had finished the Chief Constable said, "I think you should have informed us of this before, Inspector."

"I'm sorry, sir. I was in two minds about it. The Major is an old friend of the A.C. but it's years since they last met. To be frank I don't feel quite sure that he's all he seems to be. I've a feeling that he's a dark horse. Something queer about him. He keeps on hinting that he knows more than we do, but I can't pin him down to anything definite."

"You've seen him again, then, since you came down from Town?"

"I called at his place yesterday morning. I think I had better be seeing him again."

"You think he's mixed up in this business?"

"I was coming to that, sir. Roger Frere left the Court at a late hour the night before Doris was taken ill. He was picked up some time later by Major Enderby wandering along the road near White Cottage. He was wearing a dressing-gown over his pyjamas and bedroom slippers. It was a night of wind and rain and he was soaked to the skin. The Major took him home and he spent the rest of the night there. That's why he did not drink his lemonade."

"What an extraordinary thing." The Chief Constable was frowning. "How long have you known this, Inspector?"

"Not very long, sir," said Collier blandly. "Naturally it intrigued me a good deal. The Major said that Frere seemed to be all in, with all the symptoms of a man who is suffering from a severe shock, but he was not communicative, and the Major did not press him for an explanation. You see, sir, that if we assume that the arsenic was intended for Frere the pieces of the puzzle begin to fall into place."

"You mean that there was some kind of a show down, a violent quarrel perhaps, either with his step-brother before the latter went up to London, or more probably, with his wife."

"Something of the sort," said Collier. "Suppose he threatened divorce proceedings—"

Inspector Lacy nodded. "It might be. There's been a lot of talk locally, I know, about her going about as she has done with the young fellow."

"Then you suspect the wife and the half-brother of attempting to murder him?"

"It is one of the possibilities," said Collier. "In the light of what the girl said to Jessie I am looking at everything from a fresh point of view. I can't help feeling that Roger Frere knows more than he cares to admit. I may get evidence of motive from him—but can we make a move without a good deal more?"

The Chief Constable shook his head doubtfully. "I'm afraid not. What proof have we that the lemonade actually was poisoned? The girl may have been mistaken. The only proof likely to satisfy a jury would be the analysis of the dregs left in the glass—which, naturally, we haven't got. That child you brought over here is none too bright. She could easily be made to contradict herself in cross examination. On the other hand if we wait a day or two something may break. The guilty parties may get panicky and make a mistake. The wicked flee when no man pursueth. You'll want Cedric Frere followed if he leaves the Court?"

"Yes, please."

"We can manage that for you. What is your next move?"

"I'd like a few words with the Major before I go back to the Rose and Crown. There may be a report from Sergeant Duffield."

"Then we won't keep you," said the Chief Constable. His manner was quite cordial but Collier realised that he had not been quite forgiven for keeping the incident of the box of dates to himself so long. Local authorities always needed very careful handling and were apt to regard fresh developments in any case handed over as a reflection on their methods.

He had a cup of coffee and a ham sandwich at the Cadena in the High Street before starting on his twelve-mile drive back to Swain Green.

Enderby's car was standing at the gate of the White Cottage. The housekeeper answered Collier's ring.

"I don't know if the Major can see you just now, sir. He's got a visitor. He's only just got back from fetching him from Brockenhurst station—"

She was interrupted by Enderby himself, who came out of the sitting-room when he heard their voices.

"Come in, Inspector. There's somebody here I'd like you to meet. Leave your hat and coat on the stand—"

The new arrival was standing on the hearthrug making friends with his host's dog. Jock, who seemed to approve of him, left him to come and sniff enquiringly at Collier's shoes before he went to lie down beside his master's chair. The visitor was a good looking young man with a swarthy skin, brilliant black eyes and hair that shone as if it had been lacquered. He was very much wrapped up with woollen scarves and a heavy overcoat with an astrakhan collar.

The Major went to him. "Let me help you off with those. This is Inspector Collier of the Criminal Investigation Department at New Scotland Yard. This is Señor Romero, Inspector."

Señor Romero smiled as he shook hands. "I am a bundle, no? I am not used to your climate, and it was cold in the 'plane crossing the Channel."

"You come from Spain?"

"No. I am of Spanish origin, yes. Castellano. But actually a South American of the Republic of San Rinaldo. You have been, perhaps?" He spoke English fluently, with only a trace of foreign accent. His lean, clean-cut face, grave to the point of austerity in repose, lit up when he was talking.

Collier shook his head. "I've been to the States, but not yet to South America. You've come all the way by air?"

"No. Only from Cannes where I am staying with my wife and daughters."

The Major intervened. "Miss Holland has been teaching the Señor's two little girls. She is at home just now, as you know, on holiday. I thought it advisable to get into touch with Señor Romero, and he rang me up this morning from Heston to say that he was coming down to see me. I have just been over to Brockenhurst station to meet his train."

"Naturally I came at once," said Romero. "The Major said very little in his letter, but it was enough to show me that something may be developing here which you cannot be expected to understand, and that Miss Holland is in danger. I must tell you that my wife and I are very greatly attached to our little English Miss. Our children love her very much. We should never forgive ourselves if any harm came to her that we might have prevented. So I am here to tell all I know, to advise in a difficult situation. May I smoke?"

"Of course. Forgive me. Have one of mine—"

"If you will not think me discourteous I prefer my own." He held out his case to them with a very charming smile. "Please—"

Enderby took one but Collier declined. Romero hitched his chair nearer to the fire. Obviously he felt the cold.

"You said in your letter that Miss Holland had received a present of—crystalised fruit, was it not? But instead of sugar there was powdered glass?"

"Yes. Is that a thing that might happen in your country, Señor Romero?"

"Certainly. It is a recognised method of avenging a slight, an injury. Glass is easily come by. It can be hammered to a fine dust with a stone. If a girl has stolen another woman's lover she will think twice before eating *marrons glacés* if she is not very sure where they come from. In England, no?"

He looked at the man from the Yard. Collier shook his head. "Not in my experience I'm glad to say."

"*Autres pays, autres moeurs,*" murmured Romero with his engaging smile. "Will you not call me Don Juan? It is better—" He drew at his cigarette. "In your letter. Major Enderby, you said that a friend of Miss Holland is married to one of my countrywomen. But would she be jealous of our Miss Celia? I find it hard to believe. Our little Miss is serious, she is not—how do you say?—a flirt."

The room was growing dark. Enderby leaned forward and poked the fire into a blaze. The dog, who had been dozing, stirred and whimpered under his breath.

"The motive may be jealousy, but I don't think so." Enderby hesitated, choosing his words with care and glancing occasionally at Collier's attentive face. "Miss Holland's friend—his name is Roger Frere—was on a South American cruise. The boat on which he was a passenger touched at the port of San Rinaldo the day the revolution broke out last May. I understand that your country house was burned down, Don Juan?"

"Yes. My wife and I were in Paris. My child were saved by their Indian nurse. Miss Holland escaped with—I remember now, Frere was the name."

"He got away in an open boat with the help of a young lady whose house had been surrounded by the rebels. They were picked up by an English cargo boat and he brought her back to England as his wife. What is the matter, señor?" Romero had uttered a sharp exclamation and half risen from his chair. He sat down again, but Collier, watching the lean brown muscular hands gripping the arms of the chair, saw the knuckles white under the skin.

"Pardon, if I startled you, but I am beginning to understand. And yet I can hardly believe it. Can you tell me the name of my country-woman, Major?"

"I never heard her surname, but her Christian name is Nina. Wait a minute. I remember once last summer when I was up at the Court, playing tennis, and we were having tea on the terrace something was said about it being unlucky to change the name and not the letter, and Frere said that did not apply with Nina as her name was—I didn't really catch what the name was, but I know it began with an M."

The fire was halfway up the chimney and throwing out a great heat, but the two Englishmen saw Romero shiver. He muttered something to himself as he threw the end of his cigarette into the fender.

"Was the name Manara, Major Enderby?"

"Something like that."

"Santa Maria purissima—" Romero lit another cigarette. They both saw that his hands were shaking. "The Manara had an estate a few miles out of the town. In the foothills, but a long way from ours. The house was burned down that night with the old woman in it and it was thought that her niece died with her. The place had a bad name ever since Tomaso Manara built it in the eighteenth century. He came from Italy, from the Abruzzi, and there were ugly stories about him. It was said that he had narrowly escaped being arrested by the Holy Office in Rome, that he knew more than was good for him—or for others. One hears these tales as a child from the Indian servants. He married and had sons, but it was never easy for them to find wives. There was plenty of money, but there are some things that can't be bought. They went to Europe to find brides, and the women they brought back either pined and died after a year or two in that dark house, or became like the accursed family they had married into. They died out by degrees and for some years now there has been only the old woman and her niece Nina, her dead brother's only child and heiress. Nina was sent to Europe to be educated. I'll say that for Dona Eulalia. She gave the girl a chance to grow up normally. A man I know was on the boat with her going home and he said she was one of the most beautiful girls he had ever seen. She was being chaperoned by the wife of the French consul coming out from France for the first time. None of our people would have undertaken the charge. My friend kept well away from her. That was easy, he said. She had quite a number of admirers, young Englishmen and Americans on their way to the Argentine, and she behaved throughout like a well-brought up señorita. Only he, who knew what to look for, saw that she had not escaped the curse."

His listeners were so absorbed that they both started violently when Mrs. Binns put her head in at the door to say she was going home.

"Any letters for me to post, sir?"

"Not this time, thanks. Goodnight."

"Good night, sir. I'm a bit later than usual so my son-in-law has come to see me back to the village. I don't fancy that bit of road at dusk."

They heard her heavy tread going down the passage and the closing of the front door. The house seemed very quiet after she had gone. Enderby got up to switch on the lamp and draw the curtains over the window. The wind was getting up and the shrub-beries were alive with stealthy movements of branches like waving arms. He came back to the fire where the others waited for him.

"Some form of insanity, of mania—"

Romero shrugged his shoulders. "You can call it that. In Italy they have a name for it. Lupa manara."

"What's the English, sir? Though I may be no wiser. I'm no mental specialist."

"I can tell you that," said Enderby abruptly. "It's lycanthropy."

"Good Lord. Doesn't that mean animal metamorphosis, turn-ing into a wolf?"

"You've got it in one, Inspector."

"But—that's a medieval superstition, like—like flying on broom-sticks. You can't—"

Romero looked across at him with a half smile. "It is hard to believe, yes? Old stuff, but old things can be true things, Inspector. Many of our people in San Rinaldo are ignorant, but some things they know that you over here have forgotten. Ask anybody there, your taxi driver, the waiter at the hotel, the market woman, the shopkeepers, they will tell you that Dona Eulalia and her niece were witches and it was for that and not because of their politics—for they had never taken sides—that their house was burned down last May."

"I see," said Collier. "It would be a bit of luck for the niece to find an Englishman, a stranger who knew nothing of her past, to marry her."

"Of course. I wonder how she prevailed on him," said Romero thoughtfully. "To me she would be repulsive, but then I am familiar with the legend."

"But you are an educated man, what they call a man of the world. You don't believe there is anything in this story? I mean"—Collier, afraid of offending, laboured to make his point—"you have told us that this Señorita Manara and her aunt were suspected of some form of witchcraft by the ignorant and superstitious Indian population. You aren't suggesting that there was any foundation for such an accusation?"

Romero replied with another shrug, "*Quien sabe?* Perhaps over here in this so civilised country the ancient evil will die out." He glanced at Enderby who had shaken his head. "You think not, amigo? You know more of this than the Inspector—"

"I always felt that there was something queer about her," said Enderby slowly. "Lately, from what I hear, the characteristic traits known to students of the subject have become more marked. The tendency to avoid a strong light and to sleep during the day, certain other habits which are natural in nocturnal animals of a carnivorous nature and unnatural in human beings. I suspect that this young woman is responsible for all the rumours about some creature that prowls in the Forest after dark. As to whether there is any actual physical change I am not prepared to dogmatise. But you have heard that the body of a man was found in the Forest a few week ago, Inspector? The medical evidence was that he died of heart failure, possibly the result of over-exertion. But I found him, and I say that he died of shock. He was not identified, but I rather fancy you would have recognised him, Don Juan, as a former servant of yours whom you once trusted."

Romero showed a lively interest. "Caramba! Not Metcalfe?"

"I think so. I imagine that he came to the village hoping to borrow a few pounds from the vicar, and that by some chance he discovered the identity of Mrs. Roger Frere. He would know the history of the Manara family?"

"Certainly. Both Dona Eulalia and her niece were notorious."

"I expect he applied to her for a loan and got it, and then came again and again, as blackmailers will, until she grew desperate and arranged a meeting in the woods at night. He should have known better, but probably he did not realise the danger—"

Romero nodded. "I understand. She was established here, where nothing was known of her past. She must have felt safe until he came. Lately she felt safe again until Miss Celia arrived. In her she would see another enemy. She tried the old Indian trick with candied fruit and ground glass and it failed. You are right, Major Enderby. Miss Celia is in danger. I will take her away with me to-morrow."

"I hoped you would say that. Actually, of course, she knows nothing against her."

Romero glanced at the detective. "You have seen Nina Frere?"

"I got a statement from her yesterday evening. I can't say I saw her. The room was almost dark. Something wrong with her eyes. That's one of the symptoms, you say, Major. She kept on yawning and didn't seem to care much about anything. What they call hard-boiled." He leaned forward, the firelight flickering over his serious face. "Look here, sir, I remember now reading an account of witch trials—in the Pyrenees, I think it was, in the sixteenth century. The witnesses swore that these women took an actual animal shape when they roamed the woods at night, and left a shrunken simulacrum of the human body in the bed. And they—they hunted and tore their prey. A young shepherd boy was found dead—you aren't asking me to believe—"

"I don't know," said Enderby, "but I suppose that lycanthropy like other diseases may begin in a mild form and be intermittent in character. Or perhaps it may be more fairly compared to an inherited tendency to alcoholism. The horrible urge grows stronger if it is yielded to. In the dual personality the higher, the human side, grows weaker and the animal more aggressive and more dominant."

"Can doctors do nothing?"

"I shall have to talk to Roger," said Enderby. "Meanwhile I am thankful that Señor Romero is here. Celia's ignorance of the facts exposes her to very great danger. Well, you understand now, Inspector, why I've been holding back. Sir James might have heard me out if I had aired my views at the Yard, but he would have been wondering all the while whether I ought not to be certified."

"Maybe he would," Collier admitted. "I've come across some strange things myself. I was in charge of the Belgrave Manor case, you know. You mayn't have heard of that. A witch's coven on the Sussex Downs. But I'd like you to tell me one thing, Major. You know why I'm here, investigating a case of poisoning by arsenic. Speaking unofficially would you say that the same brain planned that and it attempt to get rid of Miss Holland?"

Enderby sat back and shaded his eyes with his hand. They had to wait for his answer and when he spoke he sounded very tired.

"I don't know. I should have expected her to employ the same method. But how can one be sure? I have always felt that the death of Doris didn't make sense—unless, of course, she had seen more than she should of what must be going on in that house."

"I felt that, too," said Collier, "but I'm fairly certain now that her death was an accident. Roger Frere was the intended victim."

There was a curiously tense silence which was broken by Enderby. "Good God!" He rose from his chair with the same effect of weariness that had been betrayed a moment earlier by his voice and stood with his back to them, gripping the mantelpiece with both hands and gazing down into the fire. When he turned they saw that he was very pale.

"I see," he said. "I'm sorry. I can't help you at all."

Collier took the hint and got up at once. "I'll be getting along. Good night, Major. Good night, señor."

"I'll see you out."

Collier had left his engine running. "I'll be at the Rose and Crown if you want me," he said.

"Thank you."

Enderby returned to the house, with his dog, who had followed him out, close at his heels. He walked as he usually did with his hands in his pockets and his head a little bent, a tall lean figure in his well-worn loose-fitting tweeds silhouetted for a moment against the lighted doorway before he passed in closing the door after him.

Collier let down the window on his right and admitted a breath of cold and clammy air. Well, that was that, and whether it was going to help him to make an arrest he could not tell. The wind had dropped and a thick mist was drifting in from the Solent, pouring like smoke through the wintry woods and over the desolate moorland. Collier could see only a little way before him. He drove carefully and kept his eyes anxiously fixed on the wet black surface of the road. But he was uneasily aware of the dense coverts on either side. The serried rows of tree trunks gave him the unpleasant illusion that he was driving through a hostile crowd that had divided to let him pass and was closing in again behind him.

He realised, with a touch of anger, that the strange conversation to which he had just listened had affected his nerves. Five years had passed since he had helped to break up the secret society of Satanists at Belgrave Manor and it was a case of which he did not care to be reminded.

He tried to fix his thoughts on his immediate goal, a dish of sizzling ham and eggs and a big brown pot of tea in the warm coffee room of the Rose and Crown, but even as he visualised himself enjoying his meal he was still conscious of the night outside, and unconnected words and sentences sounded in his ears, bringing little comfort.

The powers of darkness . . . the pack . . . the night of the soul . . .

CHAPTER XXII
SOMETHING WRONG

ENDERBY went back to the sitting-room where he found his visitor buttoning up his thick overcoat and winding his scarf about his throat.

"We are going to the vicarage now?"

Enderby agreed. "I'll drive you over and wait for you outside," he said. "It may be easier to persuade her if I'm not there. You see I've already tried and failed."

"You mean that she does not wish to leave? But that is strange," said Romero. "What is there to keep her here? This mist that eats into one's bones?"

"It's her home," Enderby reminded him. "She's very fond of her father."

"Leave it to me," said Romero confidently. "I will tell her that Pilar cries herself to sleep every night. It is true. We miss her terribly, all of us. My wife says, 'Does this hat really suit me? You do not know. Miss Holland would tell me. She has good taste, that little one.'"

Enderby had to bank up the sitting-room and the kitchen fires and to see that the windows and doors were fastened before they went out to the car. Romero sat beside him, and Jock, seeing his usual seat occupied, jumped in at the back. Enderby drew up outside the gate of the vicarage and stayed in the car while Romero got out and went up the drive. He rang the bell and the door was opened by a stout elderly woman.

"My name is Romero. Don Juan Romero. Can I see Miss Holland?"

Her face lit up. "Not the South American gentleman, the father of the little girls? Well, I never. This will be a surprise for Miss Celia. Come in, sir. This way—" she opened the door of the living-room, "the vicar's in here, sir. Mr. Romero, Mr. Holland—"

The vicar who had been sitting very comfortably by the fire with his slippered feet on the fender, refreshing himself after a long and tiring day with a dip into Pepys' *Diary*, laid his book down and rose to greet his visitor.

"Señor Romero, I am delighted. This is an unexpected pleasure. I had no idea, and neither had Celia, I imagine, or she would have told me. You and Señora Romero have been so very kind to her. She is so attached to you all. Do sit down. Here. Oh, dear, I'm afraid there are books on all the chairs when Celia isn't here to clear up after me. How long have you been in England? Are you staying near here?"

"I came over to-day by air."

"By air?" The vicar, a trifle flustered and uncertain, took off his spectacles and wiped them. "Can—can we have the pleasure of putting you up?"

"You are very kind, but I am staying with Major Enderby."

"With the Major?" The vicar looked more puzzled than ever. "You are a friend of his? I was not aware. Strange—"

"I very much want Miss Celia to come back to Cannes with me to-morrow, sir."

Mr. Holland's face fell. "You want her to cut her holiday short? That's—rather disappointing. But, of course, if she's really needed—you have been so kind to her—"

"Could I see Miss Celia? She is at home?"

"She is out just at present, but I'm expecting her in any moment. I didn't think she would be so late," said the vicar, glancing at the clock, "she knows I don't like her to be out after dark—but I daresay Roger will see her home."

"Where has she gone? Forgive me for asking. I have a reason—"

"I have been out myself all the afternoon and I expected to find her here, but my housekeeper told me she had gone over to Frere Court to have tea with young Mrs. Frere. The gardener brought a note, and I suppose Celia felt she couldn't very well refuse. These people are my principal parishioners, Senor Romero, but they don't come to church, I m sorry to say, and we have seen little or nothing of them—is anything the matter?"

Romero cleared his throat. "I was wondering if it would be possible to telephone and say that, if she has not already started on her way home, will she wait for Major Enderby to fetch her in his car? He could be there in a few minutes, I suppose."

"But where is the Major?"

"He is waiting outside."

"Waiting outside? Why doesn't he come in? I don't under-stand—"

Poor Mr. Holland looked more bewildered than ever and began to shake a little. "It is all so—are you trying to break some bad news?"

"No, no, everything is all right," said Romero hurriedly. If you will please telephone as I say. It is the best thing, I think—"

"Very well." The vicar went reluctantly into the hall.

"I had this put in to please Celia, but I don't like it," he complained. "My utterance does not seem to be clear enough to suit the people at the exchange, and I can't hear very well myself." He fumbled over the pages of the directory.

"I don't know their number—"

Romero stood by, trying not to betray his impatience.

At last they were put through.

"Is that Frere Court? This is the vicar. Yes, Mr. Holland. Oh . . . yes . . . will you tell my daughter that Senor Romero is here—" Romero tried to interrupt but it was not easy to stop Mr. Holland when once he had got started. "Here at the vicarage. Major Enderby will fetch her home in his car. I beg your pardon. I didn't quite catch . . . oh, in that case, of course. I must say I wish she had started earlier. I don't like her to be out alone after nightfall just now, not that I really believe . . . would you mind saying that again? I'm afraid I missed . . ."

He waited, with the instrument clamped to his ear and his charming old face, rosy and wrinkled as a winter apple, screwed up with the effort to hear. Romero, standing by, restraining himself with some difficulty from snatching the receiver, shifted his feet and glanced at his wrist watch. "What are they saying? Did they fetch Miss Celia to speak to you?"

"No. A woman's voice. One of the maids, I suppose. Not Celia. I couldn't hear very well, and now the line has gone dead. There was a sort of click—"

"They probably rang off. Did they understand that she was to wait for the Major?"

"I gathered that she had already started on her way home. I—well, really, I don't—"

Mrs. Bond, hearing the front door slam of her kitchen to find the vicar reopening it to stare after his mysterious visitor. Already the night had swallowed him up, but he could be heard running down the drive. The gate swung to after him and a minute later a car started.

"What's the matter, sir? What's wrong now?"

The vicar shook his head. "I have no idea. I—I'm not so young as I was. I—we can only wait, it seems—"

Romero, meanwhile, was trying to explain. His careful English had degenerated as a result of his growing excitement, but he did his best.

"Yes. It stands in a park. There's an avenue a mile long from the gates. But surely Celia didn't go?"

"She went. I induced Mr. Holland to make use of the telephone. He is unaccustomed, and he held it as if he thought it would bite him. I could not prevent him from blurting out my name and yours. I had asked him to say that if she would wait you would fetch her. He was told that she had already started on her way home. Can we go to meet her? Is there more than one way she could take?"

Enderby was driving slowly through the village keeping his eyes on the road. There were lights in cottage windows but all doors were closed and there was nobody about.

"I'm afraid there is. If she had been cycling or in a car she would come by the avenue to the south lodge, but if she was walking she would save over half a mile by taking a footpath that crosses the park. And there's still another possibility. Did you hear how long she had been gone?"

"No."

"There's another little used track across the park to a door in the wall just beyond the west gate which is always kept locked. It is a short cut to the White Cottage and I always came and went that way when I was asked over to play tennis last summer. If she left the Court before it was quite dark she might come that way if she wanted to see me and talk things over."

"Is that very likely, do you think?"

"It is possible."

"Then we must divide our forces. But that will be difficult. You know the ground and I do not—"

Enderby's lean face was white under the tan. "You think there is danger—"

"One cannot be certain. But we are dealing with something primitive, something that fears to be caught and caged, something that will turn and rend if it is driven to desperation—why are we stopping here?"

"This is the Rose and Crown. If the Inspector is still here I'll ask him to come with us." He sounded his horn and the landlord came out.

"What can I do for you, Major?"

"I want Mr. Collier."

"He's just sat down to a good tea. Tells me he missed his lunch."

"I'm sorry to disturb him, but it's an urgent matter. Tell him I want to take him for a ride."

The landlord laughed. "No bumping off business, I hope. Very well. I'll tell him."

"Do you mind getting in at the back with the dog, señor, and letting the Inspector sit by me? I'll have to explain the position to him as we go—"

"Certainly."

Collier did not keep them waiting. He came out still munching, and pulling on his overcoat.

"Damn you," he said, "this was going to be my first square meal to-day and I've only just started."

"Sorry, and all that. Listen, Collier, I know you're not convinced that we're right—"

"I can't say either way yet, Major. But what's the trouble? Has anything happened since I left you?"

"We have just been to the vicarage. Celia had been invited to tea at Frere Court and had not yet returned. That may sound all right to you, Collier, but we're worried. The vicar rang them up and was told that she was on her way home. Alone and on foot a night like this. Anything might happen. I want you to take the car up the avenue to meet her. Señor Romero will be with you. Jock and I will cut across the park in case she has gone by the footpath. I'll whistle three times if I need you, and you can sound your horn three times—"

"What do you anticipate?"

Collier settled himself in the seat beside the driver.

Enderby edged the car forward into the gathering mist leaving behind the warm glow of the inn's lighted windows.

"I can't tell you that. I don't know. But I'm worried. Here we are—"

The tall stone gate posts of the south entrance to Frere Court loomed before them. Enderby stopped the car and got out. Collier took the driving seat and Romero joined him. Enderby clipped the lead on his dog's collar. The big Airedale whined uneasily sniffing at the drift of dead leaves that filled the ditch at the roadside. Enderby waved to the others to go on before he turned away and was swallowed up by the darkness.

Collier drove on at a snail's pace, watching the road. "There's something wrong with the night," he said, and was startled by the sound of his own voice.

Romero glanced at him. "You feel that too?"

The car's headlamps gave them a fugitive glimpse of the banks on either side, crowned with shrubberies of rhododendron and holly, and a double row of lime trees. Once Collier checked and the car swerved.

"Something moved—"

"No. Nothing."

The great house rose up before them, a shadow among shadows, with one light showing dimly in the fanlight over the front door.

Chapter XXIII
POWERS OF DARKNESS

CELIA was alone, sitting by the fire and knitting a jumper when Mrs. Bond brought in the note. "From Frere Court, miss. Tom, the under gardener, came to the back door. I don't know if he should have waited for an answer but he was in a hurry seemingly.

Celia fumbled over opening the envelope. Her hands were shaking, her heart was thumping, too. She was angry with herself, but she could not help it. "I'm a fool," she thought despairingly. "I can't get over this complex. I'll have to go away after all—"

But the note was not from Roger, The writing, sprawling, fierce, impatient, was that of Nina Frere.

"Dear Miss Holland,

"Roger has told me that you were with us the night we escaped from San Rinaldo. I had always thought you were killed when we were attacked on the beach just as we were launching the boat. I am very glad it was not so. Roger is anxious that we should meet again and be friends. He spoke of this some days ago, but as you know, we have had trouble here, and also I have not been very well. I am better now so will you please be very kind and come this afternoon to see me, and we will have tea, English fashion, and talk together.

"Yours sincerely,

"Nina Frere."

Celia did not hesitate. Roger had said something like that to her. She had gathered, not so much from his admissions as from what he had left untold, that his marriage was not a success. He had seemed to think that she might be able to help. "Nina isn't settling down as well as I hoped. She can't get the hang of our English life," he had said. "I think perhaps if you talked to her—my stepmother doesn't bother. They get on all right, better than I expected, but that's because Nina leaves the housekeeping and giving the servants their orders to her. But they have nothing in common."

That had been some weeks ago now, when they first met in the Forest. Nothing had come of it, and lately he had hardly mentioned Nina, but Celia had not forgotten.

She would go, of course. She ran upstairs to put on her hat and wear the coat with the big fur collar that Señora Romero had given to her. Her best clothes would only be just good enough. Everyone she had heard speak of young Mrs. Frere agreed on one point. She was amazingly beautiful.

"I don't want to feel too much of a worm," thought Celia as she took a new pair of gloves from her top drawer and reinforced her self-respect by giving her nose a hurried dab with a powder puff.

She looked into the kitchen on her way out to tell Mrs. Bond that she was going to tea at Frere Court. "That note was from Mrs. Roger, asking me—"

"And about time, too," grumbled the old woman, who resented the way the Freres had ignored the vicar and his daughter. "But they might have sent one of the cars to fetch you an afternoon like this. It's coming over thick from the Solent. I've heard the syrens away out to sea, and that shows the way the wind is—"

"I shall enjoy the walk and I daresay someone will run me home," said Celia.

She met nobody in the village. The children were still in school. She heard the babel of shrill voices as she passed the little school-house. Their mothers were indoors. A mizzling rain was falling. Celia realised that it would have been more sensible to have put on her raincoat, but she would have missed the moral support derived from a garment produced by a famous firm in the Rue de la Paix. She began to know, moreover, as she trudged up the mile-long avenue to the house, that she was going to need all her courage.

She only knew Roger, not his formidable stepmother, or the film actor brother. Nina—it was strange to think that though they had spent some hours together, facing dangers unknown or half guessed at, during a night that neither of them was likely to forget, there had been no gleam of light by which one could see the face of the other. Nina had been a voice, urgent sometimes and sharp with fear, and at others merely impatient and openly contemptuous of the English girl's clumsiness, her failing strength, as, with Roger to help her, she scrambled through ditches and stumbled over rough ground, sobbing with exhaustion, drenched with sweat, while the other led the way, calling to them to follow.

"Run, can't you. Why do you linger—"

"This way, miss—" Mostyn, the parlourmaid, impeccable in her black dress and muslin cap and apron, opened the door for the visitor. Celia, following her across the hall, thought the house seemed unnaturally quiet. It had been more cheerful and homelike during old Mr. Frere's lifetime when there had always been three or four dogs of various breeds about to make a visitor welcome. She found herself wondering if their ghosts haunted their former habitation, and whether, if she were clairvoyante, she would see the tubby body of Sprats the sealyham who had always slept at the foot of his master's bed trotting towards her, and the welsh corgie rising from his place under the hall table to thrust his muzzle into her hand. They had been special favourites of hers, but she had not thought of them for years. Strange that they should be so clearly in her mind now so that she could almost see them getting in her way, trying to stop her.

It was just fancy. She did not really see them. And the parlourmaid had opened the drawing-room door and spoken her name and gone away.

Celia moved forward uncertainly, disconcerted as Collier had been before her, by the almost complete darkness. She saw something move on the sofa drawn close up to the fire and the remembered voice greeted her.

"You have come. I am glad. It was wise. Sit down over there."

She neither rose from the sofa nor offered her hand, and Celia, after a momentary hesitation, took the indicated chair. It was not an auspicious beginning, and for the first time she felt some doubt as to whether she had been right in coming. She could not see Nina's face clearly but she felt that the brilliant black eyes were observing her closely and with an unfriendly scrutiny.

"I don't know," she said. "It has begun to rain. It's beastly weather. Don't you find the lack of sunshine depressing after San Rinaldo?" Out of sheer nervousness she had pitched her voice too high and ended in a sort of squeak. Her cheeks burned and she pressed her hands together convulsively. Another voice, not her own, a warning voice, seemed to say "Steady. Steady—" Luckily she was allowed time to pull herself together for Nina did not hurry to answer.

"No," she said at last. " I do not care for the sun. I prefer the moon. A windy night, with clouds racing—" her voice rose and she checked herself abruptly with an effect of violence.

The ensuing silence was so oppressive that Celia had to break it at all costs. "It's so strange, isn't it, meeting again like this—"

"Yes. I must say I thought you were dead. You must have a very thick skull," remarked Nina.

"Roger told you I was struck on the head!"

"You call him Roger?"

"I—I've known him some time. His uncle and my father were great friends. You speak English very well, Mrs. Frere. I remember thinking that when we met that night—"

"I was sent to Europe to be educated. I was one year at a school in Eastbourne, and two years after that in a convent in Paris." Nina leaned forward deliberately and spat into the fire.

There was such rancour in the act that Celia shrank a little in spite of herself.

"You didn't like it—"

"Like it?" Nina laughed a little. "Like being in a cage? But I was so young then, I was afraid. And they—I can see it now when I look back—they were afraid of me. The fat old portress, Soeur Angelique, crossed herself when I had passed. I turned round once and caught her. It's great fun frightening people."

"Is it?"

Nina sat up with one of her lightning swift movements and rocked gently from side to side, hugging her knees. Her slim body in a dark frock merged in the shadows. The door was opened and the parlourmaid came in with the tea trolley.

"Will you pour out, madam?"

"No. Put it by Miss Holland. You will help yourself, please. There is bread and butter and cake. I do not care for tea."

Mostyn went out again.

"You shouldn't have bothered to have this for me," said Celia.

Nina answered quite pleasantly. "Why not? Most people like it. You must not mind me. Take no notice of what I say. It's all nonsense. I wasn't making you nervous, was I?"

"No, of course not—"

"The others are all out. Mrs. Frere at her bridge club, and Roger and Cedric I don't know where. I thought it would be nice to have you to myself. Because there are things, are there not, that must be said?"

Celia drank some tea and set down the cup carefully. Her hand was not as steady as she could have wished. What did Nina mean? For a minute or two she had sounded quite normal, a hostess making conversation with a caller whom she did not know very well, but already she was beginning to speak as she had done at first, betraying a harsh impatience of the ordinary forms of civilised intercourse. It was as if with every word she uttered she stripped off some of the veneer of her European education.

"Do you remember waiting in the hut of my old nurse while the roar of the crowd sounded louder every minute? I knew you were shaking in your shoes then. We were safe because they were afraid of leprosy. Does it come back in dreams?"

"Sometimes."

"I saved your life then, didn't I?"

"Yes. I'm not ungrateful. I've always wanted to thank you—"

"Then you will not join with those who want to hunt me down. If they ask you what you what you have heard about me and my aunt you will swear that you know nothing."

"It would be the truth," said Celia. "I never heard of you."

"You expect me to believe that? You were more than two years at the estancia of the Romero family. Our house was not ten miles, nearer by the jungle paths. Why, their servants—some of them— often came—" she checked herself as if she realised that she was saying too much. "They wouldn't talk, but the English manservant would. He came here to ask for money. How do I know that you and he were not in league—"

"Don't be absurd," said Celia angrily. "I don't plot with servants—"

But she was beginning to shake all over. She had remembered Major Enderby's theory that Metcalfe had died because he had been blackmailing somebody and had pushed that person past the limit of endurance. It was true then. Nina herself had admitted it. There was a secret connected with her past that had already cost a man's life, and she—Celia—was supposed to know it.

The shadowy figure on the sofa had ceased to rock from side to side and was sitting motionless, holding a fan to screen its face from the flickering light of the fire.

"I will not be spied upon," it said, in a voice grown strangely hoarse and weary.

Celia felt an unexpected pang of pity and spoke impulsively. "I don't want to do that. Please believe me when I say I want to be friends with you and help you if you will let me. You must feel lonely so far from your own people—"

But even as she said it she knew that friendship between them would be impossible while her flesh crept at the thought of touching Nina's hand. Why was it that some deep-rooted instinctive fear and disgust mingled with her reluctant sympathy?

She said, "Must we sit in the dark?" and realised with horror that her own voice was no longer quite under control.

Nina, answering, broke the increasing tension. "The light hurts my eyes." And then, after another pause, "Friends? I do not need them. I have all I need—but if they spy and pry I shall not be able to bear it. Leave me alone—that is all I ask. Go away now, please—"

"Very well," Celia stood up. "I—I can see you are not happy. I'm sorry. If ever I can be of any use I hope you will send for me. I'd like to help."

"Because of Roger?"

The challenge took Celia unawares. Her heart seemed to miss a beat, but she answered steadily. "Because of Roger. He hasn't been very lucky so far. Goodbye."

Nina made no reply. The long room was now in almost complete darkness and Celia nearly stumbled over a footstool on her way out. There was nobody in the hall and as she crossed it she had the sensation that had oppressed her on her arrival that the great house was unnaturally silent. She opened the front door and closed it after her just too late to hear the ringing of the telephone bell.

There was a faint splash of a rising fish in the moat as she crossed the drawbridge and she turned aside for a moment and leaned over the rail. It was too dark to see anything, but she was remembering how she and Roger had stood there smoking cigarettes and watching the ghostly white reflections of the sleeping swans floating on the black water below. She and her father had come to dine with old Mr. Frere and had met his nephew and heir for the first time. If she had not gone abroad then perhaps everything would have been different—and happier.

She sighed and went on her way.

She had gone a little way down the avenue, puzzling as she went over that strange interview, when what she believed must be the solution of the mystery of Nina Frere came to her like a flash. It was so dreadful that unconsciously she cried out, "Oh no—" and stopped as if the earth had opened at her feet to show her a glimpse of hell. It couldn't be, it couldn't be. And yet, if it was something must be done instantly. She must tell someone who would understand, and that person, obviously, was Major Enderby. Instead of going straight home she would cross the park by the footpath. She would have to go through Boars Spinney to the White Cottage. There was a swampy patch into which she might sink up to the ankles at this time of year, but her shoes were thick, and there was no fear of her losing herself, she had lived too long in the Forest for that. She was not deterred by the knowledge that for weeks past none of the village women had ventured out alone after nightfall. That was all nonsense. She was not afraid of a stray Alsatian dog or even of a lurking wolf or hyena escaped from a menagerie, half-starved, poor brute, in its hard won freedom, and lurking in the undergrowth.

She had to see Major Enderby at once. At once. Nothing else mattered.

She left the avenue and was crossing the open ground in front of the house. Luckily she had brought a small electric torch with her in her handbag in case nobody at the Court offered to drive her home. Its feeble ray could not penetrate the mist that covered the sodden meadows like a wet white pall but it showed her the fence enclosing the strip of woodland that lay between her and the door in the park wall, and the stile she had to climb. Unfortunately she dropped it as she was getting over and broke the bulb. She had gone another hundred yards when she heard a rustling in the undergrowth on her left.

She stopped to listen and the sounds ceased, but when she moved they began again. Something was following, keeping pace with her, unseen in the darkness.

Celia tried hard not to give way to panic. She had gone too far now to turn back, and if she called for help no one would hear her. She told herself that there was nothing to fear. The supposed tracker might be nothing more than a fox creeping back to his earth among the hollies. She thought she noticed the faint musky scent tainting the air. She glanced back over her shoulder and saw two points of greenish phosphorescent light. Eyes. But the eyes were at the wrong level for so small an animal as a fox and they were approaching, bearing down upon her.

Celia heard a high thin shriek and did not know that she herself had uttered it. The frail defences her mind had been putting up went crashing down and left her defenceless against the appalling onslaught of embodied evil.

Something leapt at her, bearing her down—

CHAPTER XXIV
JOCK AND HIS MASTER

COLLIER was first to climb the fence, but Romero was close behind him. With the inspector's powerful torch to guide them they plunged recklessly through the drenched undergrowth, snapping off the fir saplings as they ran. They had heard the three whistles, the signal agreed upon, followed by the sound of a shot and the long drawn out howl of a dog. After that, though Collier had shouted at intervals that they were coming, there had been silence.

The sodden grassland had not been easy going and both men were breathing heavily. Collier shouted, and this time they heard Enderby replying.

"Here—"

Celia was lying on the path with her head propped on Enderby's rolled up overcoat. Her face had lost every vestige of colour and her eyes were closed. The fur collar of her coat was badly torn. Romero bent over her. "She has fainted. Or it may be she is stunned. She must have fallen heavily on the back of her head. For the rest you were in time, señor. The coat alone has suffered—"

Enderby was sitting on the ground holding his dog in his arms. Jock's rough hide was smeared with blood. He was trying feebly to lick his master's hand.

"So you had to shoot him," said Collier.

Enderby answered without looking up. "Yes."

"Is he badly hurt?"

"I don't know. It way be only a flesh wound, but it's bleeding badly. Will you help me by holding him while I bandage it with my handkerchief?"

"Of course." Collier knelt on the trampled earth and took the weight against his knees while Romero held the torch. Jock began to growl, but stopped when Enderby spoke to him.

"All right, old man. These are friends—"

"What happened?"

"I heard her scream. I wasn't far off, luckily. I took Jock's lead off and told him to go ahead. I followed as fast as I could, but he had leapt at her throat. I had to shoot—"

"Good God! Then it has been your dog all the time—"

"No, no. You don't understand. He wasn't attacking Celia. It was the other. I tell you Celia was on the ground and—and something dark and shapeless crouching over her, snarling and tearing. When Jock had dragged it off I—I had to shoot. It ran off that way, I think. I couldn't go after it. I had Celia to think of and the dog. I was afraid I had killed him—"

"I see," said Collier. His tone was non-committal. "Well, we had better get this young lady home as soon as possible. Perhaps you will help me carry her back to the car, Señor Romero. I'll come back then, Major, and help you with your dog. I should think we could carry him between us using your coat as a stretcher,"

"Thank you."

"One moment," said Romero. "Celia is better—"

Celia had struggled into a sitting position. "Oh—is it you, Don Juan? How did you come here? Or am I dreaming? My head hurts. I—I was knocked down, I think. I—I was horribly frightened—"

"You're all right now, Celia," said Enderby. "You've given us all a fright, too. Damn it, woman, what do you mean by wandering about like this after dark? You've had warnings enough—"

"Don't be cross or you'll make me cry. My eyes are watering as it is. My head hurts quite a lot——"

"We are taking you home now, Miss Holland," said Collier in the fatherly tone he had used with lost children in his uniformed days. "If you go straight to bed you'll be none the worse in the morning and more able to tell us all about it."

Romero had said nothing but he had helped her to stand up and supported her with his arm. He smiled at her and his dark eyes were kind. "You are flying over to France to-morrow with me. Maria and Pilar will be so pleased—"

"No. Wait a minute. I'm all confused. Let me think. There is something important, terribly urgent—"

She stood blinking in the light of Collier's torch and frowning with the effort of concentration.

"I can't go home yet. I was coming to see you, Major. There is something I have to say. Please—"

"Very well. I will take you to the Cottage first. Do you mind if the inspector and Señor Romero come too?"

"No. It would be better if they did—"

The little party moved off slowly, Celia leaning on Romero's arm, while Collier and Enderby carried the dog between them wrapped in the latter's overcoat. They found the car where they had left it half way down the avenue.

Ten minutes later they were sitting round Enderby's fire. The men were drinking whisky and soda. Celia had refused to touch the brandy Enderby had poured out for her and asked for tea. He had gone to fill the kettle and they heard him speaking over the telephone in the passage.

"The vet's coming as soon as he can," he said when he rejoined them. He went over to speak to Jock who was lying very quietly in his basket in a dark corner.

Collier cleared his throat. "He'll have to be destroyed, you know, Major. I'm sorry. I know you're fond of him."

Enderby sat down and began to fill his pipe. His fingers trembled slightly but his voice was steady. "You're wrong, Inspector. Jock sleeps in the house. He's never been out without my knowledge. He saved Celia's life to-night."

"I've heard your story, Major. Can you prove it? Perhaps Miss Holland can settle the matter for us. Was it Jock who sprang at you and knocked you down and tore your coat collar with his teeth, Miss Holland?"

She was silent for a minute. Then she said, "I don't know. I only saw two shining green eyes and then—it's all confused. But I don't believe it was Jock. Dear old Jock. He's always so good, he and I are friends—"

"He may have passing fits of savagery—"

"If you have Jock destroyed," said the Major quietly, "I'm a lonely man, and most things have passed me by. I shall put a bullet through my head."

"That's hardly playing fair, sir," said Collier in the same tone. "I have to do my duty however unpleasant it may be. You know that."

"I know. Excuse me. I'll make your tea, Celia." Not a word was said while he was out of the room. Collier, looking at Celia, saw that her face was wet with tears. He felt very sorry for Enderby for it was obvious that if his dog was the culprit he had not known it. And yet, how was that possible?

Enderby came back with the tea tray and set it down on a small table beside Celia. "Shall I pour it out for you? Can you manage? All right—"

"Thank you." She drank some tea and set down her cup. "I had it by myself at Frere Court. I want to tell you about that. She—Nina Frere—wrote and asked me to come and see her. I went because Roger said some time ago that he wanted us to be friends. I wanted to—but I hadn't liked her that night when she helped us escape across the fields to the shore. I've been thinking about that, and I believe that she came up behind us with an oar and stunned us because she wanted to get away in a boat with Roger and leave me behind. That doesn't matter now. The point is that she's very queer mentally. She thinks I know something about her past. She practically admitted that Metcalfe had been trying to get money from her. I feel almost certain now that it was she who sent me that box of dates." Celia shuddered. "I'll never forget how I felt as we sat there, practically in the dark, while she talked in a threatening sort of way. I—I was thankful when she told me to go—"

"You were alone with her?"

"Yes."

"She actually threatened you?"

"I can't remember the exact words but that was the impression I got. And I could feel that she was terribly unhappy—lost and desolate—I couldn't understand it, but when I got outside I guessed the truth—"

"You guessed?" said Enderby. "That seems hardly possible—"

She turned to him. "I felt then that I must see you at once. You have lived in the East and you would know what must be done—"

Enderby shook his head. "You should not have gone to see her, Celia. I'm sorry you're mixed up in this."

"You know what is wrong with Nina Frere?"

"I think so, Celia. I had my suspicions and Señor Romero has confirmed them."

"You knew she was a leper?"

She was startled by the effect of her words. It was evident that they were utterly unprepared. They all stared at her. Enderby, who had been about to relight his pipe, threw the match away without using it.

"Leprosy! What put that into your head?"

"I told you she took us into a hut in which her old nurse lived. She warned us not to touch anything. Afterwards she told us that the woman was a leper. Wouldn't that explain why she lives in a darkened room? I think she found out quite lately that she has the disease—"

Enderby looked at Romero enquiringly. "What do you say, señor?"

The South American shrugged his shoulders.

"It is possible, but for myself I do not think it."

"But—don't you see?" cried Celia. "We can't leave it. We must make sure. There's the danger of her infecting others."

Collier intervened. "I think this young lady has had about as much as she can stand to-night," he said firmly. "You have to wait here for the vet, Major. If you'll let us use your car the Señor and I will take Miss Holland home. We shall come straight back to you."

"You are right, of course," said Enderby. "Go with them, Celia. Try not to worry. We'll do the best we can—"

"Thank you," she said, rather faintly now. "I do feel—I've been through rather a lot—"

Enderby went with them to the gate and saw them start with Collier driving and Romero sitting at the back with Celia. When he went back to the sitting-room he found that Jock had struggled out of his basket and dragged himself as far as the hearthrug, leaving a trail of blood on the carpet.

Enderby replaced the bandage that had slipped from the dog's shoulder and sat down on the floor beside him, lifting the shaggy head on to his knees.

"You did well, old fellow, whatever that cop may say. A bad business—and I'm afraid there's worse to come."

CHAPTER XXV
CASTING BACK

MOSTYN came into the dining-room where Roger and Cedric Frere were at breakfast. "Inspector Collier is sorry to disturb you so early, sir, but could you see him for a few minutes?"

"All right. Where is he? In the morning room? I'll come at once."

Roger threw down his paper and pushed back his chair.

"Let the fellow wait," advised his half-brother. "What a pest the police are. A set of busybodies." He paused in the act of helping himself to bacon and eggs, pushed the dish away, and reached for the marmalade jar. "I'm right off my feed," he complained. Roger, glancing at him, noticed that he was paler than usual and heavy-eyed.

"You don't look well. Cheer up. The sea voyage will put you right."

"If I ever get off," grumbled Cedric, "hanging about here waiting for the adjourned inquest. Anyone'd think I was responsible for the wretched girl doing herself in."

"Naturally, that must be one of their theories," said Roger.

"Why naturally? I never even looked at her. It might just as well have been you. And as you're taking that tone, Roger, I may as well mention that I told the Inspector that I heard you talking to her in your room only a few days before she died. He may be asking you about that. Don't say I haven't warned you."

"Thank you, Cedric. How like you. Don't go out yet. The inspector may want a word with you, especially if you have constituted yourself his assistant."

Roger found the man from the Yard standing at the window of the morning-room looking out across the park. He turned quickly as Roger entered. "I'm afraid I'm being a nuisance," he said with a disarming smile. Roger, who had been thinking something of the sort and had meant to be very curt, found himself shaking hands.

"Well, it's worrying, of course, but if you can clear up the mystery of that poor girl's death by asking me questions, I can only say go ahead. Won't you sit down?"

"Thank you. The fact is, Mr. Frere, I've got a new angle on that business, and that's why I had to see you as soon as possible."

"Really? That sounds promising. Does that mean you are about to make an arrest?" asked Roger quickly.

Collier noticed that he was gripping the arms of his chair.

"Mr. Frere," he said gravely, "I have sometimes thought that you know, or suspect, more than you have told me, that you have some theory. But your theory may be mistaken."

"I haven't one."

"Well, I am going to tell you something in confidence. It must go no further. Do you agree to that?"

"Very well."

"I must tell you for your own safety. You spent the night before Doris died at the White Cottage. When did you come home?"

"Some time between nine and half-past. I came in by the garden door. I met no one on my way up to my room. I had had breakfast with Enderby. I was wearing a suit he had lent me. I changed into one of mine. I was going on to Southampton."

"Had your room been done?"

"No. The maids would come up later for that."

"The glass of lemonade that you drink when you wake up in the morning was on your night table as usual, I suppose?"

"I suppose so. I didn't notice."

"You didn't drink it then?"

"No. I had recently had two large cups of coffee."

"Just so. That's what I wanted to get at. I think that if you had, Mr. Frere, you would not be here now."

"You don't mean—"

"I am fairly certain that Doris drank the lemonade. In fact she seems to have told the between-maid that she did. There is very little doubt in my mind that the arsenic was in the lemonade. I'm afraid this must be a great shock for you, Mr. Frere," said Collier sympathetically.

Roger looked at him steadily. "You mean that somebody was trying to get me, and missed their mark? I see you do. But you have no evidence to prove it."

"Not enough to justify an arrest. There is still a lot of routine work to be done. Normally I should be saying nothing at this stage. But I had to warn you. It is not, I hope, very likely, but there is a possibility that another attempt might be made on your life. You must be careful. I think I should feel happier about you if you went up to Town for a few days. Would you do that? You would keep in touch with us at the Yard, of course."

"I'll think it over," said Roger. "It sounds rather like running away, and I may be needed here. My wife is ill."

"I'm sorry about that," said Collier civilly. "Nothing serious, I hope, that the doctor can't put right."

"She won't have a doctor."

"I think you would be wise to exert your authority and insist on a medical examination, Mr. Frere," said Collier quietly.

"Why do you say that?"

"Well—she was good enough to see me for a few minutes the day before yesterday, and it struck me then that she was very far from well. And now, sir, about this case. Can you think of anyone with a grievance or a grudge of any kind against you?"

"I've never harmed any one that I know of, Inspector."

"Who would gain by your death?"

"The estate and the property from which the income to maintain it is derived is entailed. If I die without issue my half brother Cedric would inherit. But Cedric is too easy going to take a lot of trouble and run the risk of being hanged for committing a murder."

"Your wife will be well provided for?"

"Adequately. Yes. But then again the motive seems hardly strong enough. Don't run away with the idea that she and Cedric are the victims of a guilty passion, inspector. You can take my word for it that they are not," said Roger firmly.

"You know your half-brother well, Mr. Frere?"

"I ought to. We were brought up together and lived with my step-mother and my half-sister at a boarding house in London until I came down here."

"Could you give me the address?"

"Of the boarding house? Certainly. Twelve, Warrender Way, Earl's Court."

"Thank you, sir."

Superintendent Cardew was still in his room when Collier returned to Scotland Yard. He waved his subordinate to a chair and went on hunting for a lost form in his desk.

"All these pigeon holes," he growled, "and we haven't even any blinking pigeons to lay eggs in them. How's the case? Servant girl who took arsenic, wasn't it? Love again, I suppose. Half the trouble in this world is caused by humanity's incurably sentimental approach to the reproduction of the species."

"That may be, sir, but I haven't noticed much love about this time, and I'm afraid the suicide theory is untenable. It's a murder case right enough. Have you read my last report?"

"I have not. Going to, of course. But I've been run off my feet."

"Might I just go through it with you now, sir? Have you a few moments to spare?"

Cardew grinned. These two were old friends. "Don't ask fool questions. You know I haven't. But I know that you won't go away until you've said your piece. Carry on."

In spite of his professed indifference he listened with close attention to Collier's account of Doris Jupp's death and of the course taken by the enquiries carried on first by the local police, and then by himself.

"I think you're right," he said, after a while. "The statement of the between-maid is important. Obviously if the lemonade was poisoned it was meant for Frere and you've got to start all over again. You say there's been talk locally about the wife going about with her brother-in-law. Probably those two are your birds, but whether you'll ever get proof is another matter. The A.C. mentioned the case to me only yesterday. He seemed to think you might get some help from an old friend of his living in that neighbourhood. What's your next move?"

"I'd like a little more light on the Frere family before they went down to Hampshire."

"Well, it sounds a fairly harmless way of spending your time," said Cardew pessimistically, "but I can't think of anything better. The motive sticks out a mile, but what's the use of that? I hate these poisoning cases. Murderers who are smart enough not to try to get rid of the body are difficult, very difficult. All right, Collier. Carry on."

Warrender Way proved to be a dull grey street of tall Victorian houses, each with a basement and an area shut in by iron railings, and a flight of steps up to the front door which, in the case of Number Twelve, was badly in need of a coat of paint. The door was opened by a slatternly young servant. Collier asked for the proprietress.

"Mrs. Banks? I'll tell her if you'll wait a mo."

He was shown into a shabby dining-room. A dusty fire smouldered in the grate. The mingled smells of boiled mutton and cabbage, which had been perceptible in the passage, were stronger here. Collier, glancing up at the discoloured engraving of Landseer's *Monarch of the Glen* hanging over the sideboard thought of the oak-panelled dining-room at Frere Court with its mullioned windows, and the portrait of Mrs. Susannah Frere by Lely.

Mrs. Banks came in and looked him up and down warily. She was a thin, harassed-looking woman, worn sharp by the harsh necessities of her daily life. Shrewd and not unkindly when she could afford to be, which was not always. Collier knew the type well, and that with such a woman it is best to come straight to the point.

He produced his card.

"I see," she said resignedly. "I'm glad they haven't sent a man in uniform. It doesn't do a house like mine any good. But I hope you're making a mistake. My guests are all very quiet, orderly people, and prompt in their payments—"

"We're not interested in anyone staying here at present, Mrs. Banks."

"Well, that's a comfort. What do you want then?"

"I want to know anything you can tell me about a family that lived with you, I believe, for some years, and left about a year ago."

"You mean the Freres? Well, I'm not in the habit of gossiping about my guests."

"I had better explain," said Collier. "Could we sit down?"

"Not in here. Some of my people use the room between meals. Come into my office."

She led the way into a tiny room on the other side of the passage. Collier took a chair wedged between a roll-top desk and a sewing machine and sat there nursing his hat on his knees while Mrs. Banks ousted a sleeping cat from a basket chair and sank into it with a sigh.

"This is the only place I can call my own when the house is full as it is just now. Many's the time Sybyl Frere has sat where you're sitting now. She was a dear girl and I was very fond of her. I cried my eyes out when I heard of her being killed in that motor smash. It seemed so hard that it should happen just when there was a chance for her at last. I had been thinking she would meet some nice man who could give her a good home of her own and make her free of that mother of hers."

"Didn't she get on with her mother? I understood that she was quite broken up by the girl's death. She held the elder brother responsible and has never forgiven him."

Mrs. Banks sniffed. "That sounds just like her. She might kid herself now that she was devoted to Sybyl, but actually she was the jealous sort that grudges a daughter her youth. If you know Mrs. Frere at all I don't have to tell you that she's been a very pretty woman. She's good looking still, I suppose. I used to notice that none of the ladies staying here cared for her, but the gentlemen admired her. Old Colonel Strutt was quite silly about her and used to bring her bunches of violets, which he could ill afford. And between you and me I used to fancy sometimes that she had men friends that met outside and never brought here to introduce to her children."

"She seems very devoted to her son."

Mrs, Banks sniffed again. "That Cedric, always looking at himself in the glass! Fancying himself as a film actor. Yes. He was her darling. You're right there. And when Roger was sent for by his rich uncle she could hardly contain herself. She didn't often talk to me but she had to get it off her chest and I happened to be there. The old man was a stingy brute, she said. I'd guessed, of course, that her late husband's family didn't approve of her. My notion is that she was given an allowance and told to keep her distance. Roger went to live with his uncle, but the others didn't go down to Hampshire until the old gentleman died. Sybyl told me about it. 'We're all to live with Roger,' she said, 'it's a beautiful house full of lovely old things. I don't see why he should be saddled with the whole family, but Mother says it's the least he can do.' Roger and Sybyl were always good friends. Roger worked hard at his office, but on Saturday afternoons and Sundays he used to take her out to Kew Gardens if it was fine, or museums or the Pictures. I think he was sorry for the child. It was dull for her living here after she left school. There weren't any other young people. Most of my guests are elderly. And the post she got of reader to a blind lady wasn't very cheerful."

"And what about Cedric? Was he angry at his step-brother's being his uncle's heir?"

"Not that I know of. He seemed to take it coolly. He always seemed to despise Roger because he was just an ordinary, hard-working young fellow. 'Poor old Roger,' I heard him say. 'I can't imagine how he'll go down with the county. He's so fundamentally middle-class.' That's the way he talked. And if Sybyl stood up for him he'd say, 'My good girl, you're as bad as he is. Roger allows Mother to use him as a doormat. Stand up for yourself and don't worry about him.'"

"Were either of them the sort to get into trouble over girls?"

"Not to my knowledge," said Mrs. Banks with some decision. "Roger was what I should call a steady young chap, and Cedric was in love with himself and couldn't be bothered admiring other people."

"Thank you," said Collier. "I should say you had summed them up very well."

"I've answered your questions," said the landlady. "I haven't asked you what it's all about—"

"I'll tell you. I thought you might have seen it in the papers, but they haven't made much of it. One of the maids at Frere Court died ten days ago under rather mysterious circumstances which we are trying to clear up. We like to know something about the people we're dealing with. I'm much obliged to you, Mrs. Banks. How long were they with you altogether?"

"About seven years."

"As much as that."

"Yes, and I did my best for them. But, believe it or not, I've never had a line from Mrs. Frere from the day she left. Not so much as a card at Christmas. Too grand, I suppose. Sybyl wrote and so did Roger. When I read about the accident I wrote to say how sorry I was, and I sent a wreath for the funeral, but I didn't get even a printed acknowledgement."

Once started it was not easy to stem the flow of Mrs. Banks' reminiscences but Collier got away at last after borrowing a framed snapshot which he had noticed on the mantelpiece. It was a remarkably clear picture of the Frere family sitting on canvas deck chairs in the back garden. The inspector promised to return it within the week.

There were a few shops a hundred yards farther down the street. He called at the chemists'. The chemist, an elderly man, put on his spectacles to look at the snapshot.

"Why, this is Mrs. Frere with her sons and daughter. They lived just down the road and were customers of mine. I have missed them. A very charming lady, Mrs. Frere." His pleased smile faded. "May I ask why you want me to identify them from this photograph?"

"Just a matter of routine. Did Cedric Frere get the arsenic for the weeds in Mrs. Banks' garden from you? Your assistant may have served him, but he must have signed the book."

"Not from me certainly. I should have advised one of the patent preparations, and my assistant would have mentioned it if he had dealt with the matter. I am very particular about the sale of poisons. But I'll look at my book to make sure."

"I wish you would."

"About what time would it be?"

"About a year ago, not long before they left."

The chemist produced his register of the sale of poisons.

"They all have to sign," he said fussily. "No, it isn't here."

Collier thanked him. It had been a hundred to one chance, but it had been worth trying since he was in the neighbourhood. He foresaw that this was to be one of those cases where the police, after intensive efforts, have to rest satisfied with a moral certainty while the guilty party gets off scot free. Scot free. Collier pondered as he sat on the top of the bus taking him back to Westminster and stared with unseeing eyes at the wet umbrellas bobbing along the streaming pavements. He had to do his job and get his man if he could, but how often he had heard a prisoner say: "Thank God it's over. I was thinking of giving myself up—" The undiscovered criminal suffered prolonged agonies of fear and suspense, and in some cases, the burden of remorse.

But not poisoners perhaps. In Collier's experience they were a race apart, thick-skinned, callous, unimaginative to a degree that made them immune to pity. Roger's wife and his brother. It was not an unheard of combination. There was that Scottish case which the B.B.C. had broadcast. Collier had listened to it with professional interest. The woman had escaped from the Tolbooth and never been recaptured, but her accomplice had suffered the death penalty.

There was the box of dates stuffed with ground glass, and there were the jaunts to roadhouses that had caused so much talk locally. Yes, but still the pieces did not fit. Would Nina use powdered glass if she had access to and had already administered a dose of arsenic? The criminal mind, fortunately for the forces of law and order, was a conservative mind. Mass murderers were most often caught because they seemed incapable of varying their methods. Again, Cedric had a good deal to gain by the death of his elder brother, but no apparent interest in the attempt to eliminate Celia Holland.

Collier began to write on a blank page of his note book.

If Cedric was in love with his sister-in-law would he be so anxious to go off to Hollywood? Mrs. Banks describes him as the complete egoist. I distrust coincidences but am inclined to think that the attempts in murder Roger Frere and Celia Holland within a days of each other were unconnected. So what?

He glanced up and saw that the omnibus was crossing Parliament Square. He thrust his notebook back in his coat pocket and prepared to get off at the next stopping place. At the Yard he arranged to have Mrs. Banks' snapshot enlarged and copies sent to the Hampshire police for the men who were still engaged in tracing persons who had bought arsenic from chemists, or tins of weedkiller or fly papers from the shops who sold these commodities. It was not a very promising line, but it must not be abandoned. He was given a message that Superintendent Cardew wanted to see him before he left. He went directly to the superintendent's room.

Cardew cocked an eye at him. "Had a good afternoon?"

"Not very." He summed up his interview with Mrs. Banks. "I tried the nearest chemist but without results. It seemed to me that the idea of murder might have occurred quite a long time before it was acted upon."

"Quite likely," said Cardew. "Poisoners are leisurely people. Now if there was a knife in the business it would probably have been bought within a week of the crime being committed. How many people were there in the house the night before the girl died?"

Collier thought a moment. "Three other servants. The elder Mrs. Frere and her daughter-in-law and Cedric. Six altogether."

"Just so. And one of those six is almost certainly the guilty party. If you can find a shopkeeper who is prepared to identify that one as the person who walked into his place six weeks or six months ago and bought arsenic, or some preparation containing enough of the damned stuff to destroy a human being you can make an arrest. If not, you're sunk."

I know," said Collier gloomily. "And there's an open tin of weedkiller in the gardener's shed where any of the six could have got at it."

"So the shopkeeper with the good visual memory is more than ever a forlorn hope. Well, I'm sorry for you, Inspector, but we all have to come up against a blank wall now and then. Anyway— you'll have to talk things over with the police on the spot, but my opinion is that you should make it clear when the inquest is resumed that in your view the lemonade was doctored and that Roger Frere was the intended victim. I think that should be done for his sake. It may give the murderer a fright. The most worrying feature of the case is that if he gets off he may try again."

"I've borne that in mind, sir," said Collier. "I warned Mr. Frere before I came away. He didn't seem much surprised. I think he's known more than he is prepared to admit all along."

Cardew stared. "Do you mean that he's holding on deliberately, waiting to be murdered? It goofy to me."

"Hardly that. But I would say that circumstances and the people he is with have got him down to such an extent that he doesn't much care what happens. If ever I've met a man who's lost hope Roger Frere is that man."

"But why? What's wrong? A young man, apparently healthy, who has just come into a fortune—"

"I know. But my idea is that he hasn't reacted from a long period of bullying and brow beating. His half-sister, Sybyl, was killed while she was out motoring with him, and his stepmother seized on that with devilish ingenuity to strengthen her hold over him. If he had married the right kind of woman—some-one who would help him stand up to the rest of the family—he would probably have kicked Cedric out of the house months ago, and his adoring mother would have followed. As it is the wife is another liability."

"What is she like?"

"I don't know. They say she's beautiful."

Cardew frowned. "I don't get this. Surely you've seen her."

"I've interviewed her, but the room was practically dark. I was told she had some eye trouble. There's something queer about her. Major Enderby has a theory, but I'm trying to steer clear of it. I don't believe it has anything to do with the case I'm on."

"Sir James seemed to think the Major might be able to help you, being on the spot, and knowing the people concerned. The A.C. was telling me only to-day that he was brilliant in his own line, knows a lot of Indian dialects and was lent by the Government to more than one of the independent States to help clean up dangerous secret cults and the underground traffic in drugs, and in our Intelligence over here during the War. On the other hand, as he admitted, it's years since they met, and Sir James himself doesn't know exactly how and why he retired from the Service, except that it was said to be on account of a nervous breakdown. How does he strike you, Collier?"

The inspector hesitated. "I haven't made up my mind. Some-times I feel sure he's as straight as a die, that he may be mistaken, but that anyway it's an honest mistake; and at other times I ask myself if he isn't leading me up the garden path. There's been a panic locally about some creature that prowls about at night and scares the ponies and cattle in the forest, and it's on the cards that the Major's dog may be responsible. I'm keeping an open mind about it. But I warned him the brute would have to be destroyed if it was proved."

"What did he say to that?"

"He said that in that case he would shoot himself—and I could see that he meant it."

Cardew grunted. "I'm sorry you've got up against him. That isn't like you, Collier."

"I'm sorry, too, sir. But I don't think he bears malice. There's something fine about him. But I feel he's another man who's taken the count." He looked at his wrist watch. "If you'll excuse me, sir, the train I hoped to catch goes in twenty minutes."

Chapter XXVI
THE AVENGER

Mrs. Frere had driven in to Bournemouth that morning and garaged her car in a parking place near the Square. She spent an hour in the showroom at Bobby's choosing a hat and lunched in the restaurant. She had an appointment with her hairdresser at two for a permanent wave. The process was tedious, but not altogether unpleasant and it was followed by a special massage treatment, to soothe her nerves.

The masseuse was the girl she always had, an efficient young person with a carefully subdued voice who could talk or be silent to suit her clients. All this beauty business was expensive, but Roger could afford it. Let him pay, thought Rhoda Frere savagely.

"Madam must relax," murmured the priestess of Hygeaea.

"I know. I'm worried. Is my skin very dry, Florrie?"

The firm fingertips went on kneading the ageing flesh. "A little perhaps. I thought of trying a new cream. We have just received it from Paris. It is only thirty shillings a jar. Of course they are small jars."

"All right."

"Relax—" breathed the mellifluous voice.

"I do try to. It's difficult. It's so harassing, Florrie, to live in a world of fools," said Rhoda Frere. It was a relief to talk here where no one knew her, and to this kind sympathetic girl to whom her confidences would have no meaning. "I've been using that tonic lotion."

"I'd persevere with it if I were you. It's worth taking a little trouble, isn't it. Madam still has a beautiful line. You must take things calmly."

"I'm trying to make up my mind about something important. It means taking a risk—"

"Why don't you ask Ramona if you're undecided, madam? Lots of my ladies do."

"Ramona?"

"The palmist, madam. They say it's wonderful what she can tell you. It isn't just fortune telling, it's a science."

"You don't believe that rubbish, Florrie?"

"Well, I don't know, madam, but some of my ladies go to her regularly. You'd be surprised. I've got some of her cards here if you'd care to have one. Now, if you'll turn just a little to the left. Relax—"

Ramona. Of course it was all nonsense, but after leaving the beauty salon and spending some time in the tea-room at Beale's drinking a cup of tea, smoking a cigarette, and listening to the orchestra, she was at a loose end. She had told her friends at her bridge club that she would not be playing that day and she was in no hurry to go home. It was not very cheerful at Frere Court now with Cedric tiresome and evasive, persisting in his heartless determination to leave her and go to the States, Nina sulking in her room and pretending to be ill, and Roger going for long aimless walks or shutting himself up in the library.

She had slipped the card Florrie had given her into her handbag. She looked at it and saw that she would not have far to go if she decided after all to visit the palmist. It would pass the time and it might be amusing.

She crossed the Square, turned down a side street and presently was climbing a steep flight of stairs. Ramona lived in a flat over a shop. A scent of burning joss sticks mingled with that of Irish stew. The seeress herself, a stout dark woman in flowered cotton overall, opened the door.

"You read hands?"

Ramona's tired brown eyes rested for a moment on the beautiful arrogant face framed by the high storm collar of the expensive fur coat.

"You haven't an appointment. I don't usually see anyone after four."

Her apparent reluctance had the effect of making her would-be client more eager. After all, there might be something in it. She might be helped to come to a decision. "Can't you make an exception?"

"Very well. Come in here, please."

Rhoda Frere had expected pseudo-Oriental decorations and a suggestion of mystery, but Ramona led the way into a very ordinary and rather shabby bed-sitting room.

"Will you sit here, please, and rest both your hands here, palms upward."

She indicated a small wicker table covered with a square of black velvet and switched on a shaded lamp before she sat down facing her visitor.

Rhoda Frere took off her gloves and obeyed her instructions. She was one of those people who despise poverty and her faith in Ramona was nil. The woman was not even making a success of her business. She waited contemptuously, wondering why she had come. This room with its cheap furniture, reminded her of that ghastly boarding-house in Earl's Court from which she had escaped after so many years of bitter frustration. She closed her eyes and scarcely listened to the palmist's opening words.

". . . you have great determination. If once you set your heart on a thing you don't let go . . . almost what I should call a one track mind. You don't seek popularity. You care for one person very deeply. There are signs of recent trouble in your hand. . . ."

Mrs. Frere was listening now. All this was true enough. Could this woman know anything about her? It seemed unlikely. It might be just guesswork.

"You are about to make a decision that may have far-reaching effects. I feel that it may be a matter of life and death. I feel a very strange condition here. There has been—there still is—something evil in your surroundings. I—I can't understand it. I have never experienced anything like it before. I—I'm sorry. I can't go on—"

Ramona got up and went over to the window and opened it, letting in a cold gust of rain-laden air. The cheap casement curtain billowed out in the draught.

Rhoda Frere stared at her in angry amazement. "Well, really—" she said.

Ramona leant against the wall. Her broad swarthy face had blanched to an unwholesome shade of grey. She fumbled for a handkerchief in the pocket of her overall and wiped her forehead. "I am sorry," she said faintly. "I don't feel well."

"You don't expect a fee, I hope. You've hardly told me anything."

"No. I don't want anything."

"You shouldn't give sittings if you are subject to these attacks," said Rhoda coldly as she drew on her gloves and picked up her handbag. Ramona made no reply.

She really did look ill, thought Rhoda as she went down the stairs. Too stout to be healthy. But it was queer. She tore up Ramona's card and dropped the fragments as she walked down the street. She wished now that she had gone straight home. "The woman's a fraud," she told herself. For two pins she would complain to the police. Only—they might want her to give evidence, and she was sick of policemen. She was still in a temper when she got into her car. She spoke sharply to the car park attendant as she gave him, grudgingly, less than the usual tip.

"I'm here almost every day. I do think that you might see to it that I have a better place—"

From force of habit she drove carefully until she reached the outskirts of the town, but once in the forest she accelerated, finding relief for her nervous exasperation in speed.

She met very little traffic on the road. The December night was very dark and rain fell steadily. The screen wiper moved to and fro like the pendulum of a clock to keep the misty glass clear. Once a scutter of hooves warned her that there were ponies straying near by. She had passed through the villages of Brockenhurst and Lyndhurst when the car developed engine trouble and stopped. Mrs. Frere waited, fuming, until, after about twenty minutes, another car came by and stopped. The driver got out and came over to her.

"Anything I can do, madam?"

"If you would tell the people at the first garage you come to to send a man along—"

"Very well. But you'll get very cold sitting here. Won't you let me run you into Lyndhurst, then you can wait at the hotel and the man from the garage can bring your car there when he's put it right? Just as you like, of course."

Mrs. Frere knew the good Samaritan by sight, though she had never met him. His wife was a member of her bridge club but had shown no desire to become better acquainted. Rhoda, without knowing them, disliked them both, divining that they had been friends of her late brother-in-law and were probably prejudiced against her. She would have liked to refuse the proffered lift, but she was shivering with cold, and to wait at the hotel seemed the most sensible course.

Half an hour later she was sitting down to a solitary dinner in the coffee-room.

Her temper had not been improved by the contretemps. She had been prepared to be cool with Colonel Porter, to snub him if need be. She had soon realised that would not be necessary. He had mumbled something about needing all his attention for his driving on such a night and had driven five miles without uttering a word. When he stopped at the hotel entrance she had thanked him briefly, adding, "You need not bother about the garage. I can telephone instructions from here." The cold shoulder, she thought, as she ate her dinner and sat afterwards, sipping her coffee and smoking cigarettes. Who cared? The Porters were a stodgy elderly couple, dull as ditch water. All the same Rhoda knew that the next time she saw Mrs. Porter at the club she would have some difficulty in not acknowledging her cool little nod with a torrent of abuse. What was that fool from the garage doing with her car? It was growing late. She had paid her bill and was ready to leave. The pile of cigarette ends smeared red with lipstick was growing in the saucer of her coffee-cup.

What would happen at the adjourned inquest on Doris Jupp? Surely the jury would agree that she had committed suicide. Or they might bring what they called an open verdict. Rhoda thought she would never forget coming into the hall that night and being met by the cook, her broad face usually so red and jolly, grey and drawn with fatigue.

"Oh, madam, such a terrible thing. I tried to get you on the telephone, but you weren't at your club. Poor Doris was taken bad. She—she's dead. The doctor's been and the police, and they've taken her away—"

No need to play a part. Her sickening disappointment would pass for horrified surprise. Doris destroying herself and ruining everything through her childish greed. For it was plain to see what had happened. It just showed, thought Rhoda bitterly, that no plan was fool-proof.

But this one she had just evolved could hardly fail. She had bought the rubber gloves so long ago that they could not be traced. After they had been used they must be hidden in Nina's room, under her mattress would be best.

Only that morning Mostyn had come to her with a complaint.

"It's ten days now since I've been able to clean out Mrs. Roger's room, madam. She keeps the door locked and won't let Jessie and me in. What are we to do?"

"Is it in a very bad state? You take in her meals, don't you?"

"No, madam. We have to knock and leave the tray outside, and she puts it out when she's finished. Perhaps you could speak to her, madam!"

"I'm afraid I might do more harm than good," Rhoda had said. "You must remember, Mostyn, that Mrs. Roger is actually the mistress here."

Mostyn had looked down her long nose. "Well, it's not my place to speak, but it's plain to see that Mrs. Roger is not herself, and I don't think it ought to be allowed to go on."

Rhoda had looked at her steadily. "What do you mean exactly? Don't be afraid to speak. I shall treat anything you say as confidential."

Mostyn had answered bluntly. "Well, cook and me think she's got into such a state that she ought to be taken away. It's not a nice thing to have to do, I know. But mark my words, there'll be trouble if she isn't put under restraint."

"Very well. I'll speak to Mr. Roger to-morrow."

To-morrow. That meant that she must act tonight. Had she the strength, the courage, and the nerve? It was easy enough to drop some powder into a glass, easy to destroy from a distance, like an airman dropping a bomb from two thousand feet on a defenceless village. But this—

Thoughtfully she spanned her right wrist with the fingers and thumb of her left hand. He had not the habit of locking his door. If he woke up and cried out? Even so, no one would hear. The walls were thick, the servants were far off on the upper floor, and Cedric, a sound sleeper, at the other end of the corridor. Besides, she had studied that medical book and the other on anatomy. She must take some risks. She could not let Cedric go. He might never come back. And once the rubber gloves and the knife were planted in Nina's room she would be safe. Mostyn—Mostyn would make an ideal witness, the cook too. Their obvious honesty would make their evidence all the more damning. Nina wouldn't be hanged, of course. She might not even be tried. Unfit to plead.

It was queer about that palmist, thought Rhoda, frowning. Resentfully she remembered how Ramona had dropped her hand as if it burnt her and had rubbed her own fingers on her overall as she turned away.

"As if I wasn't clean. I think I'll write a letter about her to the police. I needn't sign it," she reflected.

There was just one moment that she dreaded, the moment when the blow must be struck. It wasn't a woman's work, she thought, pitying herself as she had often done before because all the men in her life had been weaklings. Even Cedric, her darling boy. But she wouldn't involve him in this. It was better that he should not know. It wouldn't take long. Three minutes at most from the time she left her own room.

It was like looking forward to having a tooth pulled out.

"I'll be glad when it's over," she thought.

There was that handkerchief of Nina's, drenched in her favourite scent, which she had picked up yesterday on the terrace and had the sense to keep, though then the details of her plan were still far from clear. That could be dropped in Roger's room. That would be a good bit of evidence. Nina left a trail of that scent wherever she went.

The night porter came in at last to tell her that the garage mechanic had brought her car to the door.

She dropped her cigarette, half smoked, into the fender, pulled on her fur coat, and went out.

"What an age you've been," she said angrily.

The mechanic excused himself. The car had to be towed back to the garage and it had taken him some time to locate the trouble. Mrs. Frere was a regular customer and must not be offended, so he held the car door open for her and thanked her for the proffered sixpence, waiting until she had let in the clutch and was out of hearing to say what he really thought.

Rhoda drove carefully until she had passed the outskirts of the village. After that the road lay before her apparently deserted, a wet black streak through the dense woods. The clock on the dashboard had stopped but she knew it must be past midnight. She accelerated, watching the needle mount from thirty to forty, to fifty—Murder. The ugly word crept like a cold snake through the dark channels of her mind. But it wouldn't be murder. She would be the instrument of justice, the avenger. He had killed Sybyl. There must be no faltering, no weakness now. That visit to the palmist had been a mistake. It must be her last. The woman had shrunk away from her as if—

Was it possible that she was really clairvoyante and that she had seen blood on her hands?

She had passed the White Cottage without noticing it. There were no lights in the windows. The speed at which she was travelling acted on her nerves like an exhilarating drug, giving her the illusion of superhuman power, so that she laughed as she leaned forward, gripping the wheel.

Chapter XXVII
THE CRASH

ROGER dreamed that he was lying in his coffin The lid was on and his arms were bound at his sides so that he could not push it off. He was panting, breathless, sweating with fear, vainly trying to call for help. Too late. They were hammering in the nails. He made a final despairing effort—and the hammering became a knocking on his door and the coffin lid turned into bedclothes.

He sat up and reached for the light switch. "What is it? What's the matter?"

The light went on as the door opened and Cedric came in.

"Didn't you hear the crash? It was loud enough to wake the dead. Get some clothes on. We'll have to go and see—"

He went over to the window and drew back the curtains.

"My God! There's something on fire down the avenue. Half a minute. I'll go and see if Mother heard it—"

"All right." Roger had got out of bed and was huddling on some clothes. Cedric came back while he was struggling into a pullover.

"She isn't in her room, Roger. I'd better go, hadn't I?"

"Yes, of course. I'm coming too—"

The two young men left the house together and ran towards the scene of the fire.

The branches of the limes showed like a mesh of black lace against the fierce red glow of a roaring sheet of flame. Already two trees were alight.

Cedric stared at the incandescent mass lying by the roadside.

"She—I've often warned her to be careful of skidding with all these wet leaves." He shrank back as the wind veered and a blast of hot air scorched their faces. "Roger!"

Roger laid a hand on his arm. "Steady. We can't do anything. Better come back to the house and ring up the Fire Brigade—"

"It is a car, isn't it?"

"Yes."

As they entered the hall Cedric muttered, "I feel sick. I must go and get a drink—"

"All right. I'll telephone—"

The house was very silent. The servants evidently had heard nothing. Roger leant against the wall holding the receiver and waiting to be put through.

"Hallo . . . yes . . . there's been an accident. Fire. Yes, A car and some of the trees are burning. The driver . . . I'm afraid so. We couldn't get near enough . . . as quick as you can, please."

He hung up and turned away. Cedric had left the dining-room door open. His half-brother could see him sitting with his head in his hands.

Roger went down the corridor that led into the right wing and knocked gently on Nina's door.

"Nina—"

There was no answer. He turned the handle. Useless. The door was locked. He knocked again a good deal louder.

"Nina, please. It's urgent—"

There was still no reply.

Roger went into the drawing-room and unlatched one of the french windows opening on the terrace. The red glare of the burning car could not be seen on this side of the house. He stepped out into the clammy blackness and felt his way along the wall until he came to the window of his wife's room.

It was open, as he had expected, and the drawn curtains were damp with the rain that had driven in. He passed in and found the light switch by the door. The switch clicked without effect. He remembered that he had thrust his torch into his coat pocket before he ran downstairs, and felt for it. Slowly the white ray moved round the four walls and over the muddy carpet. The bed was unmade and in the utmost disorder. Clothing was strewn on the floor and over the chairs. There was a stale and sickly smell. Roger hesitated for a moment before he went over to the big old-fashioned mahogany wardrobe and opened its double doors. Some of Nina's dresses and coats were hanging there. The hem of one dress was caked with mud. The smell in this enclosed space was overpowering. The ray of light, rather unsteady now, passed over bones and fragments of decaying skin and fur among the litter of odds and ends, the lace-edged handkerchiefs drenched with scent, the black silk and ivory fan he had bought for her in Cardiff, and which he had seen her use to shade her face with that quick Spanish turn of the wrist, that inimitable half-animal grace.

Roger left the room as he had entered it, by the window, and re-entered the house by way of the drawing-room. Cedric was still sitting where he had left him. Roger took the decanter of brandy away from him and put it back on the sideboard.

"Why don't you have some too?" mumbled Cedric. "The best thing—"

"No, thanks. Come into the hall with me. I can hear the fire engine coming up the avenue. I'm going to call the servants."

When Collier arrived twenty minutes later he came upon a scene of feverish activity. The firemen had connected their hose, drawing water from the moat. The two trees in the avenue that had been burning were hidden in clouds of pungent smoke and steam, and a steady stream was being poured on to the twisted mass of molten metal that had been a car. Police Constable Tomsett had come up from the village on his bicycle and he approached the detective from the Yard as soon as he saw him get out of his car.

"This is a shocking thing, sir. How did you hear of it?"

"I was sitting up late in my room at the inn, writing my report and going through my notes, and I saw a pillar of flame shoot up above the trees. Who is it? Not young Frere in his sports car?"

No. I've been up to the house. Both the young gentlemen are there. They were awakened, it seems, by a crash. They ran out, but couldn't get near on account of the heat. They rang up the Fire Brigade and the police at Welchester, and the police got through to me and told me to stand by until they could send someone along. We don't know yet, but we think it must be Mrs. Frere—"

At six o'clock Mrs. Bligh, fully dressed, but with her thin grey hair still in curlers, shuffled into the dining-room with a tray. The fire had been lit and Cedric sat by it, shivering and trying to warm his hands. "It's no use," he complained. "I'm chilled to the bone."

"A nice cup of tea'll warm you, Mr. Cedric. And you too, sir—" Roger, who had been pacing to and fro, stopped and sank heavily into a chair. The cook filled two cups and watched the two weary men as they sipped the hot liquid. "Help yourself to biscuits." Cedric shuddered. "No. I couldn't eat."

Roger said nothing.

Inspector Lacy came into the dining-room followed by Doctor Reed, the police surgeon, and Collier. All three were black with grime. Roger looked at them.

"Will you have something to drink?"

"Not now, thanks. Mrs. Bligh has been supplying us with jugs of barley water. Fire fighting is thirsty work. Two more trees had caught. It's definitely out now, and the men are rolling up the hose. I'm afraid there isn't much water left in the moat."

"Never mind that. Has—has anything—"

Lacy cleared his throat and glanced at the doctor.

"We have made a thorough examination of the charred mass of material," said Reed. "We—I am sorry—we found the remains of a woman still in the driving-seat. The car had struck a tree and turned over and she was pinned under the wheel. Death must have been instantaneous. Identification would be impossible, but Inspector Collier found two small diamonds, probably from a ring, and the ashes will be carefully sifted. I am afraid we must assume—"

Cedric picked up the poker and stirred the fire, sending a shower of sparks up the chimney. "I'm so deadly cold."

"It's the shock," said Reed. He turned to Roger. "I understand that Mrs. Frere left home in her car yesterday and that she has not returned?"

"That is so."

There was an awkward pause. Collier realised that Reed and the local inspector wanted him to carry on.

"No use beating about the bush," he said. "We have to tell you that we found the body of another woman crushed between the car and the tree trunk. He have examined the ground very carefully by the light of the police car's headlamps and of course it will be gone over again by daylight. There are traces of a long skid. There isn't much doubt how the accident happened. The driver braked very hard to avoid someone whom she had not seen in time. The car skidded, turned over and crashed against a tree, pinning the second victim between the bonnet and the trunk, which had snapped off ten feet from the ground. That gives some idea of the violence of the impact. I don't want to horrify you, only to show you that in either case it wasn't a lingering death. I don't know—"—he hesitated—"I don't know if there is going to be any difficulty in establishing the identity of the second person—"

Roger sat staring at the pattern of tea leaves in his empty cup. He answered without raising his eyes.

"My wife is not in her room. I went to see just now. She was a very bad sleeper, and she sometimes got up when she felt more than usually restless and went out for a walk in the park. She was a foreigner and perhaps she had not quite got used to our rules of the road. Her eyesight was bad too. She may have been dazzled by the headlights—"

"Would you recognise this?"

Lacy, moving forward, laid on the table a discoloured lump of metal from which rose a small beautifully modelled head of a snake with emerald eyes.

"I think so. Nina had a snake bracelet of native workmanship. It was the only valuable thing she possessed and she always wore it. I—I suppose that proves—"

He stumbled to his feet. Collier, who had been watching him closely, sprang forward in time to break his fall.

CHAPTER XXVIII
A RECONSTRUCTION

"GLAD to see you." Sir James Welland left his desk as Major Enderby was shown into his office and advanced with an outstretched hand. "My dear fellow, you look far from well—"

"I'm all right. You got my wire?"

"Yes. You have a statement to make in connection with the murder of Doris Jupp."

"Yes."

"Let me see." The Assistant Commissioner, who had returned to his desk, turned over some papers. "The local people called us in and we sent a couple of our men down. I gather that the case has presented considerable difficulties. I introduced Inspector Collier to you. He's a good man, though he's had his share of failures. I rather hoped you might be able to help him."

"I am afraid I let him down," said Enderby. "Is it true that there is a warrant out for the arrest of Cedric Frere?"

"How did you hear that?"

"Someone rang me up last night. He wouldn't give his name, but I fancy it was the reporter of a local paper. He seemed to think I would know. I told him I knew nothing. After thinking it over I decided to come up and see you. I want to prevent a miscarriage of justice."

Sir James looked thoughtfully at his visitor's haggard face. "I see," he said. " As a matter of fact Inspector Collier is in this building at the moment. He has come up to report to us personally. Would you be willing for him to hear what you have to say?"

"Certainly."

The Assistant Commissioner picked up the house telephone. "Put me through to Superintendent Cardew, please. . . . Is that you, Cardew? Is Collier still with you? Right. Send him to me at once."

He leaned back in his chair. Enderby had walked over to the window where he stood apparently watching the brown sail of a barge going up the river with the tide.

Collier started perceptibly when he came in and saw the lean upright figure silhouetted against the light but he said nothing.

Sir James glanced up at him. "Major Enderby has something to tell us, Inspector. As you have been in charge of this case I thought you had better hear it. Won't you both sit down?"

Enderby came slowly back to them and took the chair Collier had drawn forward for him. Collier was shocked by his appearance. He had been looking ill before, but he seemed to have aged since he last saw him.

Sir James picked up a pencil and began to draw circles on his blotting paper, wheels within wheels. It was a habit of his when he was listening.

"Please smoke if you want to, Major. The cigarettes in that box aren't bad. Give the Major a light, Collier—"

"Thanks." Enderby inhaled deeply and the tense muscles in his lean face relaxed. "I heard that you might be arresting Cedric Frere," he said abruptly. "Is that true?"

Collier glanced at the A.C. who said: "Tell the major anything he wants to know."

"Very good, Sir James. You weren't at the resumed inquest, major, but I expect you heard that it was adjourned for three months. The Chief Constable and the police under him have made up their minds that Cedric Frere is their man, but they recognise that they haven't the evidence to justify them in arresting him. My colleague, Sergeant Duffield, has worked hard but he has failed to trace any sale of arsenic or of any arsenical compound to any of the seven people who had the opportunity to commit the crime. That does not let them out because there was an opened tin of weedkiller in the gardener's shed which was accessible to them all. Their theory is that he had a double motive for killing—not Doris, of course—her death was an accident—but his half-brother. He would inherit the property, and he was in love with his sister-in-law."

"And you agree?"

"No. I had a talk with Cedric Frere yesterday evening. He was a good deal shaken by his mother's death. He's been very difficult up to now, but he's dropped some of his affectations for the time being. He told me why he was so keen to get away and I think he was speaking the truth. He said he had enjoyed taking his sister-in-law about. She was strikingly beautiful and attracted a great deal of attention wherever they went. Lots of limelight, and he's the sort of young fellow that hankers after notoriety. In spite of this, he explained that he was never attracted to her. She was a fine tennis player and a splendid dancer, but she never had anything to say for herself and she was completely lacking in what he called sex appeal. But that wasn't what upset him. Young Frere is far too much interested in himself to have much time for girls. But something happened that gave him what I could see must have been the shock of his life. He had taken her out in his car. They were passing through Wimborne and he stopped in the square and left her while he went into a tobacconist's to get some cigarettes. They kept him waiting a few minutes for his change. He happened to look out of the window and he saw that she had left the car and gone into a butcher's shop. She came out while his change was being counted out, carrying a small parcel wrapped up in newspaper. He thought she looked round in a furtive sort of way before she got back into the car and when he joined her he saw no sign of the parcel. He didn't say anything, and they went on to a road-house and danced. After a bit she said she was tired and would rest for a bit. They knew some of the people there and he found another girl to dance with. She disappeared but came back in about half an hour. While he was dancing with her he noticed a red smear on her chin. When they went out to the car park the attendant said: 'Did you find what you were looking for, miss?' She said: ' Yes,' and explained to Cedric that she had dropped her handkerchief in the car and gone out to fetch it. Later, when they were home he found a crumpled sheet of bloodstained newspaper pushed under the cushions."

Sir James stopped drawing circles. "What an extraordinary thing. I don't quite follow—"

"Well, I wasn't so much surprised, sir, because I had heard Major Enderby's theory about Mrs. Frere. But I wanted the t's crossed and the i's dotted so I asked him what he was getting at, and he said, 'Well, it's pretty horrible, and I daresay you won't believe me' and then he burst out, 'she's dead and I may be wrong, but I know I'm not. I've told you, haven't I? Can't you understand plain English—' So I said, 'She bought a piece of meat—and ate it. Is that right?' And he said, 'Yes, Oh, my God!' and jumped up and walked about the room. 'I took her out after that, and danced with her, but I couldn't forget it. I had to get away—'"

"Good Heavens!" Sir James looked across at Enderby. "Do you mind explaining?"

"Roger Frere met his wife last spring in San Rinaldo, one of the smaller and more backward of the South American republics. There was a revolution on, and he helped her to get out and married her on the ship that brought them home to give her British nationality. He hasn't said, but I gather that she worked on his feelings, his sense of chivalry. She told him that her life would be in danger if she went back, and that was true, but not for the reason she alleged. She was the last surviving member of a notorious family whose fortunes were founded in the republic about two hundred years ago by an Italian who had escaped from his native village in the Abruzzi, where he had acquired such a sinister reputation that he narrowly missed being burnt at the stake. He found his way to San Rinaldo, married, and had a family. The sons acquired land and money but they were shunned by their neighbours. Some of them married Indian women and added the native magic to their other practices. They have been dying out and this girl and the aunt who brought her up were the last of their race. The girl, Nina, had been sent to school here and in Paris, she was given a chance to grow up normally, but the taint was in her blood. I suspected something of the kind. All the symptoms were there, the alternating languor and drowsiness and intense restlessness, the dislike of any strong light, the craving for meat. A form of mania fortunately rare nowadays in western Europe, so rare that you may hardly have heard of it, Sir James, though it was well known in the sixteenth and seventeenth centuries. In a word, lycanthropy."

"My dear fellow—are you suggesting that there is any foundation in fact for the werewolf legends?"

"I certainly am."

"Let me get this straight. Are you seriously asking me to believe that this woman turned into a wild beast after night fall? That was what was supposed to happen, wasn't it? As it happens I have read some accounts of old witch trials. I always regarded them as marvellous illustrations of human credulity."

"I can't tell you how far the actual physical transformation goes. I think it is a fact that the subject acquires certain characteristics that are more noticeable at certain times. I'm not an alienist, but I think the authorities would admit that there is still a good deal that they don't know about the dark places that lie beyond the borders of what we call sanity."

"This was the young woman who was killed three nights ago in a motor accident?"

"Yes. Her husband's stepmother was coming home late, some time after midnight, driving her own car. She was nearly home, in the long avenue of limes that leads to the house. It is assumed that Nina Frere was in the road and failed to get out of the way in time. The other braked hard, skidded and overturned. The tank caught fire."

"Yes. I read the account in the papers. The inquest on both women were held yesterday, I think, and the verdict was a foregone conclusion. Death by misadventure. I noticed that one of the jury asked if the younger Mrs. Frere was in the habit of taking solitary walks so late at night."

"Yes. Roger Frere replied that she suffered from insomnia."

"How much does he know?"

"Everything now," said Enderby quietly. "He came to see me yesterday—after the funeral—you may remember that I found him wandering in a dazed condition the night before Doris Jupp's death. I took him home and he spent the rest of the night at my place. He wouldn't tell me what had happened then, but he did last night. It seems that he had gone to bed early and been asleep some time—he said he was sleeping unusually heavily and I think it just possible that one or two sleeping tablets had been dropped in his coffee. Innocuous stuff that would prevent him from waking if anybody came into his room later. I may be wrong about that, it's just a guess. In any case he did wake, fancying that he heard the howl of a dog, which surprised him as there are no dogs at Frere Court. He got up, went to the window and looked out and was just in time to see Nina run very fast across the lawn and vanish among the shrubberies. It was a raw night in December and raining steadily. He was badly rattled—there was something queer—I asked him what he meant and he said she was bent double, almost as if she was on all fours. He determined to follow her and he ran downstairs without waiting to put on anything more than a dressing-gown. He wandered through the woods, calling her by name, and finally came out on the road where I found him."

"Well—" said the Assistant Commissioner, "has this any connection with the murder of Doris Jupp?"

"I think Inspector Collier can tell you that," said Enderby.'

"A very close connection just there, sir," said Collier. "The working of Providence as they used to say. Nina Frere—if Major Enderby's right—was no wife for any man—but she saved her husband's life that night."

"How's that?"

"Frere always drank the lemonade that was made especially for him, either during the night or when he woke in the morning. He was away and Doris found it untouched when she did the room. She drank it—and died a few hours later of acute arsenical poisoning."

"I get you," said Sir James. "Providence wasn't being so kind to her. Well, now we come to it. I agree that the relations between Cedric Frere and his sister-in-law weren't what they appeared to be to the scandal-mongers, but the financial motive remains. He was in the house that night, wasn't he?"

"Yes, sir. His own account is that he drove down from London and arrived after the household had retired for the night. He garaged his car and went straight to bed."

"Opportunity?"

"Roger Frere does not lock his door. The table with the glass of lemonade on it stood between the door and the bed. There is a light with a switch within reach of the bed, but Roger Frere has told me that he tried it earlier that night, when he was awakened by the howling of a dog, as he thought, and that the bulb had gone."

"So that by opening the door a few inches the murderer could do the job without even entering the room?"

"Yes."

They were all silent for a moment, visualizing that door opening silently, inch by inch. Then Enderby spoke.

"No—" he said. "It probably happened much earlier, before Roger went up to his room. You can't arrest Cedric with nothing more than this to go upon."

"Perhaps we have more, Major," said Collier.

"You can't have. I haven't much use for Cedric, but he isn't a murderer. He hasn't got the guts. I'll have to tell you, but this— this isn't easy for me. I first met Rhoda Frere in 1917. I had been doing intelligence work in the Far Fast, never mind exactly where, and I had come home to fight in France. I was wounded and transferred to do my stuff in London. Rhoda's husband was at the front and her stepson, Roger, and her own boy were in the country in charge of an old nurse. She had a tiny flat in Westminster and was doing a bit of war work, helping at the buffet at

Victoria Station, you know the sort of thing. They called it cheering up the Tommies. She was very attractive and keen on having a good time, and she and I—"

Enderby sat with his shoulders bent and his hands resting on his knees. He was staring down at the worn pattern of the carpet at his feet and he did not lift his eyes to note the effect of what he was saying on the two men who listened to him.

"I never saw her husband. I kept out of the way, naturally, when he came home on leave. I had been sent back to India before he was demobbed. Rhoda and I had said good-bye. But she wrote to me once a few months later, after Sybyl was born and told me Sybyl was my daughter. When I came home the next time some years later Rhoda was a widow living with the children in a cheap boarding-house in Earl's Court on an allowance made her by John Frere. She wouldn't marry me—I hadn't much to offer—but she let me help her financially as far as I could, and now and then I took her to dinner and a show. I wanted a chance to make friends with Sybyl but she wouldn't have that. I used to hang about on the street corner to see her go by on her way to school. She went out with Roger on Saturdays. Once I went in the same bus with them to the Zoo and followed them about all the afternoon. I could see he was very fond of the child and my heart warmed to him. They never noticed me. I was careful. You see I had no right. My leave was up. I was sent out to the Malay States to handle a difficult job. I succeeded, but afterwards I had a bad breakdown and was ill for a couple of years. When I came back to England for good I learned that John Frere was dead and that Rhoda and her boy and girl had gone down to Hampshire to live with Roger. It seemed to me that now, at last, I could do what I had always wanted to do. The White Cottage was in the market. I bought it and settled down. Not to be near Rhoda—don't think that—I knew her too well by then. I hadn't any illusions. What I wanted was to make friends with Sybyl. Rhoda did not mind. I think she was rather glad to have me near, someone to talk to when she felt in the mood. I soon saw that I had been right in suspecting that she had not much use for a grown-up daughter. She only cared for one person and that was Cedric, and as the result of her pampering he had developed into a spoilt cub. I saw very little of him. He is the kind of boy who regards all older men as crashing bores. But Sybyl—I believe Sybyl really liked me. I was being very careful still, trying not to rush things. I hoped the liking would develop into real affection. She was starved of that at home, poor child, except from Roger. She came to tea with me once—and then Roger, meaning so well, poor fellow, gave her a car for her birthday. You know what happened—"

His voice broke. The others waited, and after a minute he resumed. "Rhoda reacted violently against Roger. Perhaps at the back of her mind she knew that she had never been very kind to Sybyl and was trying to adjust the balance by an exaggeration of her natural grief at the loss of her child. She came to me and raved about Roger having deliberately killed his sister. She came to see me fairly often, not openly, of course. It was easy for her to stop on her way to or from Bournemouth after my housekeeper had gone home. She used to park her car just off the road, behind a clump of hollies. I was a—a kind of safety valve for her violent ungovernable temper, for the expression of her acrid jealousy. Don't misunderstand me. She didn't care for me, hadn't cared since those first few hectic months during the war, but she trusted me, and—looking back I realise that she must have imagined that I was still as great a fool as I was then where she was concerned. When Roger left the nursing-home to which he had been taken after the smash he went abroad for a while. I suppose the poor fellow saw that life under the same roof with Rhoda would be impossible in the state she was in then. During his absence she calmed down. I was beginning to hope for better things when he came back bringing a foreign wife. Rhoda was furious, of course, but she showed unexpected self-control. Nina made it easier for her by not undertaking any of the duties of the mistress of the house. But the relations of those four people to one another were so strained, so uneasy and unnatural, that they couldn't last. Rhoda came to me one evening and began to talk about poisons. I had lived in the East, did I know anything about curare, the arrow poison? I said I believed curare was a South American poison and that in any case I knew nothing about it. She persisted. There were other poisons that had no taste and couldn't be traced. At last she said, 'If you don't give me some I'll go elsewhere.' I said, 'What do you want it for?' She said, 'To kill the rats that come out of the moat. Roger won't put any down for them because he thinks the swans might get it. You know what a fool Roger is.' I said, 'Not such a fool as I should be if I did what you ask.' She said, 'Very well. I'll go to someone else. There are ways. I'm not bluffing.' I knew she meant it. I pretended to give way. I left her in my sitting-room while I went upstairs and I came back with a little packet of white powder. I said, 'You see it is labelled boracic powder. One can't be too careful. For God's sake don't get it mixed with the real stuff.' She said, 'Is it quick?' I said, 'No. Just a pinch at a time. It takes weeks.' She said, 'Thank you, Geoffrey. I knew you would never fail me.' I've never been sure whether I did the right thing or not. I suppose she tried it out. Naturally, it wouldn't hurt anyone. It really was boracic powder."

"You think she believed you?"

"I am certain of it. As I said just now, she had no affection for me, but she trusted me completely."

Sir James opened his mouth to speak and thought better of it. Collier was silent. He was thinking that he was actually seeing Enderby for the first and perhaps for the last time. It is not often, perhaps not more than once in a lifetime, that a man so reveals himself. It struck him that on the whole Enderby was coming through his ordeal not too badly.

'You see how it was." He lifted his hands and dropped them again with a hopeless gesture. "What could I do? I could only trust that the impulse would expend itself, that the tension would somehow be relaxed. I had to stand by, helpless. She never again referred to the subject of poison. She told me that Nina ignored her husband and that they had occupied separate rooms from the first. That gave her great satisfaction. "At least there won't be any children to cheat Cedric out of what should be his," she said. She and Nina got on better than I had dared to expect, I suppose because they had so few points of contact. When I heard of the housemaid's death I thought the girl had had an unfortunate love affair. I did not suspect Rhoda at all until the other day when I heard from Inspector Collier that Roger had been the intended victim. Then, of course, I guessed the truth—"

"I remember," said Collier, "it was at your place. You got up suddenly from your chair and stood gripping the mantelpiece and staring down at the fire. I rather wondered—"

"You should have spoken out then, Enderby," said Sir James

"I suppose so. But it had been a great shock. I needed a breathing space. I had made up my mind though. I've been through a few things, but nothing worse than that night. You see I realised that Roger was still in danger, and I've always liked the boy. Sybyl was fond of him. Rhoda had tried and failed. Knowing her as I did I felt certain she would try again. How are you to deal with anyone utterly reckless, utterly unscrupulous?"

"I'm not blaming you," said Welland, "as man to man. But as Assistant Commissioner of police I must warn you that anything you say now may be taken down and used in evidence against you."

Enderby raised his head quickly and looked from one to the other. He smiled for the first time.

"You have a dictaphone here?"

"No. We weren't trying to entrap you. But we're coming to thin ice now, aren't we?"

"I don't quite—"

"Just a moment." Sir James looked very hard at Enderby and slightly shook his head. "I accept your statement and I will pass on the relevant part to the Welchester police. I think we may regard this case as closed."

Enderby took out his handkerchief and wiped his forehead.

"You don't want to hear any more?"

"No more," said Sir James firmly. "Thank you for coming to us. Do you feel equal to going home alone? I'll tell them to get you a taxi—"

"Yes. Thank you. I'm all right." He got to his feet and looked doubtfully at the Assistant Commissioner. Sir James left his desk and came over to him, holding out his hand.

A little colour came into the other man's grey face, a flicker of light into his weary eyes. "You're a good fellow, Welland. Good-bye."

He smiled at Collier as he went out. Collier said impulsively: "I hope your dog is recovering, sir—"

"Yes. Doing very well, thank God. Kind of you to ask—"

Collier closed the door and came back into the room.

Sir James had gone back to his desk. He sat looking thoughtfully at the intricate pattern of interlaced circles he had drawn on his blotting paper.

"I think the Welchester people will agree with me that this enquiry has gone far enough. But for my own satisfaction, Collier, I should like to hear your reconstruction of the last act. Unofficially. You know, of course, why I stopped the Major just now. I did not want him to incriminate himself. So long as certain things are merely matters of conjecture we need not take action. I have spoken the prologue. Now tell me all about it. I mean from where Enderby left off."

"Well, sir, on the face of it that accident the other night seemed straightforward enough. Mrs. Frere had had a breakdown on her way home from Bournemouth that delayed her for nearly three hours. The garage mechanic at Lyndhurst put it right and swears the car was in perfect order when he delivered it. She was a regular customer and he knew her pretty well. He says she was always very impatient and hated being kept waiting. She was a notoriously bad driver, as one would expect with that temperament, keeping to the crown of the road, pulling out to overtake just before a bend and all the rest of it. The wonder is that she's never actually been in trouble. It seemed obvious that she was going all out up the avenue when Nina Frere ran across the road, that she braked hard to avoid her, and that the car got out of control, skidded, overturned and crushed the other woman against a tree trunk. That was the theory put forward by the police at the inquest yesterday and nobody questioned its accuracy. But I wasn't altogether satisfied. I didn't say so, naturally. It wasn't my pigeon. I didn't even attend the inquest. While it was taking place in the village hall I pottered about near the scene of the accident, and eventually I found some splinters of glass on the ground at the foot of a tree on the right of the avenue as you go up from the lodge, about a hundred yards away from the place where the car crashed. There was nothing to be learned from tyre marks on the road, there has been too much traffic up there since, but eventually I found a bullet embedded in the bark of the tree five feet up from the ground. That is all, sir."

"I hope you aren't going to disappoint me, Collier. Superintendent Cardew has sometimes complained that you give your imagination too much scope. A dangerous habit perhaps, though it sometimes leads to results. But this is a private conversation. It's not going to lead to anything. Tell me what you think may have happened."

"Very good, sir, You heard what the Major said just now about how he felt when he realised that Mrs. Frere had actually tried to poison her stepson. I think that after an agonising period of indecision he determined to take the law into his own hands. He knew she had gone in to Bournemouth. He had probably seen her drive past the White Cottage. He went a little way up the avenue to wait for her. He chose that place because she would have to slow down to take the sharp turn in from the road between the gate posts. He shot her as she came level, but I fancy the bullet only inflicted a flesh wound. Whether that was the bullet I found in the tree or whether he fired again I can't say. It is possible that he missed altogether. In any case she accelerated and might have kept to the road and reached home safely if Nina had not appeared."

"Isn't it arguable that the shot killed her and that the car went on to the inevitable crash with a dead woman at the wheel?"

"I don't think that, sir. If the bullet had met with any resistance it wouldn't have gone through the window on the far side and into the tree. I think it more likely that she wasn't even wounded. The Major saw the car turn over and burst into flames. Then he went home."

"Wouldn't he be afraid of the lodge-keeper hearing a shot?"

"The gardener lives at the lodge. He's an old man and very deaf."

"Very interesting," said Sir James, "but we won't try to improve on the coroner's verdict. You and Enderby between you have spun a most unusual yarn. I don't know how much of it I believe, but it certainly sounds as if the Major had done Roger Frere a good turn."

"I was worried about Mr. Frere myself, sir. I felt that he was in danger. I tried to warn him."

"Did you suspect his stepmother?"

"I was not sure. It might just as well have been Cedric."

"Roger Frere hasn't had much luck with women so far. In his place I think I'd go into a Trappist monastery."

Collier smiled. "I don't think he'll do that, sir. I rather fancy the right girl will be waiting, and I daresay they'll settle down quite happily after a while."

"Is that so? What girl? The recipient of the box of dates? By the way, you haven't cleared that up."

"I'm afraid not, sir. I haven't any doubt in own mind that Nina Manara sent them. She jumped to the conclusion that Miss Holland knew more about her than she actually did. But I've no evidence."

"Well—" Sir James took up his pen. "What did you say to the Major as he went out just now?"

"I said I hoped his dog was better. He's been under the vet. He's very fond of his dog," said Collier quietly.

"Poor devil," muttered Sir James. "I was thinking he must be as lonely as hell. A dog. Better than nothing. Very good, Collier. That's the end for us, I hope. Report as usual in the morning."

THE END

AFTERWORD

WERE you fooled by the werewolf, dear readers? With her extraordinary denouement to her mystery in *Death in the Forest*, Moray Dalton had certain precedent for her frightful nocturnal beast. For example, there is Arthur Conan Doyle's landmark detective novel *The Hound of the Baskervilles* (1902) ("Mr. Holmes, they were the footprints of a gigantic hound!") and certain occult mysteries by such Doyle contemporaries as Sax Rohmer. However, Dalton's most immediate influence likely was a contemporary woman writer of her own, Jessie Douglas Kerruish (1884-1949). Kerruish's novel of lycanthropy, *The Undying Monster*, was originally published in England in 1922, but it appeared for the first time in the United States in 1936, where it received with much acclaim from critics. Dalton, who frequently takes note of American slang and films in her books and had Inspector Collier visit the United States for the first time in her previous Collier mystery, *Death in the Dark*, may have taken note of Kerruish's novel when it was reprinted, three years before the publication of *Death in the Forest*.

A much simplified film version was made of *The Undying Monster* in the U. S. in 1942 and the novel has been reprinted numerous times since. *Death in the Forest*, on the other hand, has now been reprinted for the first time since its publication eighty-three years ago and is making its first appearance outside the United Kingdom. It joins the ranks of Thirties werewolf novels, alongside both *The Undying Monster* and Guy Endore's best-selling *The Werewolf of Paris* (1933), while managing as well to remain within the traditional detective novel format—something of an achievement, but one not altogether unexpected from this versatile and creative author.

Curtis Evans